W9-CDW-554

AMISH CHRISTMAS TWINS

READ MORE SHELLEY SHEPARD GRAY IN

An Amish Second Christmas

MORE FROM RACHEL J. GOOD

His Unexpected Amish Twins
His Pretend Amish Bride
His Accidental Amish Family

AND MORE AMISH ROMANCE FROM LOREE LOUGH

All He'll Ever Need
Home to Stay

AMISH CHRISTMAS TWINS

SHELLEY SHEPARD GRAY

RACHEL J. GOOD

LOREE LOUGH

KENSINGTON BOOKS
www.kensingtonbooks.com

This book is a work of fiction. Names, characters, and incidents either are products of the author's imagination or are used fictitiously. Any resemblance to actual persons living or dead, or events, is entirely coincidental.

KENSINGTON BOOKS are published by

Kensington Publishing Corp.
119 West 40th Street
New York, NY 10018

Compilation copyright © 2020 by Kensington Publishing Corp.
"The Christmas Not-Wish" © 2020 by Shelley Shepard Gray
"New Beginnings" © 2020 by Rachel J. Good
"Twins Times Two" © 2020 by Loree Lough

All rights reserved. No part of this book may be reproduced in any form or by any means without the prior written consent of the Publisher, excepting brief quotes used in reviews.

To the extent that the image or images on the cover of this book depict a person or persons, such person or persons are merely models, and are not intended to portray any character or characters featured in the book.

All Kensington titles, imprints, and distributed lines are available at special quantity discounts for bulk purchases for sales promotion, premiums, fund-raising, educational, or institutional use. Special book excerpts or customized printings can also be created to fit specific needs. For details, write or phone the office of the Kensington Sales Manager: Kensington Publishing Corp., 119 West 40th Street, New York, NY 10018. Attn. Sales Department. Phone: 1-800-221-2647.

Kensington and the K logo Reg. U.S. Pat. & TM Off.

ISBN-13: 978-1-4967-1786-3 (ebook)
ISBN-10: 1-4967-1786-4 (ebook)

ISBN-13: 978-1-4967-1785-6
ISBN-10: 1-4967-1785-6
First Kensington Trade Paperback Printing: October 2020

10 9 8 7 6 5 4 3 2 1

Printed in the United States of America

Contents

The Christmas Not-Wish

SHELLEY SHEPARD GRAY

But the angel said to them, Do not be afraid. I bring you good news that will cause great joy for all the people.

—Luke 2:10

Always begin anew with the day, just as nature does.

—Amish proverb

Chapter 1

Two weeks before Christmas

"What do you think about them?" Roy asked Jemima as he wandered into her room without knocking.

Usually Jemima would have been annoyed with her little brother for disturbing her, but she wasn't asleep, either. An hour earlier, each of them had been tucked into their own beds in their own rooms by Elizabeth Anne and Will Kurtz, their newest set of foster parents.

After the children debated for a couple of seconds about whether they should risk getting E.A. and Will mad, Jemima motioned Roy to come sit beside her on the bed. She would never tell Roy, but right now, she thought she needed him as much as he needed her.

"I don't know," she replied at last. "I guess they seem nice."

Roy lifted his right thumb to suck, then tucked it under his leg so he wouldn't be tempted. "They're nicer than Dan and Shirl."

"Anyone would be nicer than them," Jemima said. They'd

only lasted at Dan and Shirl Miller's house for five weeks. Jemima personally had thought they'd been there five weeks too long. Dan and Shirl had seemed nice enough when the social worker was there, but when she was gone, Dan's and Shirl's smiles disappeared. They'd given Jemima and her little brother lots of chores, yelled at Roy every time he forgot that he wasn't supposed to suck his thumb, and weren't even very nice at Thanksgiving dinner. Shirl had gotten really mad at Jemima when she'd revealed that she wasn't thankful to be at the Millers' house on Thanksgiving Day.

So mad that Jemima had been sent to her room without any food . . . and when Roy had started crying and sucking his thumb, he'd been sent from the table, too. He'd thrown himself on the twin bed next to her and bawled. Figuring he had every right to cry, she'd curled up on her own bed in a ball and tried to pretend she was anywhere else.

Yes, it had been a really bad night. But even though her stomach had been rumbling with hunger, she hadn't regretted her honesty.

After all, how could she have uttered such a bold lie? She wasn't thankful to be at the Miller house. Wasn't thankful to be there at all. She missed her own parents and her old house and the turkey that her father had always hunted and their mother had always complained about plucking. She missed her own room and their life in the woods and the way that their *mamm* and *daed* did things.

She had not been grateful to have to share a room with Roy. She was not grateful to always be yelled at. She really hadn't been grateful when she'd eyed the watery-looking chicken, boxed mashed potatoes, and canned green beans that had been their Thanksgiving supper.

When Melanie, their social worker, stopped by the next morning, Jemima had told her everything. Melanie had hugged her tight and asked her to hold on just a little bit longer, because she was working hard to find them someplace better.

It had taken another three weeks, but now here they were at the Kurtzes' house. She was very thankful for the move, but she'd learned over the last couple of months not to expect too much . . . or to wish for things that probably would never happen.

All that did was make her feel worse.

"Are you going to call Elizabeth Anne E.A. or Mrs. Kurtz?" Roy asked, bringing her back to the present.

"I'm going to call her Mrs. Kurtz."

Roy's eyes got big. "Really?"

"I didn't like having to call Mr. and Mrs. Miller Dan and Shirl. They had friendly names, but they weren't friendly people."

"They were mean."

"All they cared about were the checks they got for watching us." She lowered her voice. "Plus, Shirl told me that she was going to put us with a babysitter on Christmas Day because they'd gotten invited to Dan's brother's house. That wasn't nice."

"But E.A. and Will don't seem like that."

"We don't really know them yet, Roy. They could act different in the morning. Some people do."

His thin shoulders slumped. "Jah. I guess you're right."

"I know I am," she replied. "It won't do us any good to get attached to E.—I mean, Mrs. and Mr. Kurtz. They might not even keep us until New Year's Day."

Roy's expression turned even more troubled. "I miss Mamm and Daed. How come they had to die?"

"Everyone said that *Got* wanted them early." She shrugged. The explanation didn't sound very comforting, but she guessed it was something they were supposed to be happy about. But even if the Lord had wanted their parents to go to heaven early, Jemima didn't think being hit by a big truck was a very nice way to die. No one wanted to hear her say that, though.

"Roy?" E.A.'s voice sounded worried. "Roy, where are . . . oh. There you are," she said as she peeked into Jemima's bedroom. "Is everything all right?"

Roy scrambled to his feet. "Jah. I'm sorry I got out of bed. I won't do it again."

E.A.'s expression softened. "Oh, honey. You didn't do anything wrong. You know, I didn't even ask if you two were used to sharing a room. Are you scared?"

Jemima spoke up before her brother could say a word. "We like having our own rooms. We're used to that."

"Jah," Roy replied, scooting toward the door. "I like my own bedroom. Danke." He darted out of her room as if he was afraid E.A. was going to change her mind.

Jemima felt her stomach twist into knots as E.A. turned to watch Roy walk down the hall. "He usually listens and stays in bed."

E.A. turned back to her. "I'm not upset, Jemima. I had a feeling that your first night here might be difficult. That's why I came upstairs to check on you."

"Oh."

"Are you all right? Do you need anything?"

"Nee. I am fine." She sank against her pillows and pulled the flannel sheet up higher on her chest. "I'm going to go to sleep soon."

"Ah. Well, I'll be on my way, then. Sweet dreams, Jemima."

"You too. I mean, *gut naucht*, Mrs. Kurtz."

Some of E.A.'s smile dimmed. "*Gut naucht* to you as well, Jemima. I'll see you in the morning."

Jemima sat perfectly still as she listened to her new foster mother walk down the hall, pause for a moment, then slowly descend the staircase. Only then did Jemima scoot farther into bed.

After turning off her bedside flashlight, Jemima closed her eyes and tried not to worry.

But, like always, attempting not to worry was as hard as wishing for sleep to come. At least she'd given up wishing for things that could never be, though.

Now she was rarely disappointed with how things turned out.

Chapter 2

"Is everything all right?" Will asked the moment E.A. walked inside their bedroom. "Are they scared? Do they need anything?"

E.A. carefully closed the door behind her before tossing her robe on the floor and crawling back into bed. "I don't know." And that was the truth. She had no idea how Jemima and Roy were feeling.

Looking even more concerned, Will sat up and faced her. "Well, what happened? You were in there for a while."

"I found Roy in Jemima's room. He was sitting on the edge of her bed and they were whispering. But the moment I showed up, he jumped to his feet and promised he wouldn't get out of bed again. Next thing I knew, he was scurrying back to his room." Hating how scared he'd looked—and how resigned Jemima had been—E.A. released a ragged sigh. "I think that boy actually thought I was going to get mad at him. Can you believe it? He thought I was going to get mad at him for talking to his sister. It makes me want to cry."

"They've been through a lot, E.A. You're still a stranger, remember?"

"I haven't forgotten. I believe Melanie said that we're the sixth foster family they've been with since their parents died three years ago."

"She also said that the couple they were with before wasn't a good fit and that the *kinner* had been especially unhappy there."

"That doesn't make me feel any better. If anything, I feel worse—like we should have filled out the paperwork months ago."

"You can't think that way. Their rough time of it isn't our fault, darling. You can't take on all their burdens, and most especially not their past."

She looked into his dark brown eyes and smiled. Will was truly one of the kindest people she knew. He'd always been that way, even back when they were children. What she hadn't known, however, was that he could be romantic, too. He'd started to call her darling when they were engaged, and though they'd been married over a year and were no longer newlyweds, every time he murmured the endearment her heart pitter-pattered a little faster.

"I know you are right, Will. It's just hard. I want them to be happy."

"They will be. Or at the very least, we'll try to help them to be happy."

"Even though they just got here and Melanie said for us to take our time getting to know each other, I already know I want more than that." She reached for his hand. "Will, I want Roy and Jemima to be with us forever."

"I'm taken with them, too. I knew it the moment Melanie introduced us to them two weeks ago and Roy asked if I liked pumpkin pie."

E.A. giggled. "Just as I was about to say that I'd make him one, he wrinkled his nose and said he thought it was yucky."

"All while Jemima was trying to get him to hush." The lines around his eyes deepened with his smile. "Elizabeth Anne, not to sound too full of myself or anything, but I think they're going to be mighty happy with us, too."

"Do you really think so?"

He nodded. "How can they not be? We already are starting to love them." He ran his thumb over her knuckles. "I bet it will just take them a while to get settled."

"I hope so."

"Come now, try to stay positive, *jah*?"

Against her will, her eyes filled up with tears. "Christmas is just around the corner. I wish those kids were only worrying about presents they wanted and how much fruitcake to eat."

Will grinned. "First, nobody sits around dreaming of fruitcake. Secondly, that's a wonderful idea. We can ask them to write a Christmas list. That will give them something positive to think about."

"I'll bring that up tomorrow."

"Gut." He ran a hand down her hair. "Does that mean you'll stop crying now?"

"Yes. I'm sorry. I don't know what's wrong with me."

"I think you do, Elizabeth," he said gently. "Ain't so?"

Feeling her cheeks heat, she nodded. Less than a week ago— just days before Roy and Jemima were scheduled to arrive— they'd gotten the biggest surprise. They were expecting a baby.

When E.A. had shared her shock, the midwife had simply raised her eyebrows. "A smart girl like you can sure be foolish," she'd chided. "I would have thought you'd have figured out how babes were made."

Yes, she had known. But she'd also learned years ago that the chances of her becoming pregnant were very slim. This

pregnancy was truly a miracle, but it was also a closely guarded secret. She and Will wanted to wait a few weeks before they shared the news. Not just to hold their secret tight for a bit before it was all of their friends' and families' news as well . . . but for the sake of Jemima and Roy.

Now all of their plans were up in the air.

"Have you thought any more about what we discussed?" Will asked.

E.A. nodded. "I've thought about it, but it doesn't feel right. We brought the children here with the intention of adopting them."

"I know we did. But the timing might not be the best. Roy and Jemima need two parents to give them all their attention. They've already been through so much. How can we give them what they need if we have a newborn?"

"Our babe won't be born for months and months. We don't need to make this decision now."

"I agree, but as soon as Christmas is over, we'll need to decide."

"That's in two weeks, Will."

He sighed in the dark. "Elizabeth Anne, I'm not trying to hurt your feelings or bring pain into those *kinner*'s lives. But one of us has to be tough. I can't think that it will be easier on those children to wait to tell them that we can't adopt them."

"If that's what we decide."

"Yes, of course. If we decide that." He ran a hand down her hair again. "Just keep an open mind, okay? At the very least, we'll be giving them a wonderful Christmas."

"At least there's that." She felt her eyes fill with tears again.

Will wrapped his arms around her. "Don't cry. Everything will work out the way it's supposed to. God has a plan, yes?"

"Jah," she whispered. But as the minutes passed and she eventually heard Will's deep, even breathing, E.A. couldn't help but think of everything the children had already been through.

How did God have a plan that included orphaning two small children? No matter how hard she tried to wrap her mind around that, it didn't make much sense.

At last, she fell into a restless sleep, finally praying that the Lord would help her be strong enough to do the "right" thing, whatever that might be.

Chapter 3

Ten days before Christmas

Jemima looked at the many sheets of paper, crayons, and colored pencils that E.A. had set out for her and Roy on the kitchen table. "Are you sure you want me and Roy to help you?" she asked.

E.A., who had been stenciling letters of the alphabet on each page, put her pencil down. "Of course, dear. It's going to be our family's Christmas present and you two are part of the family." Her smile wobbled. "I mean, you are right now."

Right now. That didn't sound very permanent. A new sense of doom settled in Jemima's chest, making it hard to breathe. Over the last few days, she and Roy had felt a little bit like they had woken up in a dream.

Everything that had been so awful and wrong at the Millers' was so right with Mr. and Mrs. Kurtz. E.A. and Will wanted to be with them and never got mad, even when Roy sucked his thumb or when Jemima accidentally knocked over her milk on the table.

Will always greeted them after he kissed E.A. hello after work. No matter how tired he seemed, he always sat down beside them and asked about their days . . . and their nights when he took the night shift.

And then there was the food! It was so good and there was lots of it. Even though it felt wrong to compare, Jemima had to admit that even their real mother hadn't cooked as well as Elizabeth Anne.

"Jem," Roy whispered. "You're daydreaming again."

Oh! She certainly had been! Right there at the kitchen table. "I'm sorry." She darted a quick look of apology at her brother before answering. "I mean, I'm not a very good artist."

"I'm not either," Roy said quickly. "Sometimes I don't color in the lines."

"But see? These pages are blank. That means anything you want to write on each page or color is the right thing to do."

"All I can think for 'C' is candy," Roy said.

"Or camels," Jemima said quickly. "The Wise Men rode on camels to see baby Jesus."

"But I like peppermint candy canes," Roy said.

But instead of saying that Jemima's was better, because it was better to think about Jesus instead of candy, E.A. frowned. "Boy, those are two *gut* things for our letter 'C,' aren't they? Hmm. Oh, how about we write: ' "C" is for Christmas candy and a camel caravan.' If the Wise Men had candy canes, they would have surely brought them for Jesus on this birthday."

Roy's eyes got big. Jemima couldn't help but gape as well. "You want to write that?"

"Why not? It uses both of your ideas." She got out a black marker and carefully printed out the sentence next to the stenciled letter "C." When she was done, she smiled. "What do you think?"

Roy said, "I want to draw a camel carrying a candy cane in its mouth."

E.A. giggled. "That sounds splendid, Roy." She slid the paper over to him. "Well, children, look at that! We already have one of our pages done."

"Only twenty-five more letters to go," Jemima said.

E.A. giggled again. "You remind me of my friend Harley, Jemima. Harley is nothing if not a realist."

"Is that bad?"

"Oh, no. A realist is simply someone who dwells on things they can see and prove. They aren't always real comfortable when it comes to considering fanciful things."

"Does that mean 'made up'?"

"Jah. Or things that might seem like just a wish."

"Oh."

E.A. stood up and walked to the stove. While Roy started drawing camels that really only looked like lumpy dogs, Jemima reached for the "W" page.

"Do you have a special wish, Mrs. Kurtz?"

"I have lots of wishes, but for Christmas, my wish is that I am able to finish sewing all my projects on time. And for snow."

"I like snow, too," Roy said as he picked up a red crayon.

"Do you have a special Christmas wish, Jemima?" E.A. asked as she poured chocolate powder into the milk she'd been heating on the stove. "Is there something special that you would love to receive on Christmas morning?"

"*Nee*," Jemima said.

"Really? Not even a new dress or maybe a stuffed animal or a doll?"

"My *mamm* gave me a *dalli* before she died," Jemima said before she realized what she'd shared. She slapped a hand over her lips. "I'm sorry. I meant, *nee*, Mrs. Kurtz. I don't have any wishes for Christmas."

E.A. was quiet as she pulled out a container from one of the cabinets, then brought over three mugs of hot chocolate. It was the fanciest hot chocolate Jemima had ever seen. In the center of each mug was a giant marshmallow and on top of the marshmallow was a sprinkling of red and green candy sprinkles.

"Wow!" Roy said.

"I've never seen marshmallows like this," Jemima added.

"That's because I make them." E.A. chuckled softly. "I'm afraid I'm not the cook that my friend Kendra is. She can make beautiful marshmallows. Mine taste okay, but they're on the lumpy side, I'm afraid."

"They're real *gut*," Roy said when he put his mug down. He smiled, showing off a marshmallow mustache.

After handing Roy a napkin, E.A. shuffled through the papers and pulled out the "M." "How about this?" she asked as she picked up the marker. "'"M" is for marshmallow mustaches'?"

This time Jemima couldn't resist giggling, too. "*Jah*, Mrs. Kurtz. That's a good one."

As she wrote, E.A. gestured toward the "W" page in front of her. "What have you decided for 'W'?"

"'"W" is for Wish and for White Christmas'?" She held her breath.

"I think that is a mighty good sentence, dear." She handed over the pen. "I'll write it down on a scratch piece of paper; then you can write the official sentence. Okay?"

"Okay," Jemima said. She would never tell Mrs. Kurtz that her secret sentence was *"W" is for wonderful parents who make wishes.* That one she was going to keep for herself. As another one of her not-wishes.

Chapter 4

Eight days before Christmas

"I'm not so sure about this," Roy whispered to Will as they climbed out of John Byler's truck. Will, John, and their friend Harley were taking Roy and Jemima turkey hunting.

Bending down to pick up his shotgun and backpack, Will fought back a smile. He didn't want the little guy to think he was making light of his concern, but boy, it was hard to keep his happiness in check. This was the first time Roy had spoken to him without coaxing.

After checking to make sure that Jemima was being occupied by Harley—he was helping her adjust her backpack—Will rested his shotgun on a knee. "What makes you nervous? The woods, the hunting, or being with me, Harley and John, and your sister?"

Roy pondered that for a few seconds before replying. "All of it."

"I understand. It's new with new friends, *jah*?"

Roy simply stared at him.

And all the unspoken words slammed into his heart. Roy didn't consider any of the men—not even Will—a friend.

"All I can offer is my opinion, Roy. And that is that it's a good thing to try something new from time to time. You won't know if you like a stranger if you don't meet them. You also won't know if you like something if you never try it at least once."

John walked to their side. "Roy, I know you and Jemima have already had your fair share of new things this year, but I promise that there isn't a one of us who would knowingly put you in danger or make you sad. Try to trust us, if you can."

"But you aren't Amish."

"*Nee*, I am not. But I used to be. And more important than that, I have known Will and Harley, here, since we were younger than you, Roy."

Roy looked up at Will. "Really?"

"Really. *Mei mamm* used to watch John and Harley in the summers from time to time. E.A., too."

This time it was Jemima who looked surprised. "I didn't know that."

"Eight of us were fast friends."

"Eight of you?"

"That's right. We took our friendship seriously, too. In fact, all of us but one are still here in Walnut Creek."

"What happened to the other one?"

"He died."

"You've known someone who died, too?"

"Jah. You aren't alone, Roy."

Roy took a deep breath. "All right."

"All right then." Will grinned. "Let's go find ourselves a turkey for Christmas."

"I'm not sure how to find turkeys," Jemima said. "What should we do?"

Harley answered that one. "You're gonna have to stay quiet, walk carefully, and try to think like a turkey."

Her lips curved up. "We're people. We can't think like *fayl*."

"Sure we can. All you have to do is look around and think about where you would want to perch."

Jemima giggled before slapping her hand over her lips. "Sorry."

"That's all right, girl. You sounded a bit like a giggling turkey. Maybe they'll think you're a friend."

Jemima giggled harder, followed by Roy, before he, too, slapped a hand over his mouth.

And so it continued.

Will, John, and Harley carried shotguns in their hands and backpacks filled with snacks on their backs. They pretended to look hard for turkeys, but in actuality, Will knew their chances of actually finding any birds were slim. What was important was that they had gotten Jemima and Roy out of the house for a little adventure. Three days before, he'd spoken to John at work about the children. When John had suggested a Christmas turkey-hunting trip, he'd been doubtful, but now he was realizing that it was good medicine for all of them.

They were all dressed in boots, layers of clothing, hats, and mittens. Harley was gifted in the way he dealt with Jemima. She responded well to his quiet, solemn ways as well as his ability to spy rabbits, deer, and bright red cardinals.

As for Roy, Will could tell that he still wasn't exactly sure what to think about John. Though Roy had been in an English foster home, Will knew that it hadn't been a very positive situation. He feared that Roy was also coming to associate Englishers with people like their former foster parents. Perhaps by the end of their adventure, the boy would warm up to John and maybe even Englishers in general.

After an hour went by, Harley stomped his feet. "I reckon it's time for a hot chocolate and cookie break." He looked around. "Anyone want to have some with me?"

"We don't have any hot chocolate or cookies," Jemima said. "Mrs. Kurtz packed us sandwiches."

"Of course we do, child. *Mei frau* Katie made it for us." Harley pointed to a rock. "Let's sit down for a spell, *jah*?"

"Does he really have hot chocolate?" Roy whispered to Will.

"Of course," Will said as he helped the boy take off his backpack. When Jemima sat on Will's other side, he felt a burst of pride. He was out with his children. Even though he hadn't known them for long and they weren't his by birth, he felt a connection to them and their well-being as strongly as if he'd held each of them in his arms in a delivery room.

"How are you doing, Jemima?" he asked. "Are you glad you decided to come out with the men today?"

She nodded. "I didn't think I would have fun, but it's nice to be out in the woods."

"I think so, too." Will smiled down at her.

"Do you think E.—I mean, Mrs. Kurtz is doing okay all by herself?" Jemima asked.

"I think so. She was going to do some cleaning around the house. Maybe sewing, too." He also knew E.A. was going to be sewing blankets for Roy and Jemima for one of their Christmas presents. She was making stuffed rabbits for each of them as well.

"She sure likes to sew," Roy said.

"That's because she has a sewing shop. Someone is managing it for her now, but for a while she worked there all the time. Ah,

here we go," he said as Harley handed out paper cups filled with hot chocolate, followed by napkins folded around sugar cookies.

Jemima gazed at the perfectly formed stars and hearts. Harley's wife, Katie, had even lined the edges with red sprinkles. They were truly works of art. "They're really pretty."

"They are, and they taste good, too," Will said.

"Why, I'd say these cookies are almost as good as my Marie's cookies," John said with a smile.

"Never say that," Harley retorted.

John laughed. "My wife Marie is a terrible cook, Jemima and Roy. That's why they're teasing about the cookies."

"You don't mind that she can't cook?" Jemima asked.

"Not a bit. We all have our gifts, *jah*? Marie is a whiz at math and all sorts of things. An' it just so happens that I am rather handy in the kitchen. I never would have known that if Marie hadn't been so terrible."

"E.A. makes good chicken," Roy said. "She bakes it with carrots and potatoes."

John's expression softened. "I bet it is wonderful-*gut*, Roy."

Just as Jemima was taking a careful sip, her eyes widened. "Oh!"

"What?"

"Look!" She pointed to a flock of four turkeys carefully pecking the ground ten or so yards away.

Even from that distance Will could tell that it was a turkey family of sorts. Three of the turkeys were much smaller than the largest one, and they were all trailing after the leader like schoolchildren followed their teacher.

"What do we do now?" Roy asked.

His eyes were wide; Jemima's were resigned. Will glanced at Harley and John, who had picked up his shotgun.

But then it became clear that none of them had the heart to shoot the mother bird. But what to do?

John jumped to his feet, somehow managing to knock over Harley's steel thermos. It fell on its side with a loud clang, ringing through the trees like Christmas bells.

The turkeys froze, all looked their way, then scurried off down a ravine.

"Oh, um, rats!" John cried.

"John, you never could stay quiet. You scared off our Christmas supper," Will said. "Now what are we gonna do?"

"I'm real sorry, everyone. I don't know what happened," John said.

Roy and Jemima turned back to Will with wide eyes. Struggling to keep a straight face again, he made a great show of looking at his pocket watch. "It's getting late. I reckon we should get on home."

"But what about the turkeys?" Roy asked. "What should we do?"

"Do?" Will asked. "Oh. Well, I think I'm going to tell E.A. that we didn't see any turkeys today."

"But we did," Roy said. "So you wouldn't be telling the truth."

"It would only be a small fib."

John winked. "I only saw a couple of birds from a great distance. I'm not a hundred percent positive they were turkeys. Are you, Harley?"

"Nee. They might have been . . . um . . . quail. Or wild chickens."

"Wild chickens?" Roy wrinkled his freckled nose.

Harley zipped up his backpack with the thermos tucked safely inside. "Ah, *jah*. And let me tell you what, I ain't about to start eating wild chickens this year for Christmas."

"Me neither," Will said. "Don't fret, *kinner*. I'll go to the butcher and ask him to put aside a turkey for us at the shop. E.A. won't care if I do that. She'll probably be pleased she doesn't have to pluck feathers."

Jemima giggled before covering her mouth again. But at the last minute, she left it uncovered and her laughter filled the air.

And Will realized that was what happiness sounded like.

Chapter 5

E.A. couldn't recall the last time she'd laughed until she'd cried. She was mighty thankful for that. She didn't want to have another memory to compete with the supper they'd just shared together.

She doubted that any other supper would come close, though. Her little family had been in fine form when they'd rushed in the kitchen door! Oh, they'd come home dirty and tired, that was for sure. But they'd also been full of stories and laughter and chatter. Roy's sweet face was flushed and his blue eyes were fairly sparkling. Will simply looked like he'd just hung the moon. And as for Jemima? Well, she looked happy.

So happy!

It had made E.A.'s heart want to sing. After she'd cajoled them all to take hot showers and put on clean clothes, they'd gathered around the table, so ready to tell her about their adventures that the children hardly took time to bow their heads while they prayed silently.

Then, the very moment after Will said, "Amen," they started talking so fast that she could hardly keep up.

Sitting around the supper table, E.A. served warm chicken and dumplings and listened with wide eyes as Jemima, Roy, and Will told her about sipping Harley's hot chocolate and about Miss Katie's cookies. About spying deer and rabbits and lots of birds and maybe even a fox in a thicket.

They also told her a rather long and convoluted tale about a mysterious flock of wild chickens that lived in the woods.

When E.A. questioned them about that—honestly, she'd never heard of such a thing—Jemima and Roy looked like they were going to bite their tongues, they were having such a time holding back their mirth.

That's when she put on her best schoolmarm expression and folded her hands in her lap. "Tell me the real story, if you please."

Her three looked at one another and seemed to come to a silent conclusion.

"Well, um, Mr. Kurtz didn't want to hurt the mommy bird," Jemima said.

"The mommy bird?"

"It was a hen, E.A.," Will said in an aggrieved tone. "The female turkeys lay eggs, you know."

"Ah, yes. I believe I heard something about that."

Just as his cheeks reddened and he looked down at his plate, it had all become so very clear. Her dear husband hadn't had the heart to shoot their Christmas supper in front of the children.

It made her love him all the more. It was things like this that made her so glad not only that they'd married but also that they'd decided to adopt. He was such a kind man. The perfect man for two children who had already lost so much. She wasn't sure why the Lord had decided that it was time for her and Will to have a baby now, too, but E.A. figured that He wouldn't give them anything more than they could handle. Maybe He thought all of them—she, Will, Jemima, and Roy—needed a baby to take care of.

And maybe they did. Caring for a helpless infant would indeed bring them all closer.

At least, E.A. thought it would. . . .

"I thought you'd have your nose in a book right now, not staring out the window," Will said as he entered their bedroom two hours later.

After E.A. had gone upstairs to read Jemima and Roy their story and put them down to sleep, Will had gone out to the barn to see to Chip and Dale, their two horses.

E.A. moved over on the mattress so he could sit beside her. "I don't think I could concentrate on anything right now."

"Why?" He played with one of the ties at her nightgown collar. "I promise, the *kinner* had a *gut* day. And I kept them safe. Neither of them ever left my sight."

"I didn't doubt that for a second." She looked at him fondly. "Actually, I guess I was just thinking about how glad I am to have married you."

He straightened. "Is that right? What made you think about me?"

"You're so silly. Of course I would be thinking of you. You're a wonderful man, Will. So caring of Jemima and Roy."

"They're good for me. E.A., when we were walking in the woods, there was a time when I had a child on each side of me. All I could think about was how proud I was that they were mine."

"Isn't that something? I had thought it would maybe take months to feel like Jemima and Roy were ours. But I love them already."

"I do, too. Now I know what it feels like to be a parent. I would do anything I could to help them."

"I would, too." She reached for his hand. "I don't know how we're going to tell them our news."

"I know. I was thinking...do you suppose maybe we could wait until after Christmas?"

"After Christmas?" She couldn't help the sound of dismay that was in her voice.

"I know it's going to be hard on you. I know you want to tell your parents, and you probably aren't feeling too good, and you're going to have to be pretending that you are just fine." He flushed. "You know? Never mind. We can do whatever you'd like."

"I don't want them to feel like they aren't important to us. I can keep the secret, but I want to tell my parents, too. Maybe I can tell them privately."

"Jah. We can do that."

He sounded doubtful, though. Was it because he knew her or he knew her parents? Was he worried that they'd spill the secret?

"I'll make sure that they know they can't tell anyone."

"If you tell your family, I'm going to have to tell mine."

"I know, Will. But I don't see any way around it." She looked down at her middle. "Especially since my body already seems to be changing."

"I didn't think you would be showing already. Is that normal?"

She chuckled. "I don't know, but I guess it doesn't matter if other women experience the same things. That's what's been happening to me."

He wrapped an arm around her shoulders. "You're right, sweetheart. Whatever is happening is the right thing for us."

She decided right then and there that she would wait a little bit longer before telling anyone else about their news. There was too much at stake.

Chapter 6

Seven days before Christmas

Unfortunately, all of E.A.'s good intentions about keeping the babe a secret flew out the window the next morning. Just as they were getting ready for church, her stomach decided that it didn't want to keep her breakfast. She barely made it to the bathroom in time.

But unlike the other times she'd gotten sick, her nauseous feelings didn't dissipate a couple of minutes later. Instead, her stomach was churning so much, she ended up sitting on the bathroom tile with her back against the wall.

"Mrs. Kurtz?" Jemima called out. "Mrs. Kurtz, are you all right?"

E.A. could hear the worry in Jemima's voice, but she didn't know what to say. She couldn't lie—and even if she wanted to, she knew a falsehood wouldn't be believed, anyway. Feeling weak and woozy all over again, she closed her eyes and let out a small moan.

"Mrs. Kurtz? Mrs. Kurtz, do you need some help?" Jemima asked. A few seconds later, she added, "Are you stuck in there? Do you need Mr. Kurtz to help you get out?"

E.A. loved Jemima. She really did. But she was so tired of being called Mrs. Kurtz. Most of the time when she heard the words on Jemima's tongue, she felt a little sad.

But today, those words felt like little jabs to her heart. When was the girl ever going to learn to trust her? She moaned again.

A couple of seconds later, Will rapped on the door. "Elizabeth Anne, you need to talk to us, please. Everyone out here is getting pretty worried."

Summoning up what she hoped was a cheery tone, she said, "I'm sorry. Jemima, please don't worry. I'm a little sick, but that's all. I'm sure I'll feel better in a few minutes." A few very long minutes.

"You're *sick*?" Roy asked, his voice sounding so close she wondered if he was leaning against the other side of the door. "E.A, are . . . are you going to go to the hospital?" His voice was frantic.

"Nee. Of course not."

"Are you sure? How come we can't go in and you won't come out?"

Oh, goodness. What a pickle.

She saw the door handle jiggle right before it opened. Will peeked in, his expression somber. When he saw her on the floor, he looked pained. "Jem and Roy, we'll be right out," he said before closing the door.

"I'm sorry about this," she whispered.

He squatted down on his haunches in front of her. "I'm sorry you feel so sick. Are you going to be okay?"

"Of course. It's just a bad case of morning sickness." She lifted a hand. "I can get up now."

Instead of taking her hand, he stared at her intently. "Elizabeth Anne, it's time to talk to them."

Her mouth watered as she tried to pull herself together. "But—"

"Keeping this secret is making things worse for the *kinner*, not better. Their lives have already been uprooted many times. Keeping this a secret is causing them more stress that they don't need."

He was right. She was being selfish and thinking only of what she wanted to deal with right at that minute. Resolving to be better, she held out a hand. "Help me up?"

Looking relieved, he stepped forward and held out both of his hands. After she was steady on her feet, he ran the faucet in the sink, put a washcloth under it, and then handed it to her.

The cool, wet fabric soothed her warm skin as well as her nerves. Just as she was about to ask where he wanted to have this conversation, the door creaked open and two dear little faces peered at her. Will had been right; they looked frightened half to death.

"See?" she said to them. "I'm okay."

Jemima just gaped.

Roy, on the other hand, wrinkled his nose in obvious disbelief. "E.A., I'm sorry, but you don't look okay at all. You look like you're gonna get sick again all over the floor."

"Don't say that," Jemima said.

"But it's true." Roy shifted from one foot to the other. "I mean, don'tcha think?"

"*Jah*, but we're not supposed to tell her that," Jemima whispered back.

As queasy as she felt, E.A. couldn't help but chuckle at their conversation. Will had been right. She wasn't going to be able to keep this pregnancy a secret any longer. "I think it's time we had a little talk."

"About what?" Roy asked.

"I'll let you know that answer in a minute. For now, you two go sit down in the living room, please. I promise that I'll be right there."

Both children waited a minute. It was obvious they were afraid to let her out of their sight.

"I promise, I'll be right there," E.A. continued in a firm voice. "But first, Will is going to help me straighten my *kapp*."

With obvious reluctance, Jemima and Roy backed away before disappearing from sight.

When she heard their footsteps fade down the hall, she said, "I hope they won't be too upset."

"They won't. A *boppli* is a wonderful thing. *Wunderbaar.*"

E.A. completely agreed.

But she also realized that sometimes babies arrived at the most inopportune times. She feared this was one of those instances.

Chapter 7

E.A. laughed softly as she finished telling Jemima and Roy the news. "So that, children, is why I was feeling so bad this morning. It wasn't because I was deathly ill—it's because I'm going to have a baby."

Will reached for his wife's hand. "I know it's a surprise, but it was a mighty big surprise for us, too," he said with a fond look at E.A. "However, I have a feeling that if you take a big breath and give yourselves some time to adjust to the idea, you both are going to feel as delighted as we do."

Though everything inside her wanted to kick and rail, Jemima only nodded. "I understand, Mr. Kurtz."

"You understand?" Will looked confused . . . and maybe sad, too?

"Jah." Remembering her manners, she smiled. "You are right, Mrs. Kurtz. This is *gut* news. I'm happy for you." She wasn't, but she couldn't really say that. Actually, she couldn't really do anything but sit there and wish she was somewhere else.

No, wish that she was back in time, sitting in her old house with her real parents. That's where she wished she was.

Beside her, Roy inhaled and exhaled noisily. Then he did it again.

E.A. looked alarmed. "Roy, what is wrong? Are you sick?"

"Nee. I'm takin' deep breaths, just like Will said I should."

Both Mr. and Mrs. Kurtz laughed. "I'm glad you're doing as I asked, but it was just an expression, Roy," Will said. "I meant that sometimes when God gives you something unexpected, it's a *gut* idea to take a moment to reflect on it."

"I'm reflectin' *real* hard."

Roy took another big, deep breath, which was really annoying. "Stop it, Roy," Jemima said.

He looked hurt. "But I'm reflecting."

"Oh, brother." He was also being stupid.

E.A. chuckled. "That's a mighty *gut* pun there, Jemima."

She smiled, even though she had no idea what a pun was, but right now she didn't care. "Is that all we needed to talk about, Mrs. Kurtz?"

Will's expression fell. "*Jah*, Jemima. Do you have any questions, though? We can talk about the baby, if you'd like. Or Christmas. We can talk about anything that might be bothering you."

She knew that wasn't true. Neither Will nor E.A. was going to like to hear about anything that she was thinking about. "I don't have any questions."

"Are you sure?"

"Yes. Can I go to my room now?"

"*Jah*, but I thought you were going to help me put together baskets for some of the widows in the area?" E.A. asked.

"I'll help you, but, um, I just need to go get something up in my room first."

Roy eyed her curiously. "What do you need to get, Jemima?"

"That's none of your business," she snapped. Why couldn't she just leave the room?

"Sorry! I was just asking!"

"I'm older, you know. You don't have to know everything that I do."

"You don't have to be so snippy, either."

"Oh, children. Let's all calm down," E.A. said.

"I am calm. I'm just trying to go to my room! Can't I leave now? Please?" Tears filled Jemima's eyes. She turned her head away before anyone else could see.

But of course they did.

Will got to his feet. "Roy, let's go to the mudroom and put on our boots and coats," he said in a tone that sounded far too chipper. "You can come help me clear off the walkway."

Roy practically slid off the couch in his haste to be Will's helper. "I'm a *gut* helper, but I'm gonna need gloves, too."

"Jah. Of course," Will said as he rested a hand on her brother's head. "We'll get gloves for both of us. Let's go. If we get our work done fast, we'll have time to make a snowman, *jah*?"

Roy practically started jumping up and down. "Jah. I'm *gut* at making snowmen, too."

As they disappeared from sight, E.A. smiled at Jemima. "I believe that brother of yours is as excited as a puppy in a field of rabbits."

The picture E.A. created was a good one, to be sure. But instead of relaxing her, it made Jemima sadder. There was no telling what her next set of foster parents would be like. Would they paint pretty pictures with their words or take the time to encourage her brother? She couldn't imagine they would be so blessed two times in a row. No, the new foster parents would probably be more like Dan and Shirl.

As her sense of doom heightened, Jemima got to her feet. She had to get out of the room before she burst into tears. "So, may I?"

"You may, but may we talk for a moment before you leave?"

"What do you want to talk about?" Jemima knew she sounded sullen and rather rude, but she didn't want to talk about the baby anymore. She really didn't want to pretend to be excited for E.A. and Will.

No, all she wanted to do was go lie down on her bed, hug her pillow tight, and try not to think about what was going to happen. Her foster parents were going to have their own children; they wouldn't need Jemima and Roy.

"If you wouldn't mind sitting down again, I'll tell you. I promise, I won't keep you here long, dear."

Dear? Did that mean she cared? Reminding herself that it was only an expression, Jemima sat back down and stared at her feet.

"Jemima, you look so worried about the future. I hate to see that."

"I'm not worried," she said quickly.

"It's okay if you are. I mean, I know that it can be hard when something occurs that seems to come out of left field. But I guess you know that."

Oh, she did. She knew far too well what it felt like to go from wishing that she could have hot fudge sauce on her ice cream to wishing that she had her parents again. There was no comparison.

But how could she put such things into words? She couldn't, especially if it risked making E.A. sad. Will would be very upset with her, and might even be so mad that he wouldn't let them stay until Christmas.

"All I want to do is get something from my room."

Looking disappointed in her, E.A. nodded. "I'm sorry, Jemima. Of course you may do that. How about you meet me in the dining room in a half hour or so? We'll work on the baskets and then maybe make some pretzels."

Jemima scooted off the couch and hurried to her room. She closed the door and leaned up against it. And then slid down the wood until her head was resting near the floor. It was uncomfortable and the wood floor was cold, but she was safe. No one could come inside without her knowing.

Only then did she start to pray for Jesus to watch over her and Roy this Christmas. She wasn't sure if He was listening, but just in case He was, she made sure to say "please" a whole bunch.

Chapter 8

E.A. waited thirty minutes, which had been difficult, since each minute felt like two hours. Then she walked back upstairs. A dozen emotions warred inside her. She didn't know how Jemima was feeling, not really. Her parents were still alive, and they were still living in the home E.A. had been born in. She'd never had a social worker assigned to her or lived with one foster family after another. She'd never even had a little brother to feel responsible for.

No, the only thing E.A. and Jemima had in common was that Jemima was nine years old and E.A. had once been a little girl as well.

But then she remembered that they had something more than that. They had love. E.A. already loved Jemima and Roy, and she wanted them in her life for years and years. She wanted to protect them and show them that even though life could sometimes be very, very hard, there were also good things that happened.

She didn't know if she had the right words to convey all that, but she knew she had to try. Feeling a little better, even though she worried that it was the exact wrong thing to do, E.A. at last knocked lightly on Jemima's door.

There was a pause and a sniff. "I'll be right out," she said at last.

The little girl's voice was hoarse, and she sounded so resigned that E.A. gave in to impulse and opened the door without waiting another second. To her surprise, the door almost hit Jemima's leg when it swung in.

Jemima scooted a few inches down.

"Oh, honey. Look at you, sitting on the floor." E.A. sat down next to her.

"You don't need to sit here, too." Jemima was looking down at a hand, which was pressed flat on the edge of the beige area rug that covered a portion of the wooden floor.

"I'm not so big that I can't sit here with you." She smiled sadly at her. "Jemima, I know we are still getting used to each other, but I think you need to know that I, um, like you very much." She almost said "love," but she was afraid to scare the child off.

"You don't have to say that."

"I am saying it because it's true, child. I do like you a lot. You're a likeable person." She smiled softly. "You are sweet, and bright, and you care about Roy so much. If you had come into my sewing shop, I would want to know you better."

"Oh."

"You know, we haven't talked a lot about your parents."

Jemima's head whipped around. "Who?"

"Your real *mamm* and *daed*. I know they were good people, and I know that they died in a car accident, but I don't know much else about them."

Jemima's blue eyes turned conflicted. "They were nice."

"I'm sure they were, but what was special about them?"

"Special? I don't know what to say."

"Why don't you tell me about Christmas?"

"Christmas?"

"Jah. What did they do at Christmastime? Did your mother like to bake cookies? Did she send Christmas cards?"

Jemima froze, then slowly nodded.

E.A. leaned back against the wall. "My mother has always loved Christmas. She's the type of person who starts making Christmas presents for other people in July or August. And, don't tell anyone, but she secretly loves to sing Christmas carols."

"Really?"

E.A. chuckled. "One time my *daed* and I caught her singing 'Rudolph the Red-Nosed Reindeer' when she thought she was alone in the house."

"I don't think my mother sang that."

"No?"

Jemima shook her head. "My *mamm* really liked Thanksgiving best. She said Christmas was for Jesus, but Thanksgiving was for everyone."

"I like that saying. It's true, too."

"Mamm used to buy lots of pumpkins and put them all around the *haus*. And she made the best apple cider and applesauce." Jemima peeked up at her. "We had an apple tree in our yard."

"Did you? I always wanted one of those. Were the apples good?"

Jemima smiled. "They were the best. *Mei daed* used to say that he didn't need to be a rich man because we had the best apple tree in the county."

"If I had an apple tree in our yard, I think I'd sneak apples all the time."

"Daed did! Mamm never even got mad because we had so many of them."

"I bet you miss that tree," E.A. said softly.

Jemima nodded. "I do." Her lip trembled. "I miss the apple

tree and our house and how our kitchen always smelled like cinnamon." Looking up at E.A., she added, "I miss my parents, too. I wish they hadn't died. Everyone says God must have wanted them bad, but I wanted them, too."

And then the tears came.

"Oh, Jemima." As the little girl let out a noise that was so full of pain it practically sliced her heart, E.A. reached out and held her close.

And then E.A. cried, too. She cried for Jemima and Roy's parents, two people who were far too young to die, . . . and for two little children who were far too young to have only memories of them.

Chapter 9

Three days before Christmas

Jemima was wearing a brand-new red dress for the Christmas party. The fabric was buttery soft and the sleeves were slightly puffed. She thought the matching red apron over it was awfully pretty, too.

Mrs. Kurtz sure could sew! Even though at first glance it looked like every other Amish girl's dress, it had a few more darts and pin tucks than others. Jemima thought it was beautiful. She also loved that the dress was fastened with straight pins in the front instead of buttons in the back like little girls' dresses.

She felt very grown-up in it. When she'd put it on, she'd spun around in it, enjoying the way the fabric fluttered around her ankles.

"When are ya going to stop fussing with your dress?" Roy complained as he watched her spin around in a circle again. "That's all you've been doing for the last hour."

She stopped abruptly. "I have not."

"You have too." He sneered. "If there was a mirror in here, I reckon you'd be standing in front of it all day long, doing nothing but staring at yourself."

She could feel her skin start to flush. "I didn't ask you to come in here. Why don't you go back to your own room?"

With a blink, his smirk vanished, and he looked once again like his usual six-year-old self. "Nee. I was bored in there. There wasn't anything to do."

Still irritated with his comments, she turned to face him. "That isn't my problem. Leave me alone. Go out and pester somebody else."

Roy glared at her. "You didn't used to talk to me like that. You're being mean, Jemima."

She knew she was, but that didn't mean she wasn't right. She didn't want to have to always entertain her little brother. "If I'm being mean, it's because you're being a baby, Roy." She was pretty sure she was right about that, too. She was still six when their parents had died and all anyone ever expected of her was to "watch out for Roy." She had, too. How come no one was asking him to do much now except a couple of easy chores and playing with the wooden farm and train sets in his room? It wasn't fair.

"I'm not being a *boppli*!"

"You are too. Now, go!"

Just as Roy stuck out his tongue at her, Will appeared in the doorway. He looked irritated and a little angry, too.

"What is the matter with the two of you?" he asked, looking from her to Roy and back again. "E.A. and I could hear you two fussing from the kitchen."

Roy's eyes widened and suddenly looked angelic.

Which really was annoying. "You should ask Roy," Jemima said. "He started it."

"I did not."

"You wouldn't l—"

"Oh, for Pete's sake. We're not starting that again," Will interrupted. "Roy, what is the matter?"

"I came in here to play with Jemima, but all she wants to do is prance around in her new dress." He lifted his chin. "And when I told her that she would probably do all that in front of a mirror if there was one in here, she told me to leave."

"Ah." Jemima noticed that Will almost smiled but then seemed to get back his composure. "Roy, I grew up with a slew of sisters. I'm sorry, but I fear you are going to have to get used to girls doing things boys don't understand."

"You mean she's going to twirl all the time?"

After giving her a quick smile, Will crooked a finger at Roy. "Come with me, boy. Let's leave Jemima alone for a moment."

Roy stepped forward but then stopped again. "But I thought we were getting ready for the party."

"Well, I'm ready, and I see that you have on your new shirt. Does that mean you're ready as well?"

Her little brother bobbed his head. "Jah."

"Then I'd say that we should go downstairs and sit patiently while the women finish, too."

"But what else do they have to do? Jemima, what do you have to do now?"

"Nothing that we need to know about, Roy," Will said easily as he guided her little brother out the door with a wink in her direction. Just before he closed it, he said, "Jemima, we'll be leaving for the Lambrights' *haus* in ten minutes. I expect you to be downstairs by then."

"I will be."

"Gut." Just before he stepped away, he lowered his voice. "You look mighty pretty, Jemima. Very grown-up."

"Danke," she said as he closed the door.

When she was alone again, she paused, and only heard silence. Then she took a moment to appreciate the fact that she was in her own room, sitting on her own bed, and Mr. Kurtz had just not only given her a few moments of privacy, but he'd said she looked pretty, too.

Swallowing the lump in her throat, she realized that she was happy. She wasn't thinking about her parents or afraid of getting yelled at or worried about where she and Roy were going to be living next week. All she felt was a beautiful sense of peace floating inside her.

She wondered if it was her guardian angel reminding her that all was going to be well. Back when she was a little girl, she used to tell her *mamm* that she was never alone because she had her very own special angel always by her side. Her mother would laugh at her comments and say that if any little girl was so blessed, it would surely be her Jemima.

After their parents went to heaven and everything had turned so wrong, Jemima had been sure she'd been stupid ever to imagine that sweet angels walked by little girls' sides. After all, how could a guardian angel really exist if both of her parents had died in an instant?

She'd decided then and there that all she'd had was a make-believe friend.

But now, maybe she'd been right all along. Maybe her special angel was looking out for her again and she was reminding Jemima that even though something very bad had happened, she was still never alone. That she was blessed and special in her own way.

The most recent turn of events seemed to say that was true. Even though Mr. and Mrs. Kurtz were having a baby, they'd said that she and Roy were still special to them and that they wanted them, too. Surely that meant something?

She didn't know everything about E.A. and Will Kurtz, but she was almost positive that they didn't lie. Not about things like that, at least.

"Jemima!" Roy called. "Everyone's waiting!"

"Sorry!" She grabbed her black bonnet, slipped it over her *kapp*, and hurried downstairs. She was ready at last.

Chapter 10

All the attention was becoming awkward. From the moment she, Will, and the children had arrived at Katie and Harley's house, all of their friends had made a beeline for E.A.'s tummy. They'd hugged her, patted her belly as if it wasn't actually a part of her body, and discussed the pregnancy in excited tones.

Any other time, E.A. would have been grateful for that. But now, while she was holding little Jemima's hand? All she wanted everyone to do was pretend that she wasn't suddenly looking very pregnant.

And "suddenly" was the key word, too. It was as if the baby had decided to grow exponentially over the last week. She'd gone from looking like she was carrying a little bit of extra weight to looking like she was four or five months pregnant. It was rather confusing.

"I don't think we have to talk about this anymore," she said when her friends Kendra and Marie started to ask her questions about how she was feeling.

"Are you sure?" Marie asked.

"Positive," she replied, hoping her quick glance at Jemima would relay what was on her mind.

"Oh, of course!" Smiling down at Jemima, Marie said, "Do you have a Christmas wish yet?"

"Nee."

"Really?" She looked up at E.A. in concern. "I know the Amish don't have Christmas trees or Santa Claus, but I thought children still got presents."

"They do," Kendra said before E.A. could. "But it's different. *Kinner* don't ask for the moon and stars, just for one or two special things."

"Oh, of course." Marie smiled again. "So, do you have one or two things in mind?"

Little Jemima looked up at E.A. with big eyes, which of course made a lump form in her throat. "You can say whatever you want to say, dear," she murmured. "I promise, both Marie and Kendra are nice women. I've known them for years and years."

Jemima seemed to think about that for a long moment, then said, "I do have a Christmas wish, Mrs. Byler. But it's a secret."

"Of course. I should have realized that. Christmas wishes are very special."

"You sound like you have experience with them," Kendra teased. "I'm going to guess that you've probably had your share of Christmas wishes over the years."

Marie's cheeks heated. "I can't deny that I have. I was a spoiled girl, and I always seemed to want just one more thing." Her green eyes lit up. "But that doesn't mean it wasn't fun to dream."

E.A. smiled down at Jemima, who was now staring at Marie as if she was some kind of Christmas angel. E.A. didn't blame her, either. Marie had an enthusiasm about her that was infectious. It had always been that way, even back when they were little girls together.

"My wish right now is to go try some of those Christmas cookies. Want to do that, Jemima?"

"Jah."

"We'll talk to you later," E.A. said to Kendra and Marie before guiding Jemima over to the long table that was filled with beautiful and tasty-looking treats. "Look, Jemima! There are the marshmallow treats that we made with Roy this morning."

The little girl smiled. "They look *shay*."

"I think they look pretty, too." They'd decorated their treats with red and green chocolate candies and cut them into stars while they were still warm. Arranged next to plates of snow crescents, gingersnaps, and other cookie cutouts, they looked perfect.

She picked up a paper plate. "What kind of cookie is your favorite?"

Jemima giggled. "All of them."

"That's the best answer, dear. How about we each pick four cookies to sample?"

"Is that really okay?"

"Jemima, you can have as many as you'd like," Katie Lambright said as she approached with her baby in her arms. "Cookies are meant to be eaten, not simply stared at."

After E.A. gave her an encouraging nod, Jemima wandered over to the opposite side of the table and slowly made her choices.

"How are things going?" Katie whispered.

"I think pretty well. Today's been a good day. Jemima and Roy seemed to like making cookies, and Jemima at least has seemed to enjoy the party. Well, once everyone stopped talking about my pregnancy."

"She and Roy are adorable, and it's obvious that they're already settling in with you and Will."

E.A. glanced over at Will, who was now carrying a sleepy-looking Roy on his hip. "I hope so. As soon as I met them, I knew I wanted to be their mother." After checking to make sure Jemima was out of earshot, she added in a whisper, "I don't know if it's going to be easy, though. By all accounts, their parents were wonderful people, and the children miss them terribly. I don't want to replace them, of course, but I'm afraid I'll never measure up."

"Oh, E.A., don't you know that you can't worry about things like that?"

"How can I not worry? Will and I are kind of like instant parents. We don't have the experience of what to say or do."

"One day soon, I want you to sit down and think about your parents. Think about what they did right . . . and what they could have done better. Then I want you to think about what would have really made a difference to you."

"I have good parents."

"You do. So does Will. But they weren't perfect, were they?"

"No, of course not."

"So, here's my question. If you didn't need them to be perfect, why are you asking yourself to be that way?"

As usual, Katie's forthright attitude made a lot of sense. "I hear what you're saying," E.A. said. "I just need to love them, right?"

Katie nodded. "That's all they need, E.A. I promise."

"Thanks. I needed to hear that."

"Any time, Elizabeth Anne. Any time at all." When her baby started fussing, she grinned. "I think I'd better take some time to be a good mother right now."

As she wandered off, E.A. stepped up to the table and chose a couple of cookies, making sure that one of her four was a star treat that she'd made with the kids.

"You took one of ours, too," Jemima said.

"I did. I thought they were mighty good."

"Me too." Her eyes lit up. "Do you have a cookie exchange party every year with your friends?"

"This was the first one, but I'm thinking we should have another one next year. What do you think?"

"I think so, too," Jemima said.

Feeling that they'd just crossed another barrier, E.A. smiled down at her. "Let's go get some punch and then sit down near Roy and Will and eat our treats."

"They saved us a spot!"

She laughed. "*Jah*, they surely did. You lead the way and I'll follow."

As Jemima carefully made her way through the crowd of thirty people, her little figure looking so proper and ladylike in her red dress, E.A. felt many of her worries fade away. Some of that was due to Katie's encouragement.

But some of it was simply due to little Jemima. She was acting like a happy nine-year-old for once.

That counted for everything.

Chapter 11

Will didn't often try to compare himself to his father, but that evening, as he drove the buggy back to their house with Roy and Jemima asleep between him and his wife, he knew his father would be looking upon him with approval.

"What are you thinking about so intently?" E.A. asked. "You've got a funny expression on your face."

"Oh, I was just thinking about my *daed*."

"What about him?"

"Well, I have lots of memories of falling asleep next to him when he was driving us home from a long day at church or from supper somewhere. I guess I couldn't help but be glad that here I am, doing the same thing."

"I've been doing a lot of that, too."

"What have you decided?"

"That I like this part of our lives. I like having to look over at you above two children's heads."

He chuckled. "I like that, too."

After directing the horse through a left turn, he smiled at her fondly. "How are you feeling?"

"Good. Tired, too."

"I noticed all the women standing around you when we got there."

"They said I looked like I was much farther along than three months." After darting another look at the *kinner*, she added, "Marie said I looked like I was closer to five months."

"Maybe she was just teasing ya."

She shook her head. "I don't think so, Will. I've read a lot of books about first pregnancies, and lots of them say the only change one might notice at this point is a thickening of the waistline. This is more than that."

Will couldn't argue with her. He'd privately been thinking that she had sure seemed to be looking rather big rather fast. "Why do you think that is?"

"That maybe we got the date wrong and I really am five months along."

He was glad it was dark because he didn't think he would be able to hide his shock. "If that is the case, our baby will be coming sometime in April."

"Jah. Practically around the corner."

April did feel like it would be there before they knew it. First they had Christmas; then it would be time to get Roy and Jemima settled in their new school. And, according to Melanie the social worker, by the end of January they might even have a court date about the adoption.

After months of simply talking about fostering children, now everything was moving at lightning speed.

Hoping he didn't sound as frazzled as he was starting to feel, he said, "We have the sonogram on Monday afternoon. I guess we'll find out then."

"Jah. I guess we will."

Seeing the gas lights flickering by their front door in the distance, he murmured, "We both know that our Lord Jesus doesn't make mistakes. If it's His will that we have our baby in April, then so be it."

E.A. reached out behind the children's sleeping forms and squeezed his biceps. "You are exactly right. There's no reason to worry."

"None at all. We need to think positive, for sure and for certain." He directed Chip, their horse, to the barn.

She laughed as he pulled up the brake on the buggy and hopped down. "Will, it's a good thing we have each other. If we didn't, each of us would be making mountains out of molehills right and left."

Walking around to help her down, he kissed her on the cheek. "You are right about that. It's a *gut* thing we have each other, indeed."

As he pulled Jemima into his arms and E.A. took hold of Roy, Will almost believed that everything was going to be just fine. That the children would adjust to both the baby and them and settle into their lives as if they'd always been there. That the adoption would go through without a hitch and that their baby would soon be born without any complications. That he and E.A. would be able to weather all these changes without getting too stressed or worried or fearful.

That everything in their future was going to be just fine.

But try as he might, he couldn't seem to shake the feeling that things weren't going to be that easy.

He really hoped he was wrong.

Chapter 12

The day before Christmas

Six hours after they left the clinic, the news still shook him to the core. They'd left the doctor in a state of shock, eaten their lunch at Josephine's in almost complete silence, and had to remind each other to look more relaxed and happy when they stopped by his parents' house to pick up the kids.

Jemima and Roy might not have noticed, but Will's mother sure did. She kept giving him worried glances while they were loading the children in the buggy.

Somehow, someway, after they'd gotten home, he and E.A. had gone about their usual routine of having supper, supervising baths, and reading a bedtime story.

Now, at long last, they were sitting together on the couch in front of the fireplace. It was finally the right time to focus on their news—it was just too bad that he still didn't have the right words.

"I don't understand how this could be," Will said for the

third time. "Do you have twins in your family that I didn't know about?"

"*Nee*," E.A. replied, "but that doesn't mean there aren't any." After another moment, she added, "My parents called while you were reading the *kinner* their story. I told them the news."

E.A. had grown up Mennonite. Since they were living as New Order Amish, they now had a phone in the kitchen. They didn't use it much—only for emergencies and special occasions.

Will guessed that their "sonogram day" counted as that.

"What did they say?"

She chuckled softly. "Will, they sounded as shocked as we are. Mamm said she'll come over tomorrow to chat."

"Just be sure Jemima and Roy don't hear you talking about it." When they were alone in the buggy, they'd decided to wait until after Christmas to tell the kids.

"Don't worry. I don't want to share the news until we've gotten our own heads wrapped around it."

"Eventually, I guess we'll have to decide the right way to tell them."

"*Jah*, but 'eventually' is the key word. The poor things are still trying to get used to the idea of my pregnancy." She frowned. "They seem okay, though neither of them seems to want to talk about it." She blinked. "Do you think we should worry about that?"

"Nee. They've accepted it already, E.A. Couples have babies all the time." Sitting beside her, he wrapped an arm around her shoulders. "We're just going to have two babes at once."

"Talk about an instant family. We're going from zero *kinner* to four in less than a year."

"You never did do anything halfway."

"Ha, ha. This is on both of us."

Will looked smug. "This is pretty special, ain't so? We're blessed."

"We *are* blessed." She smiled at him. "Next Christmas is going to be mighty special. We're going to have *kinner* everywhere."

"Two of them will likely be in our arms and the other two running around. The year after? Whoa. It is sure to be mighty busy. The twins will be crawling."

She couldn't believe he was so, so calm about all the changes taking place in their lives. Just as she was about to chide him, she gasped. "Will, where are we going to put everyone?"

He looked at her strangely. "In here with us."

"No, I'm talking about bedrooms. Where are we going to put everyone?"

"We have three bedrooms. We'll take one; the babes will be in another. And Jemima and Roy will have the third."

"That won't do."

"What won't?"

"Jemima and Roy can't share a room, Will. They like having their own rooms. No, they *need* their own rooms. Jemima, especially, needs a place of her own."

"I understand that, but they'll just have to adjust. And they will."

Her mind was spinning. It was already going to be hard on the siblings to have to deal with the new babes. "I think we're gonna need to move."

"Elizabeth Anne, we cannot."

"I know you don't want to, but it might be necessary."

"It isn't. Not right now it isn't."

"Will, lower your voice. They'll hear you."

"I'm sorry, but I don't think you are thinking clearly."

"I'm pregnant with twins, but my brain is working just fine."

"You are one of the smartest people I've ever met. But right now, you aren't sounding smart at all. We can't up and move so easily. We just got here."

They were living on his family's property. Will had saved a long time in order to be able to buy all the materials for their house. That was followed by weeks of him and his friends working on the house, then paying plumbers and other trades-people to finish out their lovely home.

She supposed he did have a point. "All right, fine. Maybe we can simply add another bedroom. And perhaps we can make the kitchen and breakfast room bigger. What do you think?"

"I think that is not going to happen. Not anytime soon."

Oh, but she hated when he got all full of himself! "Will, don't say no without thinking it through."

"I don't need to."

"Please, just think about it."

"I am, and I'm thinking that you'll be home taking care of four children and I'm going to be working to make sure every-one has shoes."

Has shoes? Goodness, but her husband could be dramatic at times! "But—"

"E.A., you're simply going to have to resign yourself to be patient. I know you want to protect Jemima and Roy from harm, but a bigger *haus* isn't what they need," he said in a new, gentle tone of voice. "I promise ya, all those children are going to need is our love and a safe, loving home. We are already giv-ing them that."

His words made sense, but just because they did, it didn't mean that all her worries were going to disappear. "I don't want them to regret moving in with us, Will. I don't want them to think they were getting one thing, but the reality is a whole lot different."

"Ah. Now I understand. So, do you regret meeting Jemima and Roy and bringing them home?"

"No. Of course not." She was shocked that he would even ask such a thing. "I love them."

"I love them, too, E.A. Now, if we already love them and consider them ours, why would you think they would feel different?"

Ooh. She hated it when he was so right. "I see your point."

"Gut. I promise, they took the news about one baby well, and they'll do the same when they hear about two."

"I hope you're right."

"I am. I promise. Life is full of changes and they'll adjust again. Moving around might be hard for them at first, but then it will all be fine. It has to be, right? I mean, they won't have any other choice."

"I hope they won't be too upset."

"If they are, I'll deal with it. Not you. I won't let them worry you. The doctor said that you need to put the babies' needs first. Remember?"

Just as she was about to respond, she heard a squeak. "Will, did you hear that?" she whispered.

He paused, tilting his head, as if he was listening hard. "I didn't hear anything. Now, can we simply just sit here and enjoy the fire and our news?"

She snuggled next to him, folding one of her hands over her belly. She was going to have twins! She was going to be a mother of four.

They were blessed, indeed.

Chapter 13

Jemima closed her eyes and counted to five. Breathed in and out, just as Will had suggested Roy do when he and Jemima had first heard about E.A. expecting a baby.

Since taking a deep breath felt as if it kind of helped, she did it again. It felt a bit silly, but she was willing to do whatever it took to get control of herself.

She had to.

But, boy, was it hard to do, because all the words she'd overheard kept zipping around in her head. *They'll adjust. I won't let them worry you. They won't have any other choice.*

You need to put the babies' needs first.

The babies were what they wanted, not two foster kids who weren't really theirs.

The *babies* were what was important.

They'd been lying to her. Mr. and Mrs. Kurtz were even worse than Dan and Shirl, because they'd only been pretending to want Jemima and Roy. At least Dan and Shirl had never acted like anything was special about them besides the checks that Social Services sent.

Sneaking back down the hall, Jemima swiped her eyes and tried to be glad that she'd wanted a glass of water. If she hadn't gotten thirsty, she would have never eavesdropped and heard what Mr. Kurtz had said about them.

He was sure she and her brother were going to adjust just fine the day after Christmas when they told her and Roy the news.

Her lungs felt heavy, and she didn't think she was ever going to be able to take a deep breath again. Standing outside Roy's room, she debated about whether to tell him the news or not.

Though it was going to be terrible to tell him, she knew she had no choice. There was no way she was going to be able to watch him be happy on Christmas morning when she knew what was going to happen on December 26. That was just too mean.

Slowly she opened his door and walked inside. Roy had a battery-operated night-light in the shape of a dog near his bed. It was a silly thing, but he loved it and it helped him get to sleep every night. As she watched him sleep, Jemima's heart felt as if it was breaking as she realized just how many things were about to change. Just like the other homes, they were going to have to leave their special belongings behind when the social worker came.

Once again, they'd be in someone else's hands, and be expected to get along, not complain, and pretend that starting all over again wasn't terrible.

But it really was.

Roy shifted in his sleep, opened his eyes, then flinched when he noticed her standing next to his bed.

"Jemima, whatcha doing?" he asked, both his expression and voice groggy with sleep.

"I just overhead Mr. and Mrs. Kurtz talking, but I've been standing here trying to figure out if I should tell you or not."

Rubbing his eyes, he sat up. "Why wouldn't you tell me?"

"Because it's not good news."

He frowned. "Am I not gonna get a new coat for Christmas?"

She sat down on his bed. "I don't know if you are or you aren't." She took a breath, then continued. "I heard them talking about what they are going to do the day after Christmas."

He smiled. "What?"

Jemima bit her lip. She didn't know whether to spoil his night or not. All she did know was that she didn't think she could keep the news to herself for the next day. She really didn't think she could face Roy when he discovered that she'd been keeping secrets from him.

"Roy, I don't want to tell you this, but I don't think it would be right to keep it from you."

"I'm not a baby. We do everything together, *jah*?"

He was right. "Fine." After peeking at the door again to make sure it was closed, she said, "I learned that E.A. is going to have twins."

Roy's eyes lit up. "Wow! We're going to have two babies around here. It's gonna be loud."

"You're missing the point, Roy. I heard them talk about our future."

"So?"

"They don't have a big enough house for four *kinner*." She looked at him meaningfully.

Her brother screwed up his face. "What are we all going to do then?" He sucked in a breath. "Do you think we're going to have to share a room with babies?"

"They're not talking about moving us around. They're talking about making room for two babies."

"What does that mean for us, then?"

"What do you think, Roy? They're going to send us away."

He shook his head. "Nee. They love us."

"They love the babies they're gonna have. They don't love us."

"Nee." His crushed expression matched how crushed she felt in her heart. "That's not right."

"Roy, I know what I heard."

He kept shaking his head. "Nee. You must have heard wrong. They wouldn't do that."

"But they are." She hated how tough she sounded; she hated that she had to be the one to tell Roy the bad news. But she had learned that it didn't make any difference how a person heard bad things. Even hearing it in a nice way didn't make it any easier.

"What are we going to do?"

"I don't want to go back to Dan and Shirl."

His bottom lip trembled. "We might go back there?"

She nodded. "They have to send us somewhere."

"But I didn't like them," Roy blurted. "They were mean."

Her brother was right. They were mean. *Really* mean. "I . . . I was thinking of running away."

"Really? We can do that?"

"I know it's scary, but maybe we could find someplace better than Dan and Shirl's house. I don't want Melanie to make us go back there right after Christmas."

He swallowed hard. "I don't want to be there ever again."

"So, it's decided?"

Roy gazed at her, suddenly looking much older. "Jah."

"Jah? Are you sure?"

"I'm sure. I'll get dressed and meet you down in the kitchen in a couple of minutes."

"Okay, but remember, it's snowy out, so we have to wear warm clothes. Lots of warm clothes."

"I'll put on the new socks E.A. knitted for me."

She noticed him looking around his room. "Don't forget, we can't take much. You can't take all your toys."

"I'm only gonna take a couple of the animals and two of the train cars."

"Put them in a pillowcase."

"Okay."

Even though he looked confused, she slipped out of Roy's room and padded down the hall. She needed to get dressed in warm clothes and gather her things, too.

They were really going to do it. They were going to run away.

Though her eyes stung, she refused to cry. Crying wouldn't do her any good.

Besides, she didn't think God cared if she cried or not.

For some reason, He had decided to stop looking out for them.

It was up to her and Roy from now on.

Chapter 14

After they made their plans, E.A. had wished Will pleasant dreams, and then gone straight up to bed.

The fire was still burning, the snow was falling outside, and Will's heart was full. Far too full to go to sleep.

He had also felt a need to give thanks. Just a few years ago, he'd been living with his family, going through the motions at his job, drifting through life. He'd felt as if something was missing, but he couldn't pinpoint exactly what had been lacking. Then Andy had taken his own life and everything had changed. That loss had made him start counting his blessings and looking around to decide what he needed—no, what he wanted—in his life.

He'd never so keenly felt the Lord at work in his life. One by one, the Lord had helped him establish his goals at work, deepen his friendships, strengthen the bonds with his family, and changed everything between him and E.A.

Now here he was, with two children snug in their beds and two tiny babes on the way. He was so blessed.

He got on his knees and stared at the dying embers in the

fireplace as he poured out his heart. "Danke, Got," he prayed quietly. "Here on Your son's birthday, I feel as if I have been given all the gifts. I praise You and give thanks."

Feeling His pleasure with the words, Will closed his eyes and continued his prayers, offering thanks for his friends and family, for the blessings of Christmas.

"Careful!" he heard Jemima whisper.

Startled, Will popped open his eyes. What in the world was she doing?

He heard the children scramble some more. It was obvious that they were now downstairs, but for what reason, he couldn't begin to guess.

Growing concerned, he got to his feet.

Then, just as Will was about to join them, the children spoke again.

"I'm scared," Roy said.

"I know, but we'll be okay."

"I wish I had the new coat that E.A. said I might get on Christmas morning. It's cold out."

"Your old coat will have to do."

"I know, but—"

"Roy, I've got on my old coat, too," Jemima said, sounding weary. "Stop complaining."

"I will. But can we get a snack before we leave? I don't want to be hungry."

Leave? Will felt his heart start beating double time.

He stood quietly, listening to them talk to each other, curious as to why they were leaving and, truth be told, curious about what they were deciding to take with them.

When he heard Roy struggle to open the jar of peanut butter, Will had heard enough.

"Those jars can be tricky to open. Do you need a hand?"

The jar fell to the floor.

"Will!" Roy exclaimed. "What are you doing here?"

"I think we all know that I need to be asking you a more important question. What are *you* doing?" Will turned toward Jemima, who was standing by the refrigerator with a stunned expression on her face. "Jemima, do you want to help me out here?"

She exchanged a panicked glance with her brother before shaking her head no.

"No?" Will couldn't believe it. "Come now. Are you two making a snack or something different?" He pointedly looked at their clothes and the shoes on their feet.

"Something different," Roy said at last.

This was one of those moments when Will felt every negative part of being a foster parent. He didn't have a lot of experience parenting, so he had no idea what to do or say.

He sure wished he did, though. It would be nice to know if he was supposed to be listening patiently or just pointing to the stairs and sending them back to bed.

Then he considered these children's history. He and E.A. were fairly certain that Roy and Jemima had had a nice life with their natural parents, but the children would hardly talk about them. Will did know that they hadn't had it easy since their parents' deaths.

Melanie the social worker had told him and E.A. that the last foster family had been particularly rough. That there might be triggers or something else that could hurt the kids that he wasn't aware of.

Finally, he wasn't used to parenting on his own. He'd found comfort in the fact that no matter how awkward he might find being a father, his wife was right next to him and she could help make things better.

But E.A. was exhausted and he knew she needed her sleep.

He was on his own.

"If you two are hungry, finish making your snacks and then come to the kitchen table. We're gonna have a talk."

Jemima hesitated. "But it's almost midnight."

"It is. It is almost Christmas morning. But that doesn't mean we're not going to talk about something so important."

"How do you know it's important?"

"Why else would you two be up and dressed in the middle of the night?"

He watched them exchange glances again. Remembering something his father used to do, he crossed his arms over his chest and stood silently. When he was but a boy, that kind of thing used to make him feel extremely uneasy.

And . . . it worked like a charm. With deliberate moves, both children finished making their sandwiches, then put them on plates and approached the table.

He walked to the refrigerator, poured three glasses of milk, and joined them.

After he sat down and took a fortifying sip, he said, "Who wants to tell me what is going on?"

"Not me," Roy mumbled as he took a big bite of his sandwich.

"And why is that?"

Suddenly looking stricken, Roy froze. "I don't know."

"You don't . . . truly?"

"It's my fault," Jemima blurted. "I told him about your secret."

"What secret is that?"

"The secret about how you and Mrs. Kurtz are going to be having twins."

"How did you hear that?"

"I was standing outside the living room and heard you two talking."

"Were you eavesdropping on purpose?"

"No. I was going to ask you something. I mean, was gonna ask Mrs. Kurtz. But then you two sounded so serious, I didn't think I should interrupt."

"And then?"

Sounding defeated, she answered, "And then I heard what you said."

"Help me understand what I said that made you so upset. What did I say that was so bad that it made you both want to leave?" When they both remained silent, Will took a stab in the dark. "Is it the twins? Is that it? Do you two really not like babies?"

Roy's eyes got as big as saucers. "Nee!"

"What is it then? I'm not a mind reader."

"I heard how you were going to change things. How you and Mrs. Kurtz were going to move us the day after Christmas."

"Maybe not that soon, but yes."

"But I don't want to do that!" Roy blurted as he started crying.

Will could hear E.A. walking down the stairs. No doubt their children's commotion had woken her up. He knew he should probably be upset with himself, but he was secretly glad.

"I know you like your room, Roy, but your next one will be all right."

"I like my night-light."

"I do, too," Will said patiently. "Roy, I'm not going to take it away from you. You can put it in your next room right beside your bed."

"But what if they won't let me have it?"

Will stared at Roy. "They?"

"Who are you speaking of?" E.A. asked as she joined them.

"The new people," Jemima said.

E.A. sent a puzzled look Will's way. "Honey, what new people?"

"The people you're gonna make us go to."

"You're going to make us leave and we won't have our things and the next people might be mean," Roy said—seconds before he burst into loud, messy tears.

Opening her arms, E.A. pulled him onto her lap. The six-year-old threw his arms around her, buried his face in her neck, and then cried even harder.

It broke Will's heart.

"I came late to this conversation, but I have to admit to being really confused," E.A. said. "Where are you two going?"

"To the next people. I heard you say you were going to send us away."

Will shook his head. "We aren't taking you anywhere."

"I heard you!" Jemima cried. "You said that we would adjust to our new place!"

"Did you hear the rest of the conversation?" E.A. asked. When Jemima shook her head, she added, "If you had, you would have heard the part about how the babies are going to need their own room. You would have heard how worried I was about making the two of you share a room again until we can afford to add another bedroom in the house."

"That's what you were talking about?"

"To be sure, Jemima," Will said. "I know you don't know us well yet, but I hope you will start learning to trust us. If we only wanted you to live with us until Christmas Day, we would have made that plain from the beginning."

"You want us forever?" Roy asked.

E.A. opened her arms. "Oh, *jah*, Roy. We want you and Jemima for a long time. Forever and forever."

Chapter 15

Thirty minutes later, with her arms firmly around little Roy, E.A. looked over at Jemima. Sitting across from them in her dress and cloak, she looked as serious as ever.

And, E.A. thought, twice as sad.

"What's wrong, Jemima?" E.A. asked softly.

"I feel embarrassed because I misunderstood everything. I'm sorry that I made everyone get up out of bed in the middle of the night."

"Hey now. Don't start making things worse than they are. I was awake already, remember?" Will asked.

"I remember."

"That takes care of that. Now, let's talk about something else."

"What?"

"Do you think it's possible for you to begin to trust us?"

"Jah."

"Are you sure?"

"Well, I want to trust you both." Her voice drifted off.

"But you've learned to protect yourself, haven't you?" E.A. said gently.

"Jah. Not everything I want to happen does."

"Nothing happens like that for anyone," Will said. "Trust and faith are a lot alike. Both mean believing in something without knowing for sure about the facts. And you can set yourself up for disappointment."

"But think about Mary when the angels and the Lord told her that her baby was special. Or when the Wise Men were encouraged to ride a great distance to see the future King. Or all the times since when miracles have happened and blessings have occurred to people who might not even have deserved them."

"You're talking about Christmas Day," Roy said.

"I am. Faith is hard. Learning to trust after one has been betrayed before is hard, too. But that doesn't mean it's not worth it."

Will studied them for a long moment before standing up. "I'll be right back," he said before disappearing down the hall.

Jemima looked at E.A. "Is he upset?"

"Nee. Will doesn't get upset about much. And especially not about things like this." Already having a pretty good idea about what her husband was doing, E.A. folded her hands neatly on the table. "I guess we'll just have to sit tight until he returns."

When Will came back, he was holding a manila folder filled with papers. "I guess I should have been listening to my own advice about having faith and trust," he said in a quiet tone. "E.A. and I have been filling out this paperwork and have been in close contact with Melanie and the lawyers, but it all takes time."

"Will, tell them what you're holding," E.A. prompted.

"Oh. Of course." He set the papers on the table. "This is the adoption paperwork we've been working on." Opening up the packet, he flipped through the papers until he came to E.A.'s favorite piece. "Look at this, you two. What do you see?"

Jemima and Roy got on their feet and studied the official-looking document. After one or two seconds, Jemima's eyes widened. "There's our names."

E.A. smiled. "That's right," she agreed, running a finger along their printed names. "Here are Jemima Mary Clark and Roland Irwin Clark."

Roy giggled. "No one calls me Roland Irwin."

"I think it's a mighty fine name, but perhaps it's a mighty grown-up name."

"I'm just a boy now."

"You are just a boy, but you're also a mighty special boy. Just like Jemima Mary here is a mighty special girl."

Jemima straightened her shoulders. "I'm named after Mary in the Bible."

"You are?" Will teased.

Jemima nodded her head fervently.

"I think that means we're supposed to open Christmas presents then."

"Right now? But it's the middle of the night."

"It surely is, but since it's now one in the morning, it actually is Christmas. And those presents do look awfully tempting. Don't you think we should see what's inside?"

Roy kept staring at him until he looked to where Will was gesturing. Then his expression was so comical, E.A. couldn't help but giggle. "I fear you have rendered our Roy speechless, Will."

"That feels like a Christmas gift in itself. Two minutes of quiet." He winked so the children would have no doubt that he was teasing, then held out a hand. "Well, let's go open presents."

But instead of taking his hand, Jemima bit her bottom lip. "We don't have anything for you."

E.A. knelt down so she could look the little girl in the eye. "That's where you're wrong. You have already given us our presents. You came into our lives, and you want to be with us forever and ever. That's more of a gift than I ever could have expected."

"Really? Do you think that's enough?"

She pressed her palm to her heart. "Here, I feel that it is enough. But if you don't believe me, then trust in His word, for it says in Psalm 127, 'Children are a gift from the Lord; they are a reward from him.'" E.A. paused until Jemima met her gaze. "Do you understand what that means, sweetheart? He doesn't say 'only the children you gave birth to are special.' He says that all children are a gift."

"He says I'm special no matter what."

"Yes, He does. You're special, no matter what, and so is Roy." Reaching for her hand, E.A. continued. "Jemima, I know you miss your parents. I know your heart aches for them and it isn't fair that they had to leave you when you are so small. They sound like wonderful people. I know they loved you and didn't want to leave you. But I can't help but think that God knew that Will and I would take care of you both, too. And that we would love you for the rest of our lives."

"Do you think it would be okay with them if Roy and I love you, too, one day?"

"Jah," she whispered, swallowing the lump that had just formed in her throat. "I think it would be just fine with them."

Jemima's eyes widened. "Are you sure?"

E.A. nodded. "I'm as sure about that as I'm sure that the sun is going to come up tomorrow . . . if we ever get back in our beds and go to sleep."

Jemima yawned. "Maybe we could open presents in the morning after all? I am kind of tired."

After reassuring Roy that they would open gifts in the morning, E.A. walked Jemima to her bed and tucked her in. "Merry Christmas, Jemima. Good night."

"Night, E.A.," she whispered, calling her by name for the very first time.

E.A. barely made it to the privacy of her bedroom before she let the tears fall. She'd just received a gift more precious than gold.

Chapter 16

Christmas Day, one year later

The house was in complete chaos, and the fact that it was Christmas Day had nothing to do with it.

Sitting on her bed with her brand-new book in her lap, Jemima Kurtz wished for nothing more than one whole hour of peace and quiet. Unfortunately, it didn't look as if this wish was going to come true anytime soon.

First, Roy had come into her room and hadn't wanted to leave. Now baby Christopher was crying in his crib down the hall. Yet again.

"I wonder what's going on now?" Roy asked.

"We'd better go check," Jemima said, leading the way to the twins' room.

"Mamm, Chris is crying again!" Roy yelled as they went.

"I can hear him!" their mother yelled back. "Go pick him up, Roy."

Roy did just that, but he wrinkled his nose. "Mamm, I think

his diaper is dirty!" he said as Chris wriggled and cried even louder.

"We both know what the answer to that is, Roy!" Daed called from down the hall. "Do it now, if you please."

Roy groaned. "Do you want to change him?" he asked Jemima hopefully.

"I do not."

"Come on. Please?"

"Nee. You change the babies' diapers less than anyone else in the house."

"Fine." He turned and walked to the changing table as if he was walking the plank. "Come on, Chris. Let's get it over with. But, Jem, stay here, wouldja?"

She knew better than to do that. If she was in "helping" distance, Roy would have her taking care of Chris in less than two seconds flat.

Instead, she darted out of the twins' room and headed downstairs. Even from the dining room, she could still hear Roy complain upstairs about Chris's stinky diaper. Thinking that her *bruder* was acting a bit like a baby himself, she started setting the table with all the plates and silverware that E.A. had put out.

In the kitchen, Elizabeth Anne was basting the turkey. "You sure got down here fast, Jem," she teased.

"I just realized that I promised you I'd set the table."

"Hmm."

Realizing she was caught in her fib, Jemima put down the last fork and joined her by the stove. Little Merry was resting in a bouncy seat on the kitchen table, no doubt watching every move E.A. made with wide eyes.

Honestly, Jemima couldn't believe how different two twins could be. While Chris was curious, loud, and demanding, Merry was quiet, attentive, and usually content. She always seemed happiest when one of them placed her in a spot where she could easily observe everything around her.

The twins were even different at night. Then they switched places. The moment either Mamm or Daed set Chris in his crib, he went to sleep—as if he was exhausted from his busy day.

Merry, on the other hand, became not very merry at all once she was in her crib. She fussed and whined whenever she was put down for the night. She liked to be in the midst of things and always acted as if they were hurting her feelings when it was bedtime.

Mamm looked up from the saucepan she was stirring on the stove. "Roy couldn't talk his way out of that diaper change, hmm?"

"Not this time. I told him that he didn't change enough diapers around here and then hurried downstairs before he could pester me even more."

"Jemima, you are sounding a bit harsh, don't you think?"

"Maybe." When E.A. raised her eyebrows, she sighed. "Okay, probably. But, honestly, I wasn't as harsh as I could've been. Roy would pass on the babies every time one of them cried if I let him."

E.A. laughed. "I suppose you might have a point, though there have been times when I wouldn't mind passing on a baby for a few minutes myself. Taking care of two seven-month-olds can be exhausting, ain't so? Sometimes even Will and me yearn for a tiny break."

Jemima walked over to Merry and kissed her forehead. "Our twins *are* draining, but they are worth it. They're adorable."

Merry responded by kicking out her feet and smiling.

After playing with her tiny sock-covered feet for a minute, Jemima sat down at the table.

Then she noticed that E.A. was smiling at her. "Uh-oh. What did I do that was funny?"

"Not a thing. I was thinking how you are pretty wonderful, too. Both you and Roy are." E.A. washed her hands and then moved next to Jemima. "When I think of all the changes you *kinner* have gone through, it boggles my mind. I'm proud of you."

Jemima knew what her adoptive mother was thinking about. They all really had been through a lot in the last year.

A few weeks after Christmas, Melanie had come to the house and escorted them to a judge's office. There he'd interviewed both Jemima and Roy separately and talked about adoption with them.

Roy never would tell E.A. what he told the judge, but Jemima had started crying when she told the man in the black robe about Dan and Shirl. He'd been so kind and patient, she had started talking a lot. A whole lot.

Before she realized it, she'd told him about how different things were with Mr. and Mrs. Kurtz. She'd even shared how she sometimes woke up in the middle of the night afraid that she would be back with one of her former foster families.

The judge had listened intently, asked a couple of simple questions, and then walked her to his chambers door with a kind smile and pat on the head. Jemima hadn't been sure what to think of that, but she took it to be a good sign.

One month after that, she, Roy, Melanie, and Mr. and Mrs. Kurtz had gone to the courthouse together. They'd all held hands while the judge talked a lot. Then, when he called them a real family, Jemima had burst into tears. That had been okay, though, because E.A., Will, and Roy had cried, too.

E.A. sat down next to her. "Uh-oh, did I say something wrong?"

"Hmm? Oh, no. Not at all. I was just thinking how different this year is from last Christmas."

"Last Christmas was certainly more exciting, I'll give it that." E.A. paused, then added, "But for all the excitement and uncertainty, I don't think I'd trade the memory for anything. It was a special time in all of our lives."

Jemima thought the same thing. It had been a hard Christmas, but it had been a good one, too. The season had encouraged her to finally break out of her shell and reveal her pain. Only then had she been able to start trusting again.

"Hey, E.A.?"

"Hmm?"

"I'm really glad I met you and Will. I'm glad you're my *mamm* now."

Reaching out, E.A. folded Jemima's hand in between both of hers. "I'm glad, too."

"I'm coming downstairs with Chris and his stinky diaper!" Roy called out. "You've been warned."

"I think I'll meet our boys in the entryway." As E.A. stood up she grinned at Jemima.

When E.A. was gone, Jemima looked at Merry, whose eyes were closed, smelled the turkey roasting in the oven, and heard E.A. walk Roy outside to the garbage cans.

Felt the warmth of the room.

And gave thanks. Thanks for everything.

New Beginnings

RACHEL J. GOOD

To all those who provide housing and care for teen mothers and for adoptive parents everywhere

Chapter 1

"Jingle bells, jingle bells," the shop owner sang at the top of her lungs as Elizabeth Yoder leaned against the door of Yolanda's Christmas Year Round Shop to push it open.

Speakers around her blasted, "Jingle all the way," and the string of sleigh bells on the knob jangled along. Cinnamon potpourri simmered in a pot near the register, and the aroma of pine garlands perfumed the air.

"Wait, let me get that for you." Yolanda dashed over. She yanked the second glass door wide enough so Elizabeth could maneuver through the opening with a large box.

"This was outside the door." Swirling snow flurries trailed Elizabeth into the store.

"Merry Christmas," Yolanda trilled. With her Santa hat tilted at a rakish angle and her round face and red cheeks, she resembled the Santa figurines scattered around the store.

Fake Christmas trees adorned every corner, their lights blinking. They pulsed off and on the way Elizabeth's head did from the loud Christmas carols. A tight band inside her temples tightened and throbbed, and her eyes stung. The closer the calendar inched to December 25, the harder it became to feign Christmas cheer.

"I'm so glad you're here early." Yolanda bounced back to the cash register. "In addition to that box, we have several new shipments and more coming later. You're going to love our new manger sets."

Yolanda's enthusiasm should have been contagious. Elizabeth did prefer the nativity scenes to all the Santa kitsch, but anything Christmas related reminded her of all she'd lost.

"Can you unpack that box and the others in the stockroom? You'll need to price the items. I have all the costs listed on the clipboard," Yolanda called. "I'll let you know if I get too busy out here."

Elizabeth set the box in the back room, hung her coat on a peg, and smoothed her black dress and apron. Then she grabbed the box cutter and slit open the carton she'd carried in. Pure white tree ornaments sparkling with glitter nestled in layers of cardboard dividers. She carried the box and a price gun to one of the undecorated fake evergreens.

After each methodical click of the gun, she dangled another ornament from an empty branch. She stood back, searching for bare spots, and squinted to be sure she'd dotted the decorations artistically around the tree. Then she lifted the packing cardboard, exposing the final layer of ornaments.

A tiny house, a reindeer, a sleigh, an angel. She reached into the box for one of the last three ornaments and pulled out . . . a sleeping baby.

Neh. Squeezing her eyes shut, she traced the indented lines of the miniature toes and fingers, the rounded bottom sticking up in the air, the soft curve of the back, the curls on the baby's head. Elizabeth stopped before she stroked the tiny eyelashes spread on the cheek.

Why did this time of year have to be so cruel?

* * *

Luke Bontrager whistled as he tied his buggy outside the Christmas Year Round Shop. He'd promised Yolanda he'd drop off these nativity sets before she opened today. He'd hoped to get here sooner, but patches of black ice made the roads treacherous. Grateful for his horse's steadiness, he'd skirted two fender benders, whose owners chattered on—or screamed into—their cell phones.

Grateful he'd made it safely, he secured his horse to the hitching post. He lifted the first box from the front seat and strode toward the door. His boots slid in the light dusting of snow on the sidewalk. He caught himself before he and the nativity set ended up on the pavement. Yolanda needed to clear that icy spot before they opened. Maybe he could do it for her before he headed down the street to his woodworking shop.

He tapped at the door with a corner of the heavy box. Yolanda stood at the cash register, singing her heart out.

The words penetrated the glass. "Hark! The herald angels sing . . ."

Nice to see someone so joyous on this overcast day. She caught sight of him through the glass and hurried over to open the door. He stomped his boots on the large green mat before stepping onto the polished wooden floors.

"I brought the nativity sets you requested. Where would you like me to put them?"

"If you take them back to the stockroom"—Yolanda waved vaguely toward the back of the store—"Elizabeth can price them."

Elizabeth. Luke's pulse picked up its pace. He'd hoped she'd be working. In fact, during his whole trip to town, he'd daydreamed about seeing her.

Despite his eagerness to spend time with her, his steps slowed when he reached the stockroom entrance. The door had been propped open with a box. He edged around it, but Elizabeth's bowed head arrested his attention. His heart went out to her. The Christmas season had to be painful.

Her eyes were closed as her fingers smoothed over all the curves and crevices of a small ornament.

Luke didn't want to startle her, but he needed to get to work. He stepped back from the doorway as silently as he could and retreated partway down the hall. Then he clomped toward the stockroom door, making sure each footfall resounded.

This time, when he got to the threshold, Elizabeth was staring in his direction. Her eyes sparkled with tears. She reminded him of an angel, one who had borne a heavy weight of sorrow.

"Luke?"

Her voice, soft and breathy, grabbed him in the gut and twisted his insides hard. All the old pain of desiring her from afar but watching her marry someone else came flooding back.

"What are you doing here?"

"I've brought the nativity sets Yolanda ordered." He carried the carton over to the workbench. "Where do you want me to put them? I have five more sets in the buggy."

His heart thundered as she moved closer. She stopped a moment, and sadness shuttered her eyes. Luke wished he could comfort her.

She gazed down at the glittering ornament she'd clutched so tightly in her hand that it left red ridges. The one she'd been caressing when he'd peeked in the door. Something about it must have touched her.

"Let me just move this box." Elizabeth motioned to the carton beside her with one hand. "Then you can put your nativity set here."

She nestled the ornament back in the box with such tenderness, Luke's chest contracted. Curious to see what she'd lavished so much care on, he leaned over. A tiny glittery baby.

She lifted the almost-empty cardboard box to make room for his carton.

Luke cast about for something to say. Something to distract his mind from thoughts of holding her. "That tree looks nice."

"*Danke*," she said without much enthusiasm. "Once all the ornaments are on, I'll have to carry it out to the store. I'm not sure where we'll find room for one more tree. We have so many already."

"Maybe you won't have room for another nativity set either."

"*Neh*, that's not a problem. Yolanda told me to clear a space for it." She attempted a smile. "Besides, it'll be great to move some Santa stuff to make a place for the real meaning of Christmas."

"True. I'm guessing many of your customers don't even know or care that we're celebrating the Savior's birth."

Elizabeth didn't answer. Instead, she stared into the box, her eyes open with wonder. She reached in and pulled out Mary.

Luke loved how Elizabeth's face glowed as she studied the carving.

She set the figure down and pulled out a camel and a wise man. "These are beautiful. I love the roughness of the wood."

She ran her hands over what Yolanda had assured Luke was a primitive style sure to attract the eyes of some of their upscale customers. It seemed his work also appealed to Elizabeth.

"They're rugged, yet each one captures real emotion. Did someone in your shop carve them?" She glanced up at him expectantly.

Luke shuffled his feet. "*Jah*. I did."

He didn't like taking credit for this work. He sold cabinets and furniture in his shop, but he'd always kept this other talent hidden.

He'd started carving to alleviate his sorrow when his best friend, Owen, started courting Elizabeth. The roughness, the primitiveness, of each figure Luke had chiseled revealed his raw emotions.

If Yolanda hadn't surprised him in the back of his shop last spring, none of his carvings would ever have been public. She'd begged him to make nativity sets for her store. Luke had demurred, but she'd insisted. To be honest, the only reason he'd agreed was because he might see Elizabeth when he delivered them.

She pulled out an angel and drew in a long, slow breath. "I never knew you did this. How long have you been carving?"

Since I lost you. Luke stopped himself from blurting out that answer, the first one that sprang to his lips. He waved a hand, trying to be vague. "Since we were teenagers."

Her eyes widened. "And you kept it a secret?"

He shrugged. He certainly couldn't tell her the truth. "They were so rough I didn't think they were good enough to sell." Even if he had believed they were, he'd never have wanted to put his deepest feelings on display.

"Did Owen know?"

Luke tried not to wince when she said his best friend's name. Owen would have been the last person Luke could have shown his work to. Owen had been the cause of Luke's carving frenzy.

Elizabeth was staring at him, waiting for an answer.

"*Neh*, Owen never knew." Not about the carving. And definitely not about the love—and jealousy—in Luke's heart.

"Oh." She breathed out the word reverently as she pulled out a shepherd. "You should have been selling these all along." Her fingers traced the contours of the tiny lamb in the man's arms. "This—this baby is so precious. And the shepherd looks so tender, so protective."

Exactly what Luke wished he could do for Elizabeth. Protect her from grief, from loss. "I, um, originally carved that to represent Jesus and the lost sheep, but Yolanda wanted me to include it in the nativity."

"It's perfect." Elizabeth sounded as if she was holding back tears.

He hadn't meant to increase her sadness, especially not so close to Christmas.

In silence, she unpacked every figure, exclaiming over each one. In the shop, the bells jangled and jangled. Business must be brisk this morning. Luke should be opening his own shop soon.

"Elizabeth," Yolanda called. "I need help."

That was Luke's cue to leave. "I need to go, but where should I put the other boxes?"

"We'll put out only one sample set, so could you put them over there?" She indicated a set of empty shelves in the back corner.

"Sure." He let her precede him out of the stockroom and followed her into the shop. "I'll bring in the rest," he told Yolanda. "But first, do you have any salt? I could sprinkle some on the ice out there."

Yolanda, who was ringing up the first customer in a long line, glanced up at him with gratitude in her eyes. "I meant to do that earlier, but I forgot. You'd be a godsend."

She gestured toward the back hallway. "Just before you reach the stockroom door, there's a small broom closet. Salt's in there next to the cleaning supplies."

Taking care of Yolanda's front walk would make Luke late opening his woodworking shop, but he couldn't leave the ice. If someone slipped when he could have prevented it, he'd never forgive himself.

He found the salt and a shovel, and headed out the door. After scraping the newly fallen layer of snow from the front sidewalk, he chopped the ice and tossed salt to prevent the dampness from freezing.

Once he finished, he carried in his other cartons, his heart lightening each time he went by Elizabeth at the cash register.

As he passed the glittery ornaments in the stockroom, he couldn't resist picking up the tiny baby. He cupped it in his palm, envisioning Elizabeth's fingers stroking it, her reluctance to release it. What had drawn her to this sleeping child?

She'd shown a similar delight in his carvings. Something had touched her about this baby and about his nativity figures.

Luke shook his head and replaced the tiny tree decoration in its box. He had to hurry in case he had customers waiting. After one quick glance at Elizabeth, who was too busy working to notice his exit, he strode down the street to his store. But all morning, his thoughts stayed behind in Yolanda's shop. He pictured Elizabeth's fingers running over his figures whose every line had been gouged out to assuage his loss of her. Had she sensed the emotions he'd carved into each one—his longing and his heartbreak?

Chapter 2

The shop's Christmas specials drew in crowds all morning. Elizabeth and Yolanda rang up sale after sale for the first three hours.

"Whew!" Yolanda wiped her damp forehead with the back of her hand. "Good thing I didn't set up any hourly specials over lunchtime."

"Your idea brought in a lot of business." If they stayed this busy until Christmas, Elizabeth might escape some of the memories flooding over her, threatening to drown her.

Yolanda beamed. "Most stores do hourly specials on Black Friday and Christmas Eve, but I wasn't sure it would work more than two weeks before Christmas. Evidently, it does."

The next special didn't start until two, so Elizabeth returned to the stockroom to finish pricing items. After she found a corner in Yolanda's shop for the newly decorated Christmas tree, she carried out Luke's carvings.

"These are so beautiful, maybe we should put them in the window," she suggested.

"Great idea!" Yolanda waved a hand at the largest display window. "Feel free to move whatever you'd like."

Elizabeth tucked the ceramic North Pole village into the shelf space she'd cleared for the nativity. That left a large space in the center of the cotton batting Yolanda had spread to simulate a cushion of snow for the window display. The perfect spot for Luke's portrayal of the real meaning of Christmas.

She cradled each figure carefully and set up the nativity set during brief breaks between customers. When she stepped outside to review her almost-completed display, her heart quickened. The figures' faces held so much longing. The expressions combined spiritual and human hunger. Exactly how Elizabeth imagined each of them would have yearned for Christ.

Only one more piece to place. Shivering from more than the cold, she headed back inside to place the last carving, the hardest one for her to touch and hold.

Reverently, she cradled baby Jesus in her hands. Tears gathered in her eyes not only for her own pain but also for what He had borne for her.

Elizabeth knelt and placed Him in the manger.

Behind her, a customer breathed out a sigh. "*Ooo.* Those are exquisite. How much is the set?"

"They are stunning, aren't they?" Elizabeth quoted the price she'd read on Yolanda's clipboard. Although it was expensive, the craftmanship made it worth every penny.

If it hadn't been so far out of her price range, Elizabeth might have been tempted to buy a set for herself. Even with her employee discount, the cost remained well out of reach.

The woman sucked in a sharp breath. "Wow." She deliberated a moment. "I'll trim down what I planned to spend on some other Christmas gifts. I can't pass this up."

"I have this set already packed in a box. I can get one from our stockroom." At the customer's nod, Elizabeth headed to the back.

As she passed the counter, Yolanda stopped her. "You never stop working. I want you to take a break. I'll take care of it." Her boss headed over and handed her a twenty. "Why don't you get us both some lunch?"

Ever since Elizabeth had started working here, Yolanda had acted like a mother hen, making sure Elizabeth ate, took breaks, and rested. Between her boss and her family, Elizabeth had plenty of people who cared about her and wanted to see her heal. Although she appreciated all they did for her, nothing could fill the hole in her heart and life.

Customers streamed in and out of Luke's woodworking shop to pick up custom Christmas gifts they'd ordered or to ensure their kitchen renovations would be completed before their holiday parties, but he struggled to focus on them. Good thing he didn't have to measure or cut anything this morning.

Starting the day by being around Elizabeth had thrown off his usual precision and attention to detail. Images of her had floated into his mind all morning. Just then he glanced up to see her walking by his shop window.

After she passed, he closed his eyes and took a deep breath.

"You okay?" one of his *Englisch* employees asked as he carried a wooden rocker to a truck outside the door.

"I'm fine," Luke tried to assure himself as well as Alan. But the words didn't ring true.

Luke had never been all right. Not since the day his best friend, Owen, asked Elizabeth to ride home in his buggy.

Over the past four years, Luke's pain had only increased, especially after Owen had married Elizabeth. Luke's heartache had worsened this past year.

"You want to go for lunch?" Alan asked. "Martin and I can mind the store."

Elizabeth might have gone to the small café in the next block.

Luke didn't want her to think he was stalking her. But if he left now, he'd probably run into her.

"*Danke.* I'll take first lunch break, if you don't mind." Luke usually waited until last, but the chance to see Elizabeth proved too much of a temptation. He hurried back for his coat.

Alan's curious look made Luke uncomfortable. He could only imagine how Alan would react if he suspected his boss intended to be a stalker. Or as Alan would call him—a creeper.

Luke pushed the thought from his mind and hurried out the door. If Elizabeth ordered takeout, he didn't have much time. He headed for the café but stopped suddenly when she emerged from the bakery across the street with a small box.

"Hey, Luke," she called, checking both ways for traffic.

She was coming to him. Struggling to breathe, he waited.

"I just wanted to tell you, we already sold one of your nativities."

"*Danke* for letting me know."

"You're welcome. They're so beautiful I convinced Yolanda to give them the best display spot in the store." She blew on her mittened fingers.

Luke wished he could hold her hands between his to warm them. He pushed aside his fantasies. "You need to get out of the cold." Although it would disappoint him to see her leave.

Elizabeth nodded. "I'm headed into the café to order lunch."

Luke realized he'd been blocking the door. "Sorry." He pulled open the door for her. "I'd been planning to come in here myself." *If I found you in here.*

"I'm getting takeout for Yolanda and me." Elizabeth got in line, and Luke followed her.

He'd get something to go too. That way he could talk to her as they waited.

"I thought maybe that was your lunch." Luke nodded at the bakery box in her hand.

Elizabeth laughed, a sweet bell-like sound that vibrated through him.

"*Neh.* Yolanda insisted on treating me to lunch, so I picked up a half dozen of the chocolate peppermint cookies she loves to snack on." Elizabeth's face darkened. "I wish everyone would stop trying to take care of me."

But you've been through a lot, Luke wanted to protest.

"Between Yolanda and my family and friends at church and Owen's family . . ." Elizabeth's voice trailed off. "Invitations and meals and worried looks. And yesterday while I was at work, someone shoveled my snow and dropped off enough firewood to last for weeks."

Luke hoped his guilty expression didn't give him away. But Elizabeth had turned toward the counter to give her order. He'd only wanted to help, not upset, her.

Elizabeth hoped Luke didn't think she was a complainer. He'd given her a strange look.

She waited until he'd ordered and paid before saying, "I didn't mean to sound like I don't appreciate everything. I do. It just makes me feel so helpless and overwhelmed." *And so guilty and undeserving.* Even more troubling, what would everyone think if they could see into her heart and soul?

At Luke's stare, she lowered her gaze. She didn't want him to read the truth in her eyes.

His quiet, "I'm sorry," touched her. She hadn't meant to accuse or blame. Least of all him. Luke had been nothing but kind. All along, he'd been a good friend to Owen and to her. Something about being in his presence always brought her peace.

And right now, she desperately needed that calmness.

"I have to get back. Yolanda's waiting for her lunch. When you have time, stop by to see how your nativity looks in the front window."

"It's in the store window?" Luke not only looked stunned, but he almost shrank back as if—Elizabeth couldn't quite identify the expression on his face. Uncomfortable? Ill at ease? Ashamed? That couldn't be right. Yet he appeared to be humiliated.

"I, um, wasn't expecting that."

Perhaps he didn't realize how good his work was. "I wouldn't be surprised if Yolanda had sold another set or two while I've been gone."

Instead of lessening his discomfort, Elizabeth's comment only seemed to make him more self-conscious.

"Maybe I shouldn't have agreed," he mumbled, rubbing the back of his neck.

"Of course you should have. Anyone would be glad to have such a beautiful reminder of Christ's birth in their home. If I could affor—I mean, they're well worth the price Yolanda's asking." Elizabeth wished she'd held her tongue. She hadn't meant to criticize the cost. He deserved to get paid for all the work that had gone into the carvings.

"I never meant for them to be on public display."

With the chattering crowds around them, Elizabeth could barely hear Luke's words. Had he said them to her, or was he talking to himself? The desperation in his eyes made her wonder if he'd come and snatch the carvings out of the window. Perhaps he worried people might think him prideful. What could she say to reassure him?

"The Lord gave you a talent, and you should be willing to share it. Think of the carvings as a gift to others." Elizabeth wanted him to realize how much his God-given ability could touch others the way it had touched her.

Luke cringed at the thought of all the passersby viewing his private emotions, his vulnerability. *Jah*, the carvings had been a gift, but he'd meant them as a symbol of his love for God and his unrequited feelings for Elizabeth, not sentiments to be blasted out into the world.

Not until she walked away did he recall her half-finished sentence. She wanted one of his nativity sets. That would give him something productive to fill his lonely evenings, although holiday orders already kept him working long hours. His only problem would be getting her to accept it.

He had another idea for a small present he'd like to give her anonymously. He kept remembering how she held that small ornament of the baby. She wouldn't have a tree, of course, but maybe she'd enjoy looking at it. He could sneak next door and put it on her doorstep on Christmas morning. She'd never guess it came from him. He hoped she'd assume Yolanda dropped it off.

Luke had dawdled long enough. His employees needed breaks, so he hurried back to the shop. But having a chance to prepare two special surprises for Elizabeth gave his steps an added bounce.

He waited until close to five to leave the shop. "I'm just running a quick errand," he told Alan. "It won't take long."

Because of Christmas, they were staying open until seven every evening. Yolanda's store stayed open until nine, but Elizabeth left at five. He stood outside the Christmas shop, pretending to be fascinated by the window display, but in reality, he had eyes only for Elizabeth.

When she opened the door and noticed him, she smiled. "Doesn't it look great?"

Jah, she did look great, but a little tired and sad. *Wait, she said "it."* He stared at her blankly until she gestured toward his nativity set.

Luke's face flamed. Did she think he'd been standing here admiring his own work? Not wanting her to think him conceited, he stuttered, "Y-you did a wonderful job arranging everything." Or he assumed she'd created a lovely scene because the whole window in front of him had blurred now that he'd caught sight of her.

Again, her lovely, trilling laugh lifted his spirits.

"No matter how I set them up, they'd look great. They really are . . ." She paused. "I don't know how to describe them." Waving a hand in the air, she said, "Even though they aren't totally realistic, their faces make me experience everything they're feeling."

Her words wrung Luke's insides. He hadn't wanted all that gut-wrenching emotion on public display. If she could read their messages, so could the rest of the world.

"There's my sister." Elizabeth waved to a girl who'd pulled a buggy close to the curb on the opposite side of the street. "I'd better go."

Although he should go inside to buy the ornament, Luke turned to watch her cross. When she stepped off the curb, she slipped in the slushy street.

A van skidded around the corner.

"Elizabeth, watch out!" Luke yelled.

Arms pinwheeling wildly, she struggled to slow her slide. The driver swerved to avoid her, hit a patch of ice, and fishtailed.

Chapter 3

Luke dashed toward her. Everything seemed to move in slow motion. He slogged through the drifts at the curb.

Like a toboggan whizzing downhill, she whooshed toward the spinning van.

God, help me.

Luke dived for her.

Grabbing her around the waist, he dragged her backward. But not fast enough. She extended one leg, kicking frantically to propel herself backward. The out-of-control van collided with her outstretched leg.

The impact would have tossed her like a rag doll if he hadn't dug in his heels and held on to her.

The driver jerked on the steering wheel. The van spun again, narrowly missing Luke. Then it jumped the curb. Slammed into a streetlight. Shuddered to a stop.

The screech of crumpling metal and the crackle of shattering glass sent shudders through him. Shrill screams split the air around them.

He clung to Elizabeth. "Don't move," he warned her as he lowered her gently to the ground. He had no idea how badly she'd been hurt.

Customers poured out of shops up and down the street. Most stood on the sidewalk, their faces startled, shocked, or scared. Others swarmed around Luke and Elizabeth or around the driver.

A teen hopped off the curb, waving his cell phone. "I called nine-one-one. Is she okay?"

"I'm not sure." Luke knelt beside Elizabeth, keeping one arm around her shoulder to support her. "Are you all right?"

Chills shot through Elizabeth's body, and her teeth chattered. She couldn't stop trembling. The places where Luke's arm touched her were the only warm parts of her body. She couldn't feel her leg. Not yet. Icy slush encased it, making it numb.

"You're shivering." Luke's warm breath close to her ear sent more tremors through her. "Here." He removed his coat and wrapped it around her.

"Y-you'll f-freeze," she protested, but he kept his hands on her shoulders to support her and prevent her from shrugging off his coat.

Her sister squatted beside her, the hem of her dress dragging in the dirty slush. Eyes wide with fear, Sarah stared at Elizabeth's leg. "They'll have to take you to the hospital."

"G-go h-home and t-tell M-mamm and D-daed."

"But who'll go with you?"

"I will." Luke's authoritative tone made Elizabeth feel warm and protected. He turned to Sarah. "Can you get your parents and head to the hospital?"

She nodded. After looking both ways several times, she hurried across to their buggy.

"Drive carefully," Luke called after her.

A siren whirred in the distance, growing louder and closer.

"They'll be here soon." Luke's voice, gentle and comforting, soothed Elizabeth's nerves.

Pain had kicked in, but she had something to say to Luke. She fought back waves of nausea as red-hot knives stabbed into her leg. "Y-you s-saved my l-life."

"Hush," he whispered. "Save your strength."

As the ambulance pulled up, her world turned into a storm of noise, confusion, and burning agony.

Sirens screamed. Strangers asked questions she couldn't answer. EMTs poked and prodded her and splinted her leg. She pinched her lips together so she wouldn't cry out. Then they loaded her into the ambulance.

Luke stayed with her the whole time. She clung to his hand as they headed for the hospital.

Elizabeth's grip tightened on Luke's fingers. Her pain must have been overwhelming, because she sucked in a breath and squinched her face. He wished he could ease her hurt.

All he could do was be there for her. At least until her family arrived.

The ambulance glided through the streets without the siren. That reassured Luke she hadn't been too badly injured.

After they arrived at the emergency entrance of the hospital, they rolled Elizabeth inside. Luke stayed beside the stretcher until a nurse ordered him to remain in the waiting room.

"We're taking her back for X-rays now," she said, staring pointedly at their entwined hands.

Reluctantly, he let go, but Elizabeth's gaze begged him not to leave. He had no intention of going anywhere. Not until he made sure she was all right. He'd wait all night if necessary.

After she disappeared down the corridor, he sank into a chair. Adrenaline drained from him. All his bumps and bruises ached. The slushy dampness that had soaked through his clothes earlier chilled him to the bone.

Elizabeth still had his coat wrapped around her, so he couldn't huddle into its warmth. Like she had after the accident, he shivered uncontrollably. He rubbed his hand, still warm from enfolding Elizabeth's, briskly up and down his arm to generate some heat, but he could do nothing about his icy wet pants and shirt back.

He needed to keep his mind off his own discomfort. Elizabeth was undergoing much worse. Luke bowed his head and prayed for her and the hospital staff.

Soon after he lifted his head, her parents and sister rushed through the door. He stood and headed over.

Small furrows between her brows, Elizabeth's *mamm* took his hands in hers. "*Ach*, Luke, how is she?"

"The EMTs put a splint on her leg. She's getting X-rays now."

"I pray it's not too bad."

Her *daed*, David, set a heavy hand on Luke's shoulder. "Sarah said you dragged Elizabeth to safety." His voice husky, he added, "*Danke.*"

"I wish I'd been faster." Luke's too-slow response still haunted him.

"You tried, Luke," Sarah pointed out. "You got her, but the van kept spinning and spinning." She pressed a hand to her mouth. "It was horrible."

Images flashed through Luke's mind of wading through the snow, fearing he'd never reach her. The front of the van loomed, coming straight at them. Then it swerved, skidded, and fishtailed into Elizabeth's leg. He squeezed his eyes shut, but the inside of his head still rang with the impact of metal against flesh.

If he'd reacted sooner . . .

If he'd been a little faster . . .

If . . .

He stared down at the floor. "I pray she'll be all right."

"Don't blame yourself, *sohn*." David squeezed Luke's shoulder. "Whatever happens is God's will. We must trust He has a reason for this."

Although Luke agreed God always had a purpose, he didn't want Elizabeth to suffer. She'd been through so much this past year. He prayed she'd have minimal injuries.

While David checked with the desk, Sarah and her *mamm* sank into chairs. Luke headed over to sit with them, but it dawned on him he'd forgotten about his business. Alan and Martin had not had their dinner breaks. And his horse, stabled in a small lean-to at the back of the building, needed to be taken home and fed.

"I have to make some phone calls," Luke told them, fishing in his pocket for some change from lunch.

Luckily, in deference to the Amish, the hospital still kept an area with pay phones. Luke got Alan on the line and explained what had happened.

"We heard the commotion and the ambulance. Someone told us you'd gone to the hospital. Glad to hear you're not hurt. Sorry about Elizabeth, though."

Alan had closed the business on other nights, so Luke left it in his capable hands. In the background, Martin called out that he'd take Luke's horse and buggy home and see to the feeding.

With thanks, Luke left the phone with a slightly lighter heart. Now all he needed was good news about Elizabeth.

Elizabeth closed her eyes as the nurse pushed her down the corridor in a wheelchair. She bit her lip to hold back the tears threatening to fall.

"You were lucky," the doctor had assured her. "It's a clean break and should mend rapidly."

Elizabeth had grown up believing in God's will rather than luck, but ever since last year, she'd struggled with doubts. Why did He allow bad things to happen?

She tried not to sink into self-pity, but it seemed as if God had given her too much to bear. Hadn't He promised an escape? So far, she'd only spiraled deeper and deeper into despair.

Tonight's accident brought memories rushing back. She relived the terror and the heartbreak of last year. It had been close to this time of year. She'd lost her husband and . . .

Last Christmas had only been a blur. Now she had this holiday season to endure.

The cast on her leg added one more obstacle. A huge one. Until tonight, she'd been able to defend her decision to keep the house she and Owen had built next door to Luke's. Working at Yolanda's allowed Elizabeth to pay the bills, but just barely. She had no emergency funds. Both her mother and her mother-in-law kept trying to persuade her to move back home.

She couldn't work at the Christmas shop with a broken leg. Not even if she mastered crutches. How could she stand on them all day? Reaching or carrying merchandise would be impossible.

After the doctor put on the cast, Elizabeth was too tired and shaky to protest the nurse's insistence on a wheelchair.

"Hospital rules," the nurse informed her.

When she pushed Elizabeth into the waiting room, Mamm, Daed, Sarah, and Luke all jumped to their feet and crowded around her.

The nurse patted her shoulder, but Elizabeth barely heard her quiet words. "Hospital staff will push you outside when you're ready to leave."

Though she should pay more attention to her family, Elizabeth couldn't take her eyes off Luke. Her mind was a bit hazy from the meds they'd given her. Had she thanked him?

With no thought for himself, Luke had saved her life.

Unable to get even a simple *danke* past the lump in her throat, she tried to convey her message with her expression as she held out his coat.

Luke's eyes flickered, registering surprise, before he took

the coat. He stepped back quickly. Had he misread what she'd intended? Before she could clear up any misunderstanding, Mamm and Sarah bent and wrapped their arms around her.

"*Ach*, Elizabeth, you're all right." Sarah teared up.

Mamm ended her hug and stood. "Not completely. What happened to your leg, *dochder*?"

Elizabeth swallowed hard and gestured toward the cast. "Only a simple break," she choked out. "Thanks to Luke. If he hadn't pulled me . . ." She couldn't go on.

Closing her eyes, Elizabeth relived those blinding headlights. Like her last accident. Except then, she'd endured it alone. This time, strong arms had encircled her, yanking her backward.

Focus on that, Elizabeth. Concentrate on safety and rescue.

Imagining the warmth of Luke's arms around her reduced her rising panic.

But it led to other dangerous thoughts.

Heat splashed up her neck and across her cheeks. She opened her eyes but kept her head bowed and avoided glancing at anyone. The merest glimpse of her face might give away her wayward feelings. She had no right to be thinking such things.

Not with Owen gone a little more than a year.

Luke convinced himself he'd mistaken that look in Elizabeth's eyes. A look he'd dreamed of seeing since he turned eighteen and longed to court her. He shook his head. *Impossible.*

After all that had happened tonight, Elizabeth had only been overwrought. She'd probably intended to convey appreciation. Gratitude for being alive. Not admiration and love.

He shrugged into his coat, still warm from her wearing it. That brought up thoughts he shouldn't be entertaining. He shook them off and tuned back in to the conversation around him.

While he'd been lost in thought, the discussion had turned into a family argument.

"No." Elizabeth's tone held steely determination.

"Be sensible, *dochder*. How do you plan to get around?" Her *mamm*'s response matched Elizabeth's resolve.

If only he'd paid closer attention, Luke would know what was going on. Perhaps, though, he had no business listening. He cleared his throat, intending to excuse himself, but the desperation in Elizabeth's eyes held him in place.

"Daed, please?"

David stroked his beard. "I know you prefer to stay in your own house, but your *mamm*'s right. You'll need someone to keep an eye on you, especially tonight."

"And how will you get to work?" Sarah asked. "Starting next week, I won't be able to pick you up in the afternoons."

Maybe he should have stayed out of the family business, but Elizabeth nibbled her lower lip, and her eyes welled with tears.

"I can pick her up and drop her off," Luke offered. "It's no trouble." After all, he lived next door, and his shop was right down the street.

Besides, spending mornings and afternoons with Elizabeth would be pure joy.

Once again, she shot him a look of gratitude that warmed his heart. When their eyes met, Luke forced himself to tear his gaze away.

"*Danke*, Luke, that's generous of you, but—" Elizabeth twisted her hands together in her lap.

Luke wanted to cover his ears to avoid whatever she planned to say next. She was turning down his offer. Just like she would have turned down his request to court her.

"But . . ." Elizabeth repeated, her attention fixed on her agitated hands. "I can't work at Yolanda's. Not on crutches. I wouldn't be much help."

Was that all she was worried about? Not about spending time with him. Not about being alone with him. He had a simple solution to her problem.

"I have some counter stools with backs. They'd be the right height for sitting at the cash register. I could also bring one for you to use at the worktable in the stockroom. They're only samples, so it's not a problem."

"*Ach*, Luke." Her voice thick with tears, Elizabeth managed a watery smile. "I hadn't thought of that. I'll have to check with Yolanda."

"I'm sure she wouldn't want to lose her best employee at this time of year."

Elizabeth giggled. "I doubt I'm the best, but it wouldn't be easy to train a new cashier when we're so busy."

Luke wanted to correct her about being the best. But with both of Elizabeth's parents examining the two of them closely, he kept quiet.

Sarah turned to her *mamm*. "I don't start at the restaurant until next week. I could spend the nights at Elizabeth's."

"*Danke*, Sarah." Elizabeth flashed her sister a grateful smile.

Luke's spirits plummeted a little. The gratitude in Elizabeth's eyes for her sister resembled the appreciation she'd flashed in Luke's direction earlier. So, it hadn't meant anything special.

Elizabeth's grogginess had started wearing off, thanks to Sarah and Luke. Her parents had never understood why she wanted to stay in her own place. In their minds, she was rejecting family and community support.

Daed clutched at his suspenders. "It seems, *dochder*, that you have friends and family willing to care for and help you."

Mamm turned imploring eyes to him as if hoping he'd tell Elizabeth to come back home.

He gave Mamm a tender smile. "Elizabeth will be all right. And she can always come home if she finds it too difficult being on her own."

"*Danke*, Daed." Elizabeth appreciated her father's support.

She doubted she'd have challenged him if he'd insisted she return to the family house.

"We should get going," he said. "We hired a car to get here as fast as we could. The driver promised to pick us up whenever we were ready to leave. I'll go call her."

"What about you?" Elizabeth asked Luke. "You don't have a way to get home, do you?" He'd come in the ambulance with her. "And what about your buggy? Is it still at work?"

"*Neh.* Martin drove it to the house for me and took care of the horse."

Daed hesitated while Elizabeth questioned Luke, waiting for the answer. "We'll drive you home." He chuckled. "It's not like it would take us too far out of our way."

Elizabeth released a soft sigh. It definitely wouldn't be an inconvenience with Luke's farm right next to hers.

She'd pushed all thoughts of Luke from her mind when she started courting Owen, but now the idea of his closeness sent a tingle through her. A reaction she should not be having about her husband's best friend.

Chapter 4

When the van arrived, Luke hung back, though he longed to help Elizabeth get in. To keep his mind from straying where it shouldn't go, Luke took the crutches from the aide.

He waited until the family had gotten in before handing the crutches up to Elizabeth. Then he climbed into the back and slid along the seat to a spot where he could gaze at her profile without her family noticing.

The air blasting from the van's heater surrounded Luke with much-needed warmth. He hunched into his coat, but his damp clothes left him shivering and clammy.

Elizabeth, her face tired and pale, revealed the fragility she'd denied earlier that day. If only he had the right to comfort her, care for her. With no one around to watch his expression, Luke imagined a nonexistent past and an impossible future. A past in which Elizabeth fell in love with him rather than Owen. A future in which Elizabeth agreed to be his wife.

Absorbed in his fantasy world, Luke barely heard the low murmur of conversation from the seat in front of him until Elizabeth swiveled her head.

Could she tell from the wistfulness on his face that she'd been featuring in his daydreams?

"Are you asleep?" Her voice, low and teasing, jolted Luke back to his surroundings. The van idled in front of his house. Everyone had been waiting for him to exit.

Grateful for the darkness hiding his heated cheeks, he mumbled, "Sorry," and headed for the door.

Sarah leaned over and slid it open.

With a quick *danke*, Luke hopped out and headed up the driveway, glad to keep his back turned as the headlights illuminated his path.

If only he had an equally clear path for his future, but Owen stood in the way of that. First, he had dated and married the woman Luke loved. Now, although Owen had been gone more than a year, Elizabeth still wore her mourning clothes.

Luke had lost her in the past and had no chance for a future with her.

Elizabeth tried not to stare at Luke as he headed up the gravel driveway to his house. Overhead, stars dotted the indigo sky. From the time she was a child, she'd always believed the beauty of creation revealed God's power, goodness, and love.

But now the splendor of that vastness took her breath away and filled her with a yearning too deep for words. Why had God denied the cry of her heart? The aching of her soul?

If she'd been alone, she'd have lifted her arms and cried out, *Why, God? Why did You take away the most precious thing in my life?*

But her family surrounded her in the van. They'd never understand her questioning God's will. She'd watched both her parents stoically accept whatever tragedies came their way with faith and trust.

Elizabeth had done the same. Until now.

The van cruised the short distance from Luke's and wound down her driveway to get as close to the house as possible.

Sarah helped Elizabeth into the house. "We missed supper. Want me to fix something?"

"*Neh.*" Sadness and exhaustion engulfed her. She only wanted to sleep. "Fix whatever you'd like for yourself, though." She tottered down the hall, unsteady on the crutches, thankful for a first-floor bedroom.

"I'm not hungry," Sarah insisted. "Need help getting ready for bed?"

Elizabeth shook her head. "I'll be fine." She needed time alone. "The back bedroom upstairs has clean sheets." So did two of the others, but she didn't want Sarah poking into the bedroom at the top of the stairs.

The heartache that had started as Elizabeth gazed at the stars increased. Owen had built this house with four upstairs bedrooms so they'd have plenty of room for children. The accident that took him from her had also stolen that dream.

Elizabeth dragged herself the rest of the way down the hall. She'd almost reached the bedroom door when Sarah spoke, interrupting Elizabeth's snail-like progress.

"Luke is really brave, isn't he?" Sarah's breathy voice revealed she was impressed.

If Elizabeth had been surer on her feet, she'd have whirled around to face her sister. She wanted to see if Sarah's eyes had gone soft and dreamy.

Ever since Luke had saved her, Elizabeth had been hiding her own admiration. A tiny bud of hope wilted inside.

If Luke had to make a choice, surely he'd prefer her pretty, vivacious sister. He'd never seemed interested in Elizabeth, despite her schoolgirl crush on him. She'd hidden her disappointment and accepted when Owen asked her out. After she'd grown fond of Owen, she'd pushed all thoughts of Luke from her mind.

Ever since he'd walked through the door carrying the nativity set, though, he'd intruded on her thoughts. And after having his arms around her, she found herself wishing for things she shouldn't. Even letting her mind stray to Luke made her ashamed of being disloyal.

Sarah's "good night" startled Elizabeth. Had her sister been standing there all that time waiting for a reply?

"Good night," Elizabeth said faintly.

Her sister padded upstairs, and Elizabeth hoped Sarah wouldn't peek into the first room at the top of the stairs.

A door snicked open. Sarah hadn't had enough time to reach the end of the hall. Elizabeth braced herself for her sister's criticism.

Sarah's voice boomed down the stairwell. "Elizabeth? I thought you were going to clean out this room."

Before her sister could question her more, Elizabeth called back, "I will, Sarah. It's just been so . . ." So hard to get up the courage to walk through that door. So hard to give up all her hopes and dreams. So hard to face a lonely, barren future.

For Luke, driving Elizabeth to work the next morning proved bittersweet. He loved being with her, helping her into the buggy, handing her the crutches, especially when their hands brushed. But being this close to her made him long for more.

"How are you doing?" he asked as he climbed into the driver's seat.

Her hollow laugh revealed inner pain. "I have bruises in places I didn't even know were hit."

Luke hoped he hadn't been the cause of any bruises. Although he suspected he might be. Heat rose from his neck and splashed across his face as he recalled holding her, tugging her to him. Last night he'd been too fearful for her safety to consider the warmth and closeness of their bodies.

And now he had no business letting his mind wander in that direction. Grasping the reins in a tight fist, he clucked to his horse.

"I hope you didn't get hurt."

His muscles ached from the suddenness of his movements. And from the force of the van almost jerking her from his arms. But that soreness would be gone within days. "I'll be fine, but I wish I'd moved fast enough to protect you."

"What?" Elizabeth's sharp question startled Luke.

She twisted in her seat so she faced him, but Luke pretended to keep his attention on the road. If his eyes met hers, he'd never look away.

"If it hadn't been for you, that van would've hit me. I'd be in the hospital or maybe even"—she shuddered—"dead."

She didn't say it, but the words *like Owen* hung between them.

Luke's resolve crumbled. He couldn't resist turning to comfort her. With the icy roads, he could only risk a brief glance. "I'm sorry."

As soon as he spoke, he snapped his mouth shut. Would she think that was an odd thing to say after her last statement? Or had she implied that unspoken meaning?

"I know. And you've always protected me whenever you could."

He'd tried, but once Owen had asked her out, Luke had backed away.

"Remember that time I got stuck in the tree when I was tagging after you and Owen?"

Luke's lips curved into a smile. Elizabeth had trailed them wherever they went, and she usually tried to do what they did. That day—they'd been eight or nine—and they'd scrambled to the top of the tallest oak in his yard.

They hadn't noticed Elizabeth until she squawked. She'd snagged the hem of her dress on a broken twig below her, but she clung to a swaying branch, too frightened to reach out and free herself.

He'd climbed down, unhooked the cloth, and guided her safely to the ground. Owen had followed them to give Elizabeth a lecture about staying home where she belonged.

"How could I forget it?" Or any of the other times he'd spent with her.

Elizabeth's voice went soft. "That wasn't the only time you took care of me."

No, it wasn't. He tried to be by her side as much as he could when they were growing up. Even as a teen, after he realized he'd fallen for her and was too shy to let her know, he watched from a safe distance. Because he'd been alert, he'd rescued her several times—once from an attacking dog, once when her *kapp* and hair had gotten tangled in brambles, and once when her horse got spooked after a singing and almost dumped her from her buggy.

That was the last time he'd come to her aid. Owen had offered to drive her home from the singing, while Luke calmed her horse and drove it to her house. Elizabeth had already gone inside by the time Luke arrived. Her *daed* thanked him, and Owen drove Luke to get the team he'd left at the singing.

The whole way back, Owen bubbled over with happiness. Elizabeth had agreed to go to the singing with him next week.

From that point on, Luke stayed away from Elizabeth. He'd never let his best friend know of his own crush on Elizabeth. A crush that hadn't diminished over time.

Even when Luke's *daed* put some of their farm acreage up for sale and Owen bought it to build a house for his bride-to-be, Luke had never admitted the truth. He'd hidden his feelings and turned them into carvings.

"What's wrong?" Elizabeth reached out and laid a gentle hand on his sleeve.

Luke forced himself to stay calm, but he had no control over his heart thundering louder than the horse's hooves or his blood pounding in his ears. He managed to shake his head, hoping she'd take it as a signal nothing was bothering him.

He'd been so caught up in trying to gain composure, he almost passed Yolanda's Christmas shop. He turned toward the curb so abruptly, Elizabeth slid toward him. Their shoulders bumped.

"I'm sorry."

Elizabeth's laughter trilled up his spine. "I think you've said you're sorry at least three times this morning. You have nothing to apologize for."

But she couldn't see into his heart. She had no idea what had caused his guilt.

Chapter 5

Elizabeth hadn't meant to upset him. She wasn't sure what she'd said that caused his look of dismay. And she'd startled him by reaching out. She should never have touched him like that.

"Wait there." Luke hopped out of the buggy and came around to her side. "I don't like you getting out into traffic like this."

"I do it all the time."

"Not with a broken leg and icy streets you don't." His brow furrowed as he stared at the stream of traffic approaching. "Let's wait for the light to change."

When traffic slowed, he slid her door open and took her hands to help her step out. "Be careful. The last thing you need is to fall."

True. But if she did, he'd catch her. She wouldn't mind that at all.

Right now, she could barely concentrate on putting her stronger foot on the ground. Her hands tingled everywhere his touched.

After she steadied herself, he let go of one of her hands to reach the crutches and close the door. She missed his warmth.

Then hooking the crutches over his shoulder, he put an arm around her waist. "Let's get you to the curb before the light changes."

A car rounded the corner and whizzed past, splattering slush. Luke turned his body to shield her, so the backs of his pant legs got soaked. She hadn't gotten splashed.

Once again, he'd been her protector. Even in small things like this, he'd always taken care of her.

"*Danke.*" She tried not to let admiration seep into her words.

"For what?" Luke looked surprised.

"You blocked the slush."

"Anyone would have done that."

Not anyone. Elizabeth could think of few people who'd do that in addition to all the other things he'd done for her—rescuing her last night, riding in the ambulance, driving her to work, assisting her to the curb. He hadn't changed from when they were young.

When they reached the curb, he held her elbow to help her up. "Ready for the crutches?"

"*Jah.*" She wanted to walk into Yolanda's on her own. She needed to prove to her boss she was capable of keeping this job despite the cast. But using crutches on a slippery sidewalk turned out to be challenging.

Luke walked beside her, one arm extended behind her, preparing to catch her if she fell. She prayed that wouldn't happen. Or maybe she should hope it did. She wouldn't mind landing in his strong arms.

Stop it, Elizabeth. You shouldn't be thinking like that.

As soon as she walked through the door, Yolanda gasped. "I didn't expect to see you today. Last thing I saw was them loading you in the ambulance."

"Only a broken leg. But if you think I'll be a problem or be in the way—"

Luke interrupted, "I told Elizabeth I can bring two high counter stools—one for the cash register and one for the stockroom."

"That would be perfect. Elizabeth can handle the cash register, and I'll do her usual running around."

Elizabeth cleared her throat. The other two were talking as if she weren't around.

A guilty expression crossed Yolanda's face. "If you want to work, that is."

"It's why I'm here." Elizabeth hadn't come all this way and struggled through ice and snow to give up and go home.

She was rewarded with Yolanda's sassiest grin. "You've got guts, girl." Then Yolanda turned to Luke. "Thank you kindly for the barstools."

He smiled at both of the women. "I'll bring them down as soon as I can."

Less than ten minutes later, he and a young boy entered the shop carrying the stools and two cushions. "Why don't you put that one behind the counter there?" he directed the boy. "I'll take this one back to the stockroom."

Luke returned with one cushion, which he tied onto the stool behind the cash register. "I figured if you're sitting most of the day, you might want a cushion."

"Well, aren't you thoughtful?" Yolanda said. "Thank you for taking care of my girl here."

Luke kept his mouth shut before he admitted how much he wished Elizabeth were *his* girl.

He'd better get out of here before he made a fool of himself. "Come on, Martin. We have plenty of work to do."

Elizabeth's quiet *danke* made his heart skip more than one beat. Instead of turning toward her, he kept walking toward the door. Better not to look her in the eyes, or he'd be lost.

"Happy to help," he said. *More than happy.* He pushed open the door.

Martin stopped in front of the window. "Didn't notice this when we were going in. It looks like the carvings you do."

Luke had tried to keep his work secret, but several times his employees had startled him by coming in early or stopping back after hours for something they'd left behind.

"It is," he admitted.

But rather than studying the nativity set the way Martin was doing, Luke tried to catch a glimpse of Elizabeth. One of the artificial trees blocked most of her face.

Yolanda headed toward the door with a shovel and a bucket of salt. He didn't want her to think he'd been admiring his own work. Or, worse yet, realize he'd been sneaking glimpses of Elizabeth.

"Come on. We need to get back to the shop." Luke strode down the sidewalk without waiting for Martin.

"Hey, wait up. What's the hurry?" Martin came pounding after him.

They'd passed three stores before jingling bells signaled Yolanda had exited the store.

Being in the Christmas store reminded Luke about his plan the previous evening. The one that had gotten sidetracked because of Elizabeth's accident. After last night, he was all the more determined to buy that ornament for her. Except now that she'd be riding with him in the morning and afternoon, he had no way to buy it in secret. If he sneaked in during a lunch break, would Yolanda mention it to Elizabeth? He had to get it soon, before it sold.

Luke mulled it over all morning. Maybe he could send one of his employees to purchase it. Not Martin, because both Elizabeth and Yolanda had seen him today. Alan might be best. An

Englischer buying a tree ornament wouldn't attract any attention.

Luke stopped Alan as he headed out the door at noon. "Would you do me a favor while you're out? Feel free to take a longer break to make up for the time."

"Sure. What do you need?"

As Luke described the decoration and handed over the money, Alan's brows drew together in a puzzled frown. "You want a Christmas ornament? Thought you Amish didn't have trees."

"We don't," Luke said. "It's not for me." He had no intention of letting anyone know who would be getting this gift.

After Alan left, Luke drifted into a daydream. Elizabeth's face lighting up when she unwrapped the tiny, sparkling baby. If only he could be there to watch, but he didn't want her to know he'd purchased the decoration for her. He only hoped it brought her joy. And it was the only way he knew to express all the love he kept bottled up inside.

During a brief lull close to noon, Elizabeth hobbled into the back and took her lunch pack from the refrigerator. She hooked the strap over the handgrip of one crutch, but before she could reach the table, the phone rang.

Elizabeth leaned against the wall to answer. A shaky voice on the other end asked for Yolanda.

"Just a minute. I'll get her." Lunch bag still dangling from her crutches, Elizabeth limped out to find the store busy again.

"Phone's for you," she told Yolanda. "I'll take over out here while you talk." Elizabeth climbed onto the stool Luke had brought and leaned her crutches against the wall behind her. Eating would have to wait.

"I won't be long," Yolanda promised.

Within minutes, the line of customers waiting to check out

snaked down one aisle and around into the next. Elizabeth flashed an apologetic smile at a woman who stared in dismay at the long line and then back at Elizabeth.

"Only one cashier?" Her incredulous tone bordered on critical.

"I'm sorry." Elizabeth took the next customer's purchases and punched in the amounts on the register. "We'll have two cashiers soon, but I'll do my best to move quickly."

The woman harrumphed and glanced at her watch. "Most of us are on lunch breaks. We didn't plan to waste the whole time in here."

Elizabeth worked as fast as she could, but she was relieved when Yolanda entered.

"My goodness." Eyes damp and voice thick with tears, Yolanda glanced at the waiting customers. "I should have come out sooner."

Elizabeth hoped Yolanda hadn't received bad news. Before Yolanda reached the counter, a young man stopped her to ask a question.

Elizabeth barely glanced at him because she wanted to rush through her checkouts, but he looked like one of Luke's employees. Yolanda pointed to a far corner of the store and then joined Elizabeth.

Once Yolanda took over the other register, the line moved faster. Elizabeth wanted to ask her boss if everything was all right, but she'd wait until they'd helped all the customers. The more buyers Yolanda assisted, the brighter and more cheerful her voice and expression became. Perhaps Elizabeth had been wrong about the call being bad news.

"It's about time." The grumpy woman who'd been at the end of the line about five minutes ago heaved an exasperated sigh and tossed her purchases in front of Elizabeth. "I have other errands to run, so I won't get time for lunch."

Elizabeth reached behind her for her bag and pulled out her sandwich and apple. "Here." She handed them to the woman.

The woman's eyes widened. "You'd give up your lunch after I've been so crabby?"

Her words hit Elizabeth hard. Hadn't Elizabeth herself been doing the same with God? Complaining and criticizing?

Humbled, Elizabeth admitted, "I've been complaining a lot recently, but I'm grateful that didn't stop God from sending us the greatest Christmas gift of all—His Son."

The woman's eyes grew misty. "I've been so frazzled trying to finish all my errands and shopping, I almost forgot why we're doing all this." She waved a hand around the shop. "Thank you for the reminder."

Actually, the woman had helped Elizabeth by revealing her ungratefulness.

Before Elizabeth could thank her, a Mennonite girl in a calf-length flowered dress barged through the door, setting the bells jangling. In her arms, she carried a huge stack of papers. "Hi, I'm Melva. My parents run New Beginnings just outside of town." She flicked her chin to the left.

Without stopping for breath, she rambled on. "We're having a benefit auction on Saturday. Would it be all right if I put a flyer in your window?" She stopped and gulped in some air. "I could also leave some for your customers."

"What's New Beginnings?" Yolanda sounded suspicious.

"It's a shelter for teens who are expecting babies. Some are runaways, but many teenagers come to New Beginnings if they've been kicked out of their homes."

"And you're having an auction?" Yolanda's tone had softened.

The girl approached the counter and held out a flyer. "We're also asking for donations of items, if you have anything to give."

The customer Elizabeth had been waiting on stepped forward. "I assume you also take donations." She pulled two twenties from her wallet.

After the girl took the money, the woman turned back to Elizabeth. "It can't compare with what God gave us, but maybe it will help a little."

Elizabeth forced a smile. When the teen passed the flyer with its baby-in-a-cradle logo to Yolanda, Elizabeth winced. She gritted her teeth and fought off the self-pity that threatened to overwhelm her.

No husband. No babies. No future. A lonely Christmas.

Hadn't she just reminded this woman—and herself—about being grateful for the true meaning of Christmas? Elizabeth tried to focus on that rather than her loss.

Several others followed the woman's lead and held out fives, tens, or twenties. Grumbling turned to generosity.

The teen's eyes widened. "Oh, wow! Just wow! Thank you all."

Yolanda skimmed through the flyer. "The shop will donate a nativity set like the one in the window and two of our decorated Christmas trees."

Elizabeth gasped. She must have misheard. Those trees were expensive, and all the ornaments on them represented a huge portion of the shop's income.

Yolanda caught Elizabeth's eye and whispered, "I just received the best Christmas gift ever. More precious than money can buy." At Elizabeth's questioning look, she explained, "That phone call. Tell you later." Then she went back to waiting on customers.

"That's so generous of you." The girl held out a small stack of flyers. "Is it all right if I leave these here?"

"Of course." Yolanda cleared a space for them on the counter between the registers.

"My dad will stop by on Friday to pick up donations."

Yolanda nodded. "That'll be fine."

The young man Elizabeth thought she recognized from Luke's shop headed for her register. As he passed the girl, he said, "Be sure to stop at Bontrager's Woodworking Shop down the street. I know my boss will donate. He's always generous."

So, he did work at Luke's store. And he was right about Luke's generosity. If anyone could attest to that, she could. And Luke was also kind, thoughtful, caring . . .

When the customer handed her his purchase, Elizabeth halted, hand frozen in midair. She didn't take the white, sparkling ornament he held out. *A baby.*

The baby she'd held that day Luke had dropped off the nativity sets. The baby that had brought back all her pain. The baby she'd hidden on the back branches of the tree, so she wouldn't have to see it.

"Are you okay?" the man asked. "You look like you might faint."

Yolanda whipped her head around to study Elizabeth. "As soon as you check out this customer, go back and eat your lunch. Can't have you fainting behind the counter and causing a scene." Although Yolanda barked out the words as an order, the worry in her eyes made it clear she cared.

"I'll be fine," Elizabeth managed to say. Once she finished with this customer, she'd think of something besides husbands and babies.

"I shouldn't have made you work so hard after your accident last night. Maybe we should cut back your hours until your leg heals."

"No, please don't do that. I'm all right." Or she would be soon.

"Oh, are you the one who was hit by the van last night? My boss called about that. He went to the hospital with you, didn't he?"

Elizabeth nodded and forced herself to reach for the ornament. She pinched the very edge between two fingers as if it were on fire. Then she dropped it onto the small stack of tissue paper beside her register and wrapped it. Even after she slid it into a small gift bag, her fingers still burned. And the shape of the baby remained imprinted in her memory.

A baby. A family. Something she'd never have.

Chapter 6

Alan returned with a small bag and handed it to Luke. "Here's the change."

Luke set the ornament gently in the drawer of his worktable. Then he waved away the change. "Keep that for your trouble."

"You sure?" Alan asked.

After Luke nodded, Alan pocketed the money and said, "The girl that works there—the one with the crutches. She's the one you took to the hospital last night."

"Elizabeth? Yes, she ended up with a broken leg."

"She's awfully brave to come into work the next morning. Most people I know would have taken time off and made their employers pay sick leave."

That made Luke smile. He couldn't imagine Elizabeth ever considering that. "I don't think she'd do that."

Alan grinned. "I wouldn't either."

His comical expression made Luke laugh. "I know. That's why I hired you."

Before Alan headed to the workroom, he remarked, "She's something else, that girl."

Luke had always believed that, but Alan's remark made Luke curious. He raised an eyebrow to encourage Alan to continue.

"You should have seen the way she dealt with this grumbling lady. The woman reamed her out for taking so long." Alan waved a hand to indicate the length of the store. "They had a superlong line that stretched all the way to there and then some."

Luke's hackles had risen when Alan mentioned someone yelling at Elizabeth. "That wasn't her fault."

"I know, but the woman was upset about wasting her whole lunch break in the store." Alan stopped to explain, "That's what took me so long."

"I figured." Luke wished Alan would stick to the story.

"Anyway, when the woman complained about missing lunch, that girl—Elizabeth—reached behind her, took her own lunch out of a bag, and handed it to the woman. Can you believe it?"

Knowing Elizabeth, *jah*, he could. But did that mean she went without lunch herself?

"Can you keep an eye on things out here for a few minutes?" Luke asked Alan. "I need to run into the back to make a phone call."

Alan gazed at the phone on the counter with a questioning look, but he only nodded. "Sure."

Luke hurried to the back, ran a finger along the list of nearby businesses posted on the wall beside the phone, and dialed. "I'd like to order a large pizza with double cheese to be delivered to Yolanda's Christmas Year Round Shop. I'll send someone over in a few minutes to pay for it. Please don't tell them who ordered it."

After pulling money from his wallet, he put it in an envelope with a note saying that it was for Yolanda's pizza, and then he sent Martin over with the envelope and extra money for another pizza for the three of them. Alan had already eaten, but Luke had no doubt both of his employees would be happy for a snack later that afternoon.

While they waited for Martin to return, Alan pulled a crumpled flyer from his pocket. "That reminds me. This girl came into the Christmas shop. I told her to stop by here for some donations. I know how you like to help worthy causes."

Luke read the flyer. "Did she want items for the auction?"

"Yep. And people gave her cash donations."

"Hmm." Luke looked around the shop. Most of the items on display had *Sold* signs on them. He had a few unfinished samples in the back.

"There she is now." Alan pointed to a Mennonite teen emerging from the store across the street.

The girl glanced at the sign over their door and, after looking both ways, crossed and headed into Luke's store.

"Good afternoon!" she called out, her voice filled with cheer. "I'm Melva Hess."

"I understand you're here for donations." Luke wished he had more money in his wallet, but paying for the ornament and pizza left him with only two tens. He pulled those out and handed them to her.

"Thank you." Her bright, enthusiastic smile made Luke glad he'd decided to contribute more than money.

"That's all the cash I have, but if you can use items to auction, we can donate this grandfather clock and"—he led the girl to the store's showpiece—"this armoire."

Elaborately carved, the massive piece of furniture stood almost nine feet tall, with double closet doors in the center and narrower doors on each side that opened to reveal shelves and deep drawers.

Melva sucked in a long breath. "It's beautiful." She stood

staring at it for a long time. "I don't know how Dad will get that in his pickup truck, though."

"We can deliver it," Luke said. "And we'll also take it to the winner's house."

"That's so awesome of you. I know my parents will be thrilled."

"I did have one other question." Luke motioned for her to follow him to the workroom. "I've started two cradles. They won't be ready in time for the auction, but would some of the new mothers want one?"

"Oh." Tears sprang to Melva's eyes. "Not many of the mothers keep their babies, but a few do. Having a cradle would be helpful."

Luke nodded. "Then I'll plan to finish these by Christmas or soon after."

With all their orders, he didn't want to promise something he couldn't deliver. He'd take these to his home workshop tonight so he could work on them in the evenings. The shop had way too many orders for him to do anything but customer work while he was here.

"Everyone in town has been so generous." Melva beamed at him. "I can't thank you enough. Dad will stop by on Friday to pick up the clock and make arrangements for the armoire."

Luke followed her to the front, and she held out a thin stack of papers.

"Could I leave some flyers here and put these two in the window?"

"Of course." Luke set the flyers on the counter while Melva hung back-to-back posters on the glass pane in the door.

"Thanks ever so much." She waved and skipped next door.

Luke smiled at her energy. Elizabeth had been lively and cheerful like that as a teenager. Always leaving sunshine behind wherever she went.

In fact, until she'd lost Owen, Luke had never seen her depressed or discouraged. Seeing her still wearing black mourning clothes made him ache for her. Would she ever get over Owen?

The lunchtime rush had slowed to a trickle when a pizza delivery arrived. The warm yeasty and tomato-y smell set Elizabeth's stomach rumbling. She'd already nibbled the few carrot sticks left in her lunch bag.

Yolanda laughed. "I bet that irritated lady this morning told customers to order lunch because they'd be waiting in long lines."

Elizabeth giggled. "It's a good solution."

But the deliveryman didn't hand the pizza to a customer. He headed straight to Yolanda. "A gift for you."

Yolanda's eyes widened. "For me? I can pay you."

The man shook his head. "Already been paid. Tip too."

"Well, God has certainly blessed me today." Yolanda patted the counter beside her. "You can put it right here." Turning to Elizabeth, she said, "Let's eat it here. Then you don't have to drag that broken leg back to the lunchroom."

Between customers, they ate the pizza. Cheese pizza was Elizabeth's favorite, but she rarely had it.

As they ate, Yolanda teared up as she told Elizabeth about the phone call that morning. "It was my daughter."

Elizabeth stared at her. "I didn't know you had a daughter." She'd often heard about the problems her boss had with her rebellious teenage son, but Yolanda had never mentioned a girl.

Dabbing her eyes with a napkin, Yolanda swallowed hard before speaking. "I never talked about her because she hasn't spoken to me in five years. I didn't even know where she was living."

"*Ach*, Yolanda, that must have been hard."

"It was, but God is good. Today she called to tell me she has a little girl of her own. I'm a grandma, and I didn't even know it."

Elizabeth's jaw clenched. The pizza in her mouth tasted like cardboard. Babies seemed to be everywhere today.

Yolanda didn't notice Elizabeth's distress. As a new grandmother, she was so caught up in the wonder of her news. "Anyway, my daughter said taking care of the baby made her appreciate how hard it had been for me as a single mom. She called to apologize."

"That's wonderful." Elizabeth tried to inject cheer and excitement into her words, but they fell flat.

Yolanda studied her. "You okay?"

Instead of answering, Elizabeth lifted a pizza slice and forced herself to take a bite.

"If you need a break, just let me know. You've been working nonstop all morning. Or if you want to go home early, that's fine."

"I'll stay for my shift." Besides, Luke wouldn't come for her until five. Even if she wanted to leave, she had no transportation.

The bells jingled cheerily several times in a row, and customers browsed the aisles.

Yolanda lowered her voice to a whisper. "I wish I hadn't put out the two o'clock coupons. We'll be busy from now until seven."

Elizabeth's full mouth prevented her from speaking.

Leaning over, Yolanda kept her voice low, but she couldn't keep excitement from leaking into her words. "I didn't tell you the best part. My daughter wants to come for Christmas and bring the baby. I'll get to hold my three-month-old granddaughter."

Elizabeth choked on her pizza, and tears sprang to her eyes. Yolanda pounded her on the back. Elizabeth mopped the wetness running down her cheeks, hoping Yolanda would assume it came from the near choking.

"You want any more?" Yolanda gestured to the last few slices of pizza.

Elizabeth shook her head. She'd had enough. Enough of pizza. And enough of baby stories.

"If you wait on the customers, I'll clean this up." Yolanda gathered the pizza, paper plates, and napkins. But just before she headed for the lunchroom, she said over her shoulder, "Isn't God wonderful?"

Elizabeth didn't respond, but her conscience pricked her. God had given His Son as a gift to the world. She was grateful for that.

But she still harbored doubts and—she had to admit it—anger. Why were others being blessed with happiness and babies while she dealt with loneliness and loss?

A little before five, Luke told Alan and Martin he'd be gone for an hour. At their surprise, he explained he'd agreed to drive Elizabeth to and from work until she got her cast off. "She lives next door, so it makes sense."

Alan waggled his eyebrows. "Just being neighborly?"

"Someone needed to help. And I'm right nearby, so it only makes sense."

"*Um-hm.*" Alan didn't sound convinced. "Does she realize you have to take time off work to take her home?"

"*Neh.*" He flashed Alan a warning look. "And I don't want her to know."

Throwing his hands up in surrender, Alan pretended to be hurt. "I would never dream of telling her." Then he added with a sly smile, "Not about that nor about your interest in her."

Luke tried not to let his embarrassment show. "The Amish believe in helping others in the community," he said stiffly.

"Especially when they're pretty widows."

No point in sparring with Alan. Most likely he had plenty more barbs. Better just to change the subject. "I'm sorry this'll delay your supper breaks, but there's still pizza back there."

"You going to buy us pizza every day until Elizabeth's cast comes off? Or should we plan to bring snacks from now on?"

"We can discuss that when I get back." He didn't want to be late to pick up Elizabeth.

She was already outside when he arrived.

"Sorry," he said as he hopped from the buggy.

Elizabeth rolled her eyes. "Here we go again."

"What?" Luke had been so busy banishing memories of holding her close last night, he hadn't been paying attention to her conversation.

"You're always apologizing."

"Sor—"

She laughed as he pinched his lips shut on the word.

"I don't like thinking of you out in the cold because I was late."

"You weren't late. I was early."

"Even so—" Luke lost his train of thought as he took her ungloved hand in his to help her into the buggy. That drove everything from his mind except the softness of her skin.

Once she settled onto the seat, he had no excuse to keep holding her hand. Reluctantly, he let go. Then he set her crutches beside her, careful not to brush against her arm. He needed to have some powers of concentration left to drive.

Elizabeth regretted teasing Luke when he stayed silent for most of the ride home. She hadn't meant to hurt his feelings. Only now if she said she was sorry, he might interpret it as her mocking him.

She strained to find something to say that would sound friendly. Something that would erase her cutting remark. But the day had been too filled with baby-related angst.

Sadness engulfed her as the events washed back over her. At five, she'd been so grateful to escape the shop and Yolanda's baby joy. Despite being thrilled for her boss, Elizabeth's own pain kept her in a dark place.

Then when she left the shop to wait for Luke, she couldn't avoid the flyers taped in the window. Melva had placed one facing out toward the street and another facing in, so Elizabeth passed the baby logo going in and coming out. She'd have to walk by it several times a day until Saturday.

The last thing she wanted to see this close to Christmas was a picture of a baby. Even worse, she couldn't bear to read about young mothers who were giving their babies up for adoption.

Although she'd reminded that customer today of God's love, a sharp pain stabbed through Elizabeth at the thought of unwanted children. How could God allow such injustice? Teens who couldn't or wouldn't want the babies they bore, while she, who desperately wanted a child, had lost her chance to be a wife and mother?

Luke broke into her gloomy thoughts. "How did your day go?"

Startled, she tried to say something upbeat. "We had an unexpected pizza delivery today. And it even was my favorite—double cheese."

He smiled. "And that was the highlight of your day?"

"Pretty much. It came at the perfect time, because I was really hungry." Maybe she should be thanking God for that instead of grousing about what she couldn't have. "Yolanda had a great day, though."

She filled him in on Yolanda's daughter and new grandchild, trying not to wince when she mentioned the baby.

"That's wonderful. She's such a hard worker. When she opened that shop ten years ago, my *daed* wondered if a Christmas store would make it. She's done well."

Elizabeth had passed the store many times as a teenager but

never had a reason to go inside. Not until after Owen died and she'd noticed the *Help Wanted* sign in the window. She'd been desperate for a job and had taken to Yolanda right away. Even more important, Yolanda had taken to Elizabeth and hired her on the spot.

"You look far away." Luke studied her as they waited at a red light. "I guess this time of year is hard."

A lump in her throat, Elizabeth nodded.

"I miss my best friend." Luke's voice, low and husky, strummed a chord deep in Elizabeth's soul. "I can't even imagine what it's like to lose a husband."

"It's so hard to be around all the Christmas shoppers. Smiling people buying gifts for loved ones, happy tunes blasting from speakers, and Yolanda's always so cheerful." Maybe she shouldn't have admitted that.

"I understand." His eyes and expression revealed that he truly did.

"I know the accident was God's will and I should accept it, but . . ." No matter how understanding Luke was, Elizabeth didn't want to reveal the bitterness in her heart.

"But it can make you question God."

Elizabeth's gaze flew to his face. He sounded as if he'd experienced the same doubts. Had he been questioning Owen's death too?

Her voice barely a whisper, she confessed, "Deep inside, I'm still angry at God for all He took away."

"*Ach,* Elizabeth." Luke reached out and squeezed her shoulder. Then he yanked his hand back, his face red. "Sorry," he muttered.

This time Elizabeth didn't call him on his apology. Mainly because she wasn't sorry. His touch had been healing. And it stirred something deep in her soul.

Chapter 7

A horn honked behind them, and Luke jumped. He'd been so absorbed in Elizabeth he'd forgotten they were on the road. All the cars in front of him had pulled through the green light while he'd dawdled.

His face, already burning from touching her, turned fiery. He flicked the reins and steered the horse to the shoulder to allow the drivers behind him to pass. Most whipped around him so fast, the sides of the buggy shook.

He started to apologize but held his tongue. No need to start her on another lecture. Not that he minded. But right now her thoughts seemed to be elsewhere. And so were his. A place he had no right to go.

Instead, he should be trying to help. "Sometimes it's hard to accept God's will." He should know. "You're not the only one who's gotten upset with God."

Luke hadn't, but he'd directed his irritation and jealousy toward a human target—Owen. That had left Luke wrestling with guilt and shame. If he hadn't surrendered that in prayer after Owen married Elizabeth, he never could have lived next door to them and remained friends.

Elizabeth tapped her fingers on the door, and her eyes held a faraway look. "I feel so guilty about my anger." She hung her head. "I haven't told anyone, not even my family."

He could understand that. They'd been taught to trust God in all circumstances, but it wasn't always easy. Sometimes God's will led along an unknown and twisty path. But holding on to guilt and shame tied you in knots. And it put a barrier between you and God. Luke had experienced that too. But how could he help Elizabeth?

The last thing he wanted to do was act judgmental. That made people close down. Maybe if he opened up about his own pain, she'd listen. Was it possible to share without revealing that she'd been the cause of his own loss of faith?

"I understand how you feel. I went through something similar years ago. I didn't lose a spouse like you have, but I did lose out on something very precious."

Elizabeth's nervous movements stilled, and she turned to stare at him. "I didn't know that. What was it?"

Luke kept his eyes on the road but waved a hand. "I'd rather not talk about it. But that event was the most painful one I've ever been through."

"I'm sorry, Luke."

Her soft, almost-breathless words touched him. How would she feel if she knew he was talking about her?

"It was a rough time." *Sometimes it still is.* "I couldn't understand why God let it happen. I questioned Him, which kept me from His comfort." Comfort he'd needed often, especially this year.

Elizabeth's eyes welled with tears, and she stayed silent the rest of the way home.

Luke hoped he hadn't hurt her. She'd been through enough this year.

He pulled the buggy close to her house. Then he turned to her. "I didn't mean to be critical. I know what you've been going through is one of the most difficult things anyone ever has to face."

A single tear trickled down her cheek. "What you said helped. At least a little. I need some time to think about it."

And pray about it. If she wasn't ready to do that, he could do that for her until she was.

He started to get out to help her, but she shook her head. "I want to do it on my own."

She'd have an easier time if he helped, but he respected her wishes and stayed where he was. He didn't drive away until she was safely in the house. Then he headed back to work.

Before she opened the door, Elizabeth dabbed at her eyes. Luke's words had affected her deeply. If only she could tell him the whole truth. She had a feeling he'd understand and comfort her.

Right now, though, her heart and soul felt too exposed, too raw, to talk about it. And she didn't want her sister to see the tears.

As soon as she entered the house, Elizabeth sniffed the air. Something smelled different. It took her a moment to place it. *Pine.*

She hobbled down the hall and into the living room. Her sister had draped a fresh garland on the fireplace mantel. Elizabeth's stomach clenched.

No.

After being surrounded by holiday items all day, she hadn't wanted any reminders of Christmas in her own home.

Their *mamm* usually put pine boughs and candles on the mantel at home and strung Christmas cards on the wall nearby.

Elizabeth had done the same for her first Christmas with Owen. That was the last thing she wanted to be reminded of today.

"I'm making supper," Sarah called from the kitchen.

Elizabeth didn't need her sister's announcement. The scent of frying onions almost overpowered the evergreens.

She guessed Sarah was making onion patties, one of Elizabeth's favorite foods.

"Everything's almost ready." Sarah clanged a pot lid and opened the oven door. "Why don't you sit at the table? I'll bring it out."

Not used to being waited on, Elizabeth stood where she was, swaying on the crutches. She hadn't realized how tired she was. Yesterday had been traumatic, and the store had been packed all day.

Sarah came up behind her. "Sit. Sit. I can take care of everything." She set meatloaf on the table next to the bowl of applesauce.

Elizabeth tottered toward a chair and eased herself into it. "You didn't have to make a big meal. Soup and salad would have been fine."

Sarah looked a little hurt. "I thought it might make you feel better. Besides, once I finished the chores, I didn't have much else to do." She bustled out to the kitchen and returned with green beans and onion patties.

"*Danke.*" Although her stomach rebelled at all that food, Elizabeth tried to act grateful.

The pungent aroma of pine brought up too many memories. Her eyes burned with unshed tears. Grateful for the silent prayer, she bowed her head to hide them.

But as she'd told Luke on the ride home, she wrestled with anger. She'd never confessed that to anyone. Not even her family. Why had she trusted him with her darkest secret?

Sarah moved restlessly across from her, and Elizabeth sat up with a start. Prayer time was over, and she'd wasted it thinking of something else entirely. She always tried to pray, but since . . . Well, since then, it had been difficult.

Sarah passed her the bowl of green beans. "How did things go at work?"

"We had lines the length of the store. The customers never stopped." Because they had to eat everything on their plates, Elizabeth dished out only tiny amounts.

"What's the matter? Don't you like my cooking?" her sister demanded.

"I do." Elizabeth cast about for a reason that might satisfy her sister. "Someone delivered a huge pizza to the shop today. I ate way too much."

"I see."

"Don't worry. I'll enjoy all the leftovers. I can even take some to work with me."

That perked Sarah up, and she smiled. "Well, if I don't have to do much for meals the next few days, I could help you out by cleaning out that room."

Sarah didn't have to say which room. Elizabeth had been fearing this. Keeping her eyes on her plate, she tried to steady her voice, but it came out shaky. "I plan to do it after my cast comes off."

"At least let me pack things up. I could take the boxes over to the Re-Uzit. That'll make it easier for you."

Nothing would make it easier. So far, Elizabeth hadn't been brave enough to deal with it. "I'll do it myself." *Later. Much later.*

Elizabeth was so lost in thought she missed what her sister said after that until Sarah mentioned Luke's name.

"You know, I keep thinking that you might not be alive if it hadn't been for Luke." Her eyes filled with tears. "It was hard enough losing Owen, and I remember how hard we prayed for your recovery after that accident. I'm so grateful to God for healing you."

Outwardly, Elizabeth appeared to have recovered, but inwardly, she was still a mess. *I'm not sure I'll ever fully heal.* But Luke's words helped.

Sarah tilted her head to one side. "I've always been curious about Luke. He's very handsome, kind, and a good, hard worker. I wonder why he never married."

Elizabeth stabbed two green beans with her fork. The tines screeched across the plate, and Sarah glanced at her.

"Do you need help?"

"I'm fine." Elizabeth pushed out the words despite clenched teeth.

Sarah leaned across the table as if to take Elizabeth's silverware. "I can cut things for you, if you want."

"I don't need help." At the sharp edge in Elizabeth's voice, Sarah sank back into her chair. Elizabeth attempted to lighten the mood. "It's my leg that's broken, not my arms."

Sarah's reproachful look increased Elizabeth's guilt.

"I know." Her sister bit her lip. "I thought maybe you had bruises or something."

"*Ach*, Sarah. I'm sorry. I didn't mean to snap at you." At least not about helping with the meal. Being interested in Luke was a totally different matter.

For more than a week, Luke drove Elizabeth back and forth to work. It meant losing more than an hour of work every evening and then spending long hours in his workshop once he got home. But he didn't want Elizabeth to know he returned to the store after dropping her off, or she might find another way home. And he'd lose the best part of his day.

So far, she hadn't brought up the serious conversation they'd had, and Luke didn't want to push or pry. He helped the only way he could—by praying.

Often it was after nine before he got into his home workshop. He'd brought the cradles home last week because with all the Christmas rush at work, he had no free time. He should be working on them, but he'd spent most nights working on the nativity set for Elizabeth.

Luke hadn't given Yolanda his original carvings, because they revealed too much emotion. He intended to give some of those to Elizabeth, but a few were too rough and revealed too much of his inner angst, so he'd been making replacements. Once he completed those, he'd planned to finish the cradles.

The auction had gone well for New Beginnings last weekend, and his armoire had brought in a huge amount of money, much more than he'd have charged if he'd sold it in the store. Most of the money would cover feeding and clothing the girls as well as keeping a roof over their heads. But the shelter had few supplies for the teen moms who decided to keep their babies. Now that the Christmas rush was over, he'd see about making other furniture to help.

Last night he'd worked until almost midnight to complete the final nativity figure. Barely able to keep his eyes open, he added the final coat of white paint to one cradle, but the other still needed more work. He might have to deliver them a few days after Christmas unless he got that one done today.

All the holiday orders for his woodworking business had gone out yesterday, so he'd scheduled today off. Alan's brother had offered to help out in the store, and unlike some of the other stores that had long hours on Christmas Eve, Luke had told them to close by three.

But when he awoke to eight inches of snow, he was tempted to head into town to help Alan clear the sidewalks outside the business. Luke usually took care of several neighboring stores, particularly the ones with elderly owners. First, though, he'd have to shovel out his driveway and Elizabeth's.

He'd almost reached the end of his driveway when he heard the scream.

Chapter 8

*W*as that Elizabeth?

Luke rushed toward her house. Elizabeth lay in a heap at the foot of her porch steps.

He knelt beside her. "What happened?"

Half-laughing, half-crying, she waved an arm in the air. "I wanted to sweep off the porch, but I slipped on a patch of ice and bumped down the stairs."

"Are you hurt anywhere?"

"Besides my pride? No, but I'll probably have a few bruises tomorrow on my back and"—her cheeks flushed a becoming shade of pink—"and . . . never mind, I'm fine."

He was pretty sure he knew which part of her had taken the most bruising. "If you're sure nothing is broken, I'll take you inside." He bent to lift her.

"Luke, no. Just hand me my crutches. I'm fine."

Ignoring her protests, he lifted her gently in his arms and carried her inside. Kicking off his snow-encrusted boots on the doormat, he took her into the living room. After he lowered her onto the sofa, he went outside to retrieve her snow-covered crutches. He wiped them off and brought them to her.

She acknowledged him with a quick *danke*. Then she added, "I'm not an invalid."

Her attempt to look indignant didn't match the longing for care in her eyes. Luke's heart went out to her. She tried so hard to cover up her neediness.

"I know you're not. I only want to help."

Elizabeth bit her lip. "I didn't mean to be so *murrish*. It's just that . . ." She dipped her head and avoided meeting his eyes.

"It's all right." Luke's words came out too stiff and formal. He'd hoped to hide his hurt. Instead, he sounded miffed.

"*Ach*, Luke. I'm sorry. I'm grateful for all you've done—driving me to work, replenishing the firewood, shoveling my driveway." When he cleared his throat as if to deny it, she waved it away. "I know it was you. You've done so much. I can never repay you."

"I don't expect to be repaid." The gruffness of his voice came across as annoyed. Could he ever manage to say what he meant without giving off the wrong message? It would be easier if he wasn't trying to hide his feelings.

He tried to soften his tone, but this time, he sounded robotic. "God wants us to help others." That hadn't been his sole motivation, but he couldn't share his deeper reason.

"I know, but I have to learn to take care of myself."

Elizabeth may have intended to appear independent and capable, but Luke detected a quaver in her voice under that show of strength. Did she feel that she needed to go through life alone?

He'd be happy to assist her with anything she needed and more, but he couldn't say that. Not now. Not when she was still dressed in black. Not when she was still mourning. And maybe not ever.

He choked back the lump in his throat and tried to add lightness to their dark memories. "So, you planned to shovel your own sidewalk and driveway on crutches?" He lifted one eyebrow to show he was teasing.

Elizabeth stared at him for a long moment. Then she burst out laughing.

At the sudden change in her expression, Luke's heart contracted. Then it began beating double time. Her beauty took his breath away.

"*Neh.* I only planned to sweep and salt the porch. Just enough so I can get out to the buggy for church tomorrow morning."

He waved toward the driveway covered with eight inches of snow. "And how would they get to the house?" He kept his tone joking rather than critical.

But she sobered. "You must think me the most prideful and stubborn person you've ever met."

"Well, not the most," he teased. "I've met worse."

Planting her hands on her hips, Elizabeth demanded, "Like who?"

"I can't tell you. I refuse to gossip."

"Oh, you." But her smile had returned.

"Just to be clear," Luke said, "I don't think you're prideful or stubborn. I see you as a woman trying hard to cope in difficult circumstances. But accepting help from others is not a sign of weakness."

Another lesson Elizabeth needed to learn. This holiday season had been filled with them. Right now, she could practice graciously accepting the many things he'd done for her.

"*Danke.* Not just for the rides to work and for this"—she waved toward the freshly stocked woodpile—"but for everything. You've done so much for me."

"You don't have to thank me." His words came out gruff.

She must have embarrassed him by calling attention to his good deeds. Of course he wouldn't want praise for kindness. She should have thought of that.

He blew on his hands and shuffled his feet. "I'd better get going. I still have projects to finish in my workshop." He made himself turn and head for the door. If he didn't, he might spend all day staring at her.

"Wait," Elizabeth called after him. "When you're done, why don't you come in and warm up? I can make some hot chocolate."

Luke turned and smiled at her. "You have to return my favor?"

"*Neh, neh.*" The only things on her mind had been the length of the driveway and the below-freezing temperatures.

Come on, Elizabeth. Be honest. Wanting his company didn't enter your mind?

Luke was still waiting for her answer.

"I thought you might be cold after shoveling." Her answer sounded lame and defensive.

He stared at her for a moment. "It is pretty cold. I might want something to warm me up." His face blazed at how that sounded. He quickly added, "Hot cocoa is always good for that."

Elizabeth glanced down at the wooden floorboards, hoping he couldn't hear how her heartbeat had quickened. She tried to keep her tone neutral. "Just knock whenever you're finished."

"I will."

Her eyes misty, Elizabeth stared after him as he headed back outside. He took such tender care of her. As much as she appreciated it, it reinforced her loneliness.

Shaking off the thought, she picked up her crutches and eased herself off the couch. Maneuvering into the kitchen and getting all the ingredients took longer than she expected. She'd complained about her sister coddling her, but having her here had made life much easier. Sarah had moved back home last weekend to be closer to her new job, and Elizabeth missed the company.

With today being a Saturday, she didn't need to go into work, so she'd missed her usual drive with Luke this morning. Because she'd expected him to work on Christmas Eve, she'd offered to help at the store. But Yolanda had refused. She'd insisted Elizabeth needed to stay at home and enjoy her holiday weekend.

Now Elizabeth was glad she had. She'd get more time with Luke than she usually did, and his attention wouldn't be distracted by traffic. That thought made her insides flutter.

She went over to the window. Luke's back was to her, so he couldn't see her staring out the window. He lifted heavy shovelfuls of snow and easily tossed them aside. Woodworking must have given him those strong muscles, that brawny body.

He finished the last of the driveway and turned so suddenly she had no time to step back from the window. Had he seen her?

She clicked into the hallway and pulled open the front door. She didn't want him to forget her invitation.

Before he climbed the porch steps, he lifted the tarp over the woodpile and picked up some of the firewood he'd stacked there. "Nothing like a fire on a freezing day." He stepped onto the porch and stomped the snow off his boots.

Elizabeth shuffled backward on her crutches to pull open the door. When he walked in, he filled the entryway. She backed against the wall as he bent to set down the firewood. Then he removed his boots and hung his coat on a peg.

His deep blue work shirt highlighted the blue of his eyes. She forced herself to look away as he lifted the logs.

When he stood, Elizabeth sucked in a breath. She'd never been this close to his chest, his broad shoulders. Not while she was facing him. He'd pulled her against him when he'd rescued her, but then she'd had her back to him. Even in the ambulance, he'd been nearby, but not this close. Or if he had, she'd been too dazed to notice.

In her narrow hallway, she couldn't scoot away, so she rocked unsteadily on her crutches. Maybe this hadn't been such a *gut* idea.

"Lead the way." He motioned for her to precede him down the hall.

Her usual step-lift-*clunk* gait grew even more awkward with him behind her.

"Take your time." His breath lifted the tiny loose hairs on the back of her neck and sent shivers down her spine.

Was he afraid she'd fall again?

His nearness made her even more clumsy. She had to stop and steady herself several times.

"It's hard to use crutches, isn't it?"

"I guess," Elizabeth murmured. She didn't add that right now his presence made it even more difficult.

While she went to the stove to heat the milk, Luke tore a few sheets of paper from the old phone book she kept by the fire and wadded them up. After he lit those, he made sure the kindling caught before he joined her in the kitchen.

She'd propped herself up near the stove. Steam rose from the mugs she was stirring. Chocolate and— Luke inhaled deeply. *Peppermint?*

"Umm. That smells delicious." He couldn't wait to wrap his hands around the hot mug. Although he'd rather wrap his arms around Elizabeth. He shoved his hands into his pockets to keep himself from acting on that impulse.

"Would you like a lemon bar? Sarah made some when she stayed last week."

"Why don't I carry all this into the living room so we can sit by the fire?" Luke offered.

On second thought, maybe that wasn't such a wise idea. Relaxing together in front of the fire brought up too many of his fantasies. He reminded himself Elizabeth was still a grieving widow.

And today was Christmas Eve. He should be in his shop working on the second cradle. He'd intended to do that as soon as he'd finished shoveling, but he couldn't resist spending time with Elizabeth.

Besides, she seemed lonely and sad today. Perhaps she needed company.

Or maybe he was creating excuses.

Her grateful smile chased away all thoughts of leaving. After she pointed out a tray, he loaded it and carried it to the table by the couch. Once Elizabeth had settled onto one end of the sofa, he brought her a mug and a lemon bar. Then he sat on a wooden rocking chair across from her.

Luke sipped the steaming chocolate and appreciated the warmth flowing inside. The fire hadn't caught yet. Even so, his toes and fingers stung as they thawed. But the rest of him remained much too hot.

Elizabeth floated off into daydreams. Sitting by the fire with the man she loved. She sat up so abruptly her hot chocolate sloshed in the mug. Where had that thought come from?

Struggling to tamp down the old feelings rising inside, she gulped a large sip of cocoa and choked. She pinched her lips together so she didn't dribble chocolate all over her. She managed to swallow the mouthful of hot liquid scorching her tongue.

"Are you all right?"

Something about the warmth of the fire and Luke's accepting expression made Elizabeth lower her guard. He'd only been asking about her choking, but she answered honestly, "I don't know. I'm not sure if I'll ever be all right again."

Luke's eyes filled with sympathy, and she dropped her gaze. Her attraction to him added to her guilt.

"I understand."

She appreciated his attempt at comfort, but no one else could really know. Only someone who'd been through what she had could truly comprehend her grief. Or her guilt.

"I mean, I can't understand what it's like for you," he said, "but if you ever feel like talking about it . . ." The anguish in his words told her he was dealing with his own sorrow.

"Maybe sometime." If she could talk to anyone, it would be him. She had no idea why, but she'd never trusted anyone the way she trusted Luke.

He cleared his throat. "So are you going to your parents' house for dinner tomorrow or . . ."

Elizabeth hesitated. He'd been trying to change the subject. Instead, he'd hit on a different guilty secret. She might not have been honest with her family, but she decided to be truthful with Luke.

"I told my parents"—she clenched her hands in her lap—"I was invited to Owen's family dinner. That much was true."

Luke waited, as if sensing her need to unburden herself.

"Except I thanked Owen's parents for their invitation but said my parents wanted me to come home for the holiday. That's true, but I didn't tell them or my parents I don't plan to go to either house." Her hands grew more agitated.

"You're spending Christmas alone?"

Elizabeth hung her head. "I can't sit across the table from my family and try to act cheerful, and I don't want to drag down their day. And being with Owen's family would remind me—and them—of all we've lost."

Luke longed to clench his own hands, but he forced himself to listen. Hearing the pain underlying Elizabeth's words stabbed his already-bloodied heart. But she needed comfort.

He pushed aside his own hurt to concentrate on hers. She'd been through much more than he'd endured. At least Elizabeth was alive and he could see her, even if her heart still belonged to another man.

When she started talking again, her words were so quiet Luke could barely hear them. "The accident took away something precious. Precious and irreplaceable. I've been struggling to accept it ever since."

"It's not easy losing someone you love." Luke should know. He'd been through that heartbreak. But his loss didn't compare with knowing you'd never see the person you loved. Not ever again.

Unless they both went to heaven, he corrected himself.

But sometimes that felt so far away when you needed and wanted that person in your life, experiencing the day-to-day activities. Talking, touching, connecting . . . Comforting, embracing . . .

All things he wanted to do with Elizabeth.

To keep from reaching out, he clutched his suspenders.

"Everywhere I go, I'm reminded of . . ." Elizabeth stumbled to a stop. She couldn't tell Luke. It wouldn't be proper.

But the past few weeks at the Christmas shop had been hard. First Melva with her New Beginnings flyers, then Yolanda with her baby news.

Melva had collected the flyers on the door last Saturday after the auction, so Elizabeth didn't have to face them, but she couldn't escape Yolanda's baby joy. Every day, Yolanda bubbled over with excitement as she shopped for presents for her new granddaughter.

"Look at this." Yolanda held up a miniature Santa suit along with a hat that matched the one she always wore. "Isn't this the cutest sleeper? I ordered some for the store."

A wave of sadness engulfed Elizabeth. Her own baby wouldn't have worn an outfit like that, but each reminder of babies hurt. Perhaps she should explain her deep ache to her boss. If Yolanda understood, maybe she'd stop bringing in baby toys, clothes, and accessories. But Elizabeth couldn't bring herself to dim Yolanda's exhilaration over reuniting with her daughter or meeting her first grandchild.

"I decided we should do a Santa baby corner," Yolanda said. "You're so good at decorating, I'll put you in charge."

Elizabeth shook her head. "I don't think—"

Yolanda interrupted her. "I know you worry about that pride stuff, but you do have a talent, and you should use it." Her face fell. "I wish I'd thought of it earlier, though. It's too late to stock up for Christmas, but we can plan a baby special for our Christmas-in-July sale."

Maybe by then Elizabeth would have come to terms with her grief. If she ever did.

"Elizabeth?" Luke said gently.

She looked so sad and far away. He didn't want to startle her or bother her, but he wanted to console her.

"The first Christmas after my parents died," Luke said, "I didn't feel like going anywhere either. It was my hardest holiday ever."

Elizabeth focused on him as if his story had become a lifeline. If it helped, he'd keep talking.

"I refused to spend the holiday with my brothers in Indiana. I stayed home alone, walking through the house, touching special things that belonged to Mamm or Daed, reliving memories."

Her sharp indrawn breath told him she'd felt the same. "I didn't know you went through that." A look of guilt crossed her face. "We should have invited you over."

Luke shook his head. The last place he would have wanted to be that Christmas—or any Christmas—was at the newlyweds' dinner table. "I didn't want to be with anyone, so I understand why you don't want to go to your family dinners."

"*Danke* for saying that." Elizabeth looked relieved. "I've felt terrible about not wanting to be with my parents. But how did you get over it?"

"I'm not sure you ever do. You learn to live with the loss, and the ache lessens over time. I also remembered something Mamm always said: 'When you're lonely, focus on others rather than yourself.' I took her advice, and it did help."

So that's why he was always so generous. Elizabeth bit her lip. She'd been so busy feeling sorry for herself, she'd closed off her heart.

Forgive me for my selfishness, Lord. Please show me someone in need.

Then a still, small voice inside answered her prayer. *You already know who to help.*

Elizabeth shook her head. *No*, she screamed inside. *Please, Lord, anything but that.*

God had been nudging her to do this for months. He'd even brought the perfect person into her life a few weeks ago. But she'd turned away.

Luke sat silent while she fought an internal battle. Across from her, he'd bowed his head and laced his fingers together as if in prayer. Was he praying for her? If so, he needed to pray harder and longer, because God had asked her to do the impossible.

Chapter 9

Elizabeth's face revealed his words had made an impact. She sat rigid and tense as if fighting a war within. Unsure what to do, Luke kept praying.

He entrusted her to God. And at the same time, he surrendered his own human desires and will.

Lord, please help and comfort her. I'm willing to do whatever You ask, even if it means staying out of her life forever.

After his surrender, peace flooded his soul. If God wanted him to walk away and not come back, it would be the hardest thing he'd ever been asked to do, but Luke meant every word. Even so, he'd never stop loving her or praying for her.

When he opened his eyes, Elizabeth had scrunched up her face and she'd squeezed her eyes shut. Her head twisted back and forth as if she were saying no.

Luke kept praying. He couldn't bear to see her suffering. *Please, Lord, help her to surrender to Your will.*

Then he prayed for her peace and comfort. He still had his head bowed when Elizabeth's soft voice called his name.

"Luke?" she said again, hesitantly.

He looked up.

"I-I have something I need to do, but I can't do it alone. Would you be willing to help?"

"Of course." He'd do anything she asked.

"It means climbing the stairs, and I'm really slow."

Luke wanted to offer to carry her, but he sensed she'd want to get upstairs on her own. "We can go as slowly as you need to."

Elizabeth bowed her head, and her reply came out muffled. "It might . . . take time . . . upstairs too."

"I have all day. Whatever you need."

Elizabeth stayed seated for so long Luke wondered if she'd given up on her idea. Then with a sigh that seemed to come from the depths of her soul, she clutched her crutches and pulled herself shakily to her feet.

Luke inched along behind her, careful not to get too close. He only stayed near enough to catch her if she fell.

She stopped at the first door at the top of the stairs. "In here," she said, her voice barely above a whisper.

He stepped to the side and pushed open the door to let her enter first, but she wobbled on her crutches, her face drained of color. He stepped forward to catch her if she fell. Or fainted.

She squeezed her eyes shut as if in unbearable pain.

"Elizabeth, what's wrong?"

She didn't answer. Only stared past him into the room beyond. Luke turned to see what had caused her distress.

Behind them lay a nursery. A hand-carved wooden cradle rocked ever so slightly from the vibrations of the old reclaimed wooden floorboards they'd stepped on. A low dresser topped with a plastic pad held stacks of diapers along with an assortment of creams and ointments. A rocking chair, also disturbed by his heavy footfalls, creaked back and forth.

Shell-shocked, Luke tried to wrap his mind around this. She'd been expecting a baby? He'd never known.

That wasn't surprising. Amish women never talked about

their pregnancies in front of men. But he and Owen had been close. Closer even than brothers. Owen might have hinted at having his firstborn.

"*Ach*, Elizabeth," Luke breathed. He hadn't known she'd lost her husband and a child.

"I-I want to give all of this away. New Beginnings needs *baby*"—the word dripped with agony—"items."

"Are you sure you don't want to keep some of it?" Perhaps she'd marry again. Have more children.

Luke wished he could be that lucky man, but most of all, he wanted her to be happy. That's why he'd backed away when she'd chosen Owen. And now he'd just made a promise to give Elizabeth up if God willed.

She buried her face in her hands. "*Neh*. Everything has to go. I want to clear out the room."

"But—"

"You don't understand," she said almost savagely. Then she softened her voice until he could barely hear it and choked out, "I may . . . never have . . . children."

Although she wasn't looking at him, his cheeks heated to hear her talk about something so intimate, so personal. But her grief overshadowed his uneasiness. She needed comfort. How would she ever get over her losses? No wonder she'd been in such agony. She'd lost her husband, her child, and her future.

Luke wished he could wrap his arms around her, pull her close, reassure her everything would be all right. Even if he gave in to temptation and did the forbidden, he could never make up for all she'd lost. Never.

Powerless to stop the tears trickling down her cheeks, Elizabeth turned her back to Luke. She'd just let him see into the most private part of her life, the deep source of her grief. She'd not only lost Owen; she'd also lost her unborn child.

This Christmas she should have been holding a baby in her

arms. A tiny little one. Elizabeth wrapped her arms around herself, but nothing could lessen her loss.

Why, God, why?

Downstairs, she'd asked for God's forgiveness for her selfishness. But standing in this room surrounded by her baby's things, the agony pierced her, fresh and intense.

Until the accident, she'd always believed in God's perfect will and accepted both blessings and hardships. Whatever had come her way, she'd trusted He had sent it. But this? This she struggled to accept. Her heart and spirit rebelled. Everything in her railed against this tragedy.

Why did You take my baby? My little one?

No answer.

A huge, thick wall blocked her words from flowing upward. No healing or peace flowed downward. Trapped in a cage, bound by bars of grief, anguish pressing in from all sides, Elizabeth struggled to follow through with her decision.

If she let go of all these baby things, it would mean this loss was real.

But it already was real. Hanging on to all these things would only bring more grief.

Elizabeth steeled herself. New Beginnings had teens who could use these things. She'd been raised to be giving. To donate to charity. To help others. But clearing out this room would be a constant reminder of her empty arms.

Please give me the strength to do this, Lord.

Did she have any right to call on God for miracles when she raged at Him inside?

Luke stood nearby as Elizabeth's gaze moved from item to item in the room. Her eyes revealed she was conflicted. He wanted to suggest she give herself more time to heal.

But this was between her and God. So, he waited. And asked the Lord to help her make her decision.

She squeezed her eyes shut for a few moments and heaved a huge sigh. When she opened them, tears sparkled on her eyelashes, but her face appeared calm. "I'm ready."

"Are you sure?" Luke didn't want her to do something she'd later regret.

Elizabeth hesitated only a second before nodding. "Would you be able to take these to New Beginnings today?"

All thoughts of finishing the other cradle fled. Elizabeth needed him, and he wanted to be here for her. "I can go and get the farm wagon. We should be able to fit everything in there."

She headed for the wooden dresser that would have served as a changing table and leaned down to open the bottom drawer.

Luke rushed over to assist her so she didn't fall. "I can get that." He waited until she'd stepped back to pull open the drawer. It was empty.

"I-I thought I'd put everything up here"—she fluttered a hand toward the diapers and baby products—"in the drawer."

He removed the drawer and packed everything neatly inside. Elizabeth bit her lip as he took out and stacked several filled drawers. "I'll carry these down first."

"Wait!" Elizabeth's heartrending cry stopped him as he reached the top of the stairs.

Had she changed her mind?

He set the drawers down on the landing.

Her face ashen, she clicked her crutches on the wooden floor and shuffled forward, making her way toward him. "I . . . there's something in that top drawer I want to, need to, keep."

Hoping to save her some steps, he asked, "What is it?"

She stopped and kept her eyes shut for a long moment. "Under the blankets," she whispered.

Luke lifted the small stack of blankets and extracted a large padded book. A scrapbook.

His sisters kept scrapbooks for their miscarriages and stillborns. They filled the pages with footprints and keepsakes. Sometimes, if they'd been close to delivery, they had a viewing and funeral, so the book was filled with cards and pressed flowers from sympathy bouquets.

He'd thought it a bit macabre. But his *mamm* gently explained that each child God brought into the world should be honored. No matter how brief the life.

Aching for Elizabeth, he handed over the scrapbook. Unlike his sisters' thick books, this one had few pages. She must not have been far along when she lost the baby. But the fancy script on the cover read: *Matthew James*. So, she'd known she'd have had a son.

Wobbling on her crutches, Elizabeth clutched the scrapbook with one hand. Shifting her weight onto her good leg, she cradled the book close. A cold, empty substitute for the baby who should have been in her arms.

What could he say to help, to comfort? Words failed him.

Lord, please wrap Your arms around her. Comfort her. Give her peace.

He sent her a sympathetic look. "I'm sorry." His words came out husky but heartfelt.

She tipped her head up and down in a barely perceptible nod. Then she turned and, shoulders slumped, leaned on the crutches, not moving.

"Do you still want to"—Luke waved a hand uncertainly toward the dresser drawers even though she couldn't see him—"move all these things?"

In the silence that followed, she rocked back and forth as if she were rocking a baby. Luke couldn't bear to watch. He longed to hug her, hold her. But he had no right.

Elizabeth had to do this. If she didn't, she'd never again find the strength. If she sent Luke away now, she wouldn't feel right asking him to come back another time. It had been hard enough showing him the room, watching his reaction, seeing the pity in his eyes.

Besides, how could she be so selfish? Keeping all these baby things when many young girls at New Beginnings had nothing.

The scrapbook burned against her chest. God had taken Matthew James before she'd had a chance to mother him, but she should be an example of the mother she'd prayed to be. A mother who put a child's needs ahead of her own. A mother who opened her heart, no matter how painful. A mother who shared God's love.

He gave His only Son. The least she could do was give up a few worldly possessions.

After a long period of deliberating, one word exploded from Elizabeth's lips, "*Jah.*" The answer had been torn from the depths of her soul.

She stayed frozen in place until Luke's soft grunt indicated he'd picked up the dresser drawers. As much as she yearned to stare as he carted them downstairs, she forced herself to hobble to the nursery.

By the time Luke returned, Elizabeth had put the scrapbook on the closet shelf and started packing the contents of the closet into the diaper pail and hamper. He gave her a gentle, caring smile that thawed the ice around her heart.

"I can set that in the cradle"—he pointed to the almost-full diaper pail—"and take both of them down."

Elizabeth managed a nod. She set one more pack of diapers inside and handed him the lid. The rest of the diapers and most of the clothing fit into the hamper. She waited until Luke had gone downstairs before struggling to her feet, using the door-jamb for support.

Balancing precariously on one leg, she lifted the two cross-stitch wall hangings of Bible verses and tucked them into the hamper. She barely had time to steady herself before Luke bounded up the stairs.

"Is that everything?" He indicated the hamper.

Elizabeth swallowed hard. "The rocker too."

"You sure?" Luke studied her.

She stared at the rocker where she'd dreamed of rocking her little one. The baby she'd never have. Her *jah* came out hesitant, uncertain.

"I could move it somewhere else if you'd like."

Elizabeth tore her gaze from his questioning eyes. "You can take it," she said in a tear-clogged voice.

Luke set the hamper on the rocker seat and headed out of the room. Rather than following, she stood and glanced around, remembering her joy as she and Owen had painted and furnished the room. Now it was bare.

Leaning against the wall for support, Elizabeth picked up the last of the baby clothes in the closet and hugged them to her chest. Then stuffing them into her generous coat pockets, she clomped to the door.

She took one last look back before she closed the door on the room that was as empty as her life.

Chapter 10

That seemed to be the last load, but he should check to see if Elizabeth had anything else that needed to go. Luke hesitated before climbing the stairs again. She might need some time and privacy. She had to say good-bye.

He cleared the thickness clogging his throat and called up to her, "I'm going to get the wagon now. I won't be long. Please don't come down until I get back."

No answer.

Luke hoped she'd heed his advice and wait. The thought of her tumbling to the bottom of stairs increased his worry. He put on his boots and jogged across their snow-crusted lawns to hitch up the team. His icy fingers fumbled with the too-stiff leather. The faster he worked, the clumsier his attempts. Finally, he succeeded in connecting everything and hurried back.

He rushed up the stairs. Elizabeth had stayed where he'd left her, staring at the door of the now vacant room. He hated to disturb her, so he stood silent, giving her time to grieve.

"Luke?" she said, her voice low and soft. "I'd like to go with you."

For a moment, Luke's heart beat wildly. She wanted to go with him? Then his soaring spirits crash-landed. She meant go to New Beginnings.

As much as he'd like her company, he'd rather not see her suffer. She'd been through so much already. "I can do it myself."

She turned anguished eyes to him. "I have to do this."

No, you don't. He wanted to argue, but the tenseness of her jaw told him she'd made up her mind.

She waved away his offer to help her downstairs. Instead, she sat and bumped down each step, propelling herself with her hands and good leg, her cast sticking out in the air. He walked backward a few stairs below her to be sure she made it safely.

Her gaze far away and distracted, she didn't protest when he helped her into her coat or held out his hand to assist her into the wagon. She even let him wrap her in blankets, but she seemed lost in another world.

Frigid winds whipped past their faces as they traveled the icy roads to New Beginnings, the furniture rattling behind them. When they pulled in front of the building, Elizabeth huddled deeper into the blankets, her face grim. If only he could erase the agony swimming in her eyes.

Elizabeth's teeth chattered from more than snow as Luke helped her down from the wagon. *I'm not sure I can do this.*

If she could turn around now, she'd do it. She shook her head. Holding on to baby things she couldn't use when someone else needed them was selfish.

Lord, I can't go through with this unless You help me.

Once again, she doubted God would hear her after she'd spent so much time blocking Him from her life. But as soon as she prayed, a deep inner peace flowed over her. No matter how painful, she was doing the right thing.

"You're trembling." Luke's concerned gaze probed deep

into her soul. "*Ach*, Elizabeth, we can go back home if you want."

She wavered on her crutches, but not in her decision. "*Neh*, I need to do this." Her words lacked the conviction she carried in her heart.

Luke studied her closely. "Let's get you inside to warm up. If you change your mind when we go in, we can turn around and leave."

Elizabeth had no intention of doing that. She just had to get through this ordeal.

The gray-haired Mennonite lady behind the counter greeted them with a cheerful smile. "Welcome to New Beginnings. I'm Elvira Hess."

In the large, sunny living room to their left, pregnant teens chatted or texted on cell phones. One curled on a window seat reading a book. Another cradled a newborn.

A sharp, swift arrow shot through Elizabeth. She turned away so quickly she wobbled on her crutches. Luke put a hand on her shoulder to steady her. He stayed close behind her, his body heat radiating into her back, giving her much-needed support.

"I, um, have a donation of baby things. If you want them, that is."

"Of course we do. So many of the girls here have nothing, and no one to help them feed or clothe their little ones."

The sound of squalling infants floated down the hallway. A young girl, her eyes red and swollen, appeared in the doorway behind Mrs. Hess. "I need help feeding the babies."

Babies, babies, and more babies. All these young girls all have children. But I don't.

"I'll be right with you, Aubrey, as soon as I finish with this donation." Mrs. Hess slid a ledger across the counter. "If you'll just record your contact information and the items you plan to donate, I'll prepare a receipt."

Elizabeth's hand shook as she jotted down the items. A tear dripped onto the paper. She lifted the pen, trying to blink away the blurriness in her eyes.

Luke leaned closer to whisper in her ear, "And the cradle."

He must think she'd forgotten. But she hadn't. She only needed time to compose herself.

"Do you want me to write it?" he asked.

She surrendered the pen and blinked hard while Luke added the cradle and rocking chair.

"Furniture?" Mrs. Hess asked when Luke turned the ledger toward her.

"You don't take furniture?" After not wanting to give it up, Elizabeth dreaded the thought of having to carry it back upstairs, of having to face emptying the room another time.

"We most certainly do. It's just rare to get such a large donation. Are you both sure you want to do this?"

Luke cleared his throat, but before he could correct Mrs. Hess's mistake, Elizabeth cut him off.

"*Jah*—yes." Elizabeth's lips trembled. "I lost my unborn baby last year, and . . ." She couldn't push out any more words.

Luke squeezed her shoulder gently. She glanced back at him gratefully and stayed focused on the reassuring pressure. His tender touch was the only thing keeping her from falling apart.

Mrs. Hess glanced at him, a question in her eyes. To Elizabeth's relief, he only nodded.

"You're both young. Perhaps God will bless you with more children."

"*Neh*, I can't have another one." How could she with no husband? And she'd never marry again. Not when she couldn't have the man she loved. She should correct the woman's mistake about Luke, but she couldn't bear any more pity.

The woman's face softened, and her eyes filled with sympathy. "I'm so sorry." She reached across the desk and grasped Elizabeth's hands. "Sometimes we don't understand the path

God has chosen for us, but remember He loves you dearly and His grace is all-sufficient."

Although she nodded, Elizabeth hadn't found that to be true. But the Lord had answered some of her prayers. And deep inside, she recognized that she'd been the one blocking His grace and His comfort.

Melva bounced into the room. "Luke, what are you doing here? I mean, it's lovely to see you. Did you know how much your armoire sold for?"

The price she named made Elizabeth gasp. He'd given something that valuable to the auction? Her own donation today paled in comparison.

Mrs. Hess's eyes rounded. "You're the Luke who donated the armoire. We're ever so grateful." She turned to her daughter. "And he's back with more donations."

Luke started to correct her, but Elizabeth shook her head. She didn't want credit for this donation. He appeared uncomfortable, but he complied.

"Melva, can you help Aubrey with the babies while I finish up here? And please ask your father to come out and help unload the furniture."

"Sure, Mom," Melva said, and flashed Luke and, by extension, Elizabeth a broad smile. "Come on, Aubrey."

But the girl kept her gaze fastened on Luke and Elizabeth as Luke leaned down to whisper, "Melva reminds me of you as a teenager. Always so bright and cheery."

Elizabeth turned to look at him. "She does?" How far had she come from that young, enthusiastic girl who trusted God in everything to a depressed twenty-two-year-old who resented God's decisions?

A secret smile played on Luke's lips. The smile that had made her fall in love. The smile that often haunted her dreams. The smile she wished—

She turned back around. Melva and Aubrey had gone, and Mrs. Hess was too busy writing the receipt to notice Elizabeth's dejected expression. Her spirits had been damaged enough. She didn't need to fall back in love with the man who'd broken her heart.

Luke couldn't even imagine how difficult this must be for Elizabeth to see all these girls, hear babies crying, and know she couldn't have a child of her own. He hadn't realized that was the case.

Now the tears in her eyes as she stroked that sparkling baby ornament took on a different meaning. He'd tenderly wrapped the little decoration and planned to put it on her front steps tomorrow. At least he'd discovered all this before he caused her even more heartache.

As soon as he got home, he'd put the ornament in the finished cradle and give it to New Beginnings. It would look nice hanging on the small Christmas tree in the lobby.

"Hey, Luke. Good to see you." Mr. Hess pumped his hand. "Thank you both for your generosity." With a smile as broad as his daughter's, he included Elizabeth. "Let's get going. It's cold out there."

In less than ten minutes, the wagon was unloaded and the furniture placed in the lobby. "I'm pretty sure I know which girl we'll be giving these to. Right, Elvira?"

His wife nodded and smiled. "I can't thank you all enough." As her husband passed, she remarked, "That means the only other thing we need is one more cradle."

Elizabeth had started toward the door, but Luke stopped. "I did tell Melva I'd make two cradles for you. They're almost done."

"That would be perfect. She won't need them until next week. God is so good."

Mrs. Hess didn't see Elizabeth wince, but Luke did. He reached for her hand, and she didn't pull away after he squeezed it. She clung to his fingers.

Heavenly Father, please comfort her broken spirit and show her Your love.

When Elizabeth woke on Christmas morning, the sad, dull ache she'd gone to bed with the night before cast a pall over the day. Rather than scrambling out of bed the way she usually did, she stayed under the covers.

She could spend the day in bed. Nobody would know. No one at all.

Her family and Owen's each assumed she'd gone elsewhere for the meal. And she'd made it clear to Luke yesterday, when he'd offered to come over to keep her company, that she needed a day by herself to come to terms with the empty room upstairs. Too bad it had to be Christmas Day.

With nobody stopping by, would it hurt to leave her daily chores undone?

After lying there for a while, Elizabeth scolded herself, *You made this choice to be alone. You could get dressed and go to either house.*

Luke's words about helping others came back to her. She'd spent so much time pitying herself, she'd neglected God's command to care for others. *Jah*, she'd donated the precious items she'd spent so much time making and selecting to New Beginnings, but she hadn't given her time or shared her love. Instead, she'd focused inward. It had all been about *me, me, me*.

Talk about *hochmut*. Wasn't feeling sorry for yourself a form of pride? She'd been putting her needs and feelings first.

God, please forgive me for being self-centered. Help me to think more about others rather than dwelling on my own pain.

As she prayed, some of her gloom lifted. And she saw even more clearly her sin of pride. Not only had she been immersed in self-pity, but being angry at God also stemmed from the same root.

Realizing this, Elizabeth wished she could fall to her knees to cry out to the Heavenly Father for forgiveness. But her cast kept her confined to bed for prayers. Surely God would understand. She prostrated her heart before Him.

Oh, Lord, I see now that my rage and my refusal to submit to Your will also stems from pride. I thought I knew better than You how my life should run. I wanted to take control and refused to accept this path You've led me down. I may never know why everything happened, but I surrender to You. Not my will but Yours be done.

A tidal wave of God's love and forgiveness engulfed her, washing away her anger and replacing it with acceptance. And God's comfort enveloped her. She'd blocked His love and support by refusing to surrender to His will. The sadness and heartache hadn't been totally erased, but it had become more bearable because now she could lean on Him.

Elizabeth lay there for a while, basking in the warmth of God's love and the wonder of Christmas.

Her heart lighter, she reached for her crutches. She selected a black dress from habit, then stopped. Today she was celebrating Christ's birth.

Pushing aside her three black dresses, she reached to the back of the closet, where she'd shoved her four other dresses, the ones she'd worn when she was younger. Maybe the bright pink wasn't suitable, but only family would see her today.

Putting on a cheerful color improved her mood even more. As a child of the King, she could celebrate today. She clicked down the hallway and out to the kitchen.

Cooking wasn't easy when she was on crutches, but with her heart clean and light, Elizabeth set dough rising and started a batch of cookies before she made breakfast. Humming a hymn, she hobbled around preparing the recipes.

Once she finished baking the sticky buns, she'd call her parents to let them know she was coming for the meal. Her sticky buns and cookies were family favorites. She'd take those to make up for not helping to cook the dinner. Besides, with her crutches she'd only be in the way of all the hustling, bustling aunts and cousins in the kitchen.

She'd have to trek to Luke's and ask to use the phone he kept in his backyard woodshop for business. Someone from her family would drive over to get her. She owed them all an apology for the fibs she'd told. She'd confess to Owen's family too and spend Second Christmas with them tomorrow.

Two hours later as Elizabeth was balancing on one leg to pull the sticky buns from the oven, three loud raps on the front door startled her. She nearly dropped the pan and went tumbling after it.

She grabbed the edge of the counter to stay upright and slid the pan onto the wooden cutting board. She'd turn the sticky buns out after she answered the door. Most likely, Luke had broken his promise and come over to check on her. The thought made her spirits even lighter.

Sidling over to where she'd leaned her crutches, she almost tipped over a cooling rack of cookies. She shuffled to the door as quickly as she could, but when she opened it, nobody stood there. Instead, a carved wooden cradle sat gently rocking on the porch, the back of its rounded wooden hood facing her. Diapers, blankets, and baby clothes had been piled in the cradle.

Elizabeth squeezed her eyes shut to hold back the pain. How could anyone be so cruel?

Then her eyes flew open. That was her cradle. The one she'd donated to New Beginnings. Why had someone put it on the porch?

Tracks in the snow led to the woods at the side of Elizabeth's house. There someone in a dark coat stood watching.

"Hey!" Elizabeth called out, but the figure turned and fled. "Wait!"

Elizabeth ventured a little farther out onto the porch. She slid on an icy spot and clung to the doorknob, hoping it would prevent a fall.

And then the bundle of blankets moved.

Chapter 11

A baby. There was a baby in that cradle under the mound of clothes and diapers. Taking a few cautious steps, Elizabeth moved forward to peek under the wooden hood.

She sucked in a breath. *Not one baby. But two. Twins.*

Why had they been left on her porch? She'd discover that answer later. Right now, she needed to get them out of the freezing weather.

After hobbling back to the doorway, she leaned her crutches against the house and used the doorjamb to lower herself to the porch. Because of the cast, her leg stuck out in front of her, but she managed to lean forward and pull the cradle toward her.

Then she wriggled backward, dragging the cradle with her. After it bumped over the threshold, it moved more smoothly on the polished wooden floorboards.

As soon as the cradle was far enough inside, Elizabeth kicked the door closed.

After it banged shut, a voice called, "Elizabeth, are you all right?"

Luke. She'd slammed the door in his face.

She'd also left her crutches on the porch. *I need to get up. But how?*

Maybe she could pull herself upright by leaning against the wall. As she started sidling in that direction, Luke hammered on the door.

One of the babies wailed. The pounding must have startled the little one. Elizabeth scooted back to the cradle and lifted the crying infant.

A piece of paper fluttered to the floor.

Elizabeth put the baby over her shoulder and rubbed the little girl's back. At least she assumed it was a girl from the pink sleeper. "Are you hungry, little one?" She didn't even know the baby's name.

She leaned over to see if the cradle contained bottles. A can of formula and several bottles had been tucked under the diapers and clothes.

A muffled "Elizabeth" penetrated the door.

She'd forgotten all about Luke. "Come in," she called. "The door's open."

He must not have heard her, because he didn't enter.

Elizabeth didn't want to yell louder and disturb the sleeping baby. The one she held was still whimpering. Wrapping one arm tightly around the little girl, Elizabeth pushed herself toward the door with her other hand.

As she passed, the paper on the floor beside the cradle caught her attention. In bold printing, it said:

> *Elizabeth,*
> *The day you came to New Beginnings, I was debating about giving my daughters up for adoption. When I overheard you say you'd lost your own baby, it broke my heart. I could tell you'd be a car-*

*ing, generous mother because you spent so much
time making all those baby clothes and because you
donated all you had to New Beginnings.*

    *I want my daughters to experience something I
never had—two loving parents. I'd like my little
girls to grow up in a stable home where they'll be
cherished by a couple with loving and caring hearts.
It's clear you and your husband have a deep bond.
I've never seen two people so much in love.*

    *This is the hardest thing I've ever done in my
life, but I cannot do for my twins what the two of
you can do. If you're willing to adopt them, you
can contact me at New Beginnings any time before
the New Year to sign the adoption papers.*

    Prayerfully yours,

    Aubrey Lundeen

Elizabeth's hand shook as she reread the letter. Aubrey wanted her to adopt the twins? But the teen mother thought Elizabeth was married. To Luke.

"Elizabeth?" Luke sounded frantic.

Too stunned to answer, Elizabeth sat there in a daze, holding the letter. Adopt these babies? She'd love to keep the darling little twins, but would Aubrey give her daughters to a single mother? Most likely not. She wanted them to have two parents.

From the depths of her heart, Elizabeth cried out in silent anguish, *Not again, Lord. I've already lost one baby. Now I'm given a chance to have two, only to have them snatched from me.*

The baby in the cradle yowled. The little girl in Elizabeth's arms fussed louder. Elizabeth cuddled her close. After stuffing the letter into her pocket, Elizabeth picked up the other twin.

Right now, these little ones needed her. Elizabeth pushed aside her own pain. She might only have these small girls for a day, but she'd pour out all of her love. Just like God had when

He sent baby Jesus. As Luke had pointed out, sacrificial giving was the real meaning of Christmas.

Elizabeth had sacrificed when she'd donated her baby things to New Beginnings. But that was nothing compared to the heart-wrenching sacrifice of giving up the chance to keep these two precious children.

The doorknob rattled.

Elizabeth croaked out, "Come in," but her too-tight throat choked off the words. She swallowed hard to try again, but before she could answer, the door crashed open.

Luke had been outside getting firewood when Elizabeth cried out. He couldn't make out her words, but she sounded upset. He dropped the logs and rushed toward her house.

In the distance, she hunched over a large object on her porch. Most of it—possibly a large wooden box filled with stacks of cloth—seemed to be inside the open front door. But Elizabeth was on the floor, her leg with her cast stuck straight out on the porch.

Had she fallen? Or had that large object knocked her over?

Luke sprinted through the snow, his boots churning up the powdery snow on top and crunching through the icy layers beneath. He had to help her.

Puffing out white clouds of breath, he'd almost reached her front door when it slammed. He stood on the porch. Had she seen him and shut him out?

Yesterday she'd made him promise not to come over, but what if she needed someone to lift that big box? She might also need assistance to stand.

"Elizabeth?" he called through the door. "Are you all right?"

No answer.

Luke spied her crutches leaning against the house. She couldn't get around without those.

He knocked. A cry penetrated the door. A combination of mewling and yowling. Was she hurt?

He called again. But only silence greeted him.

She could be lying there unable to move. Maybe even pinned under that box or whatever it was. He had to help her.

When she didn't answer his third call and the cries grew louder and shriller, Luke rattled the doorknob. He hated to barge in uninvited, but he couldn't let her cry. Besides, she needed her crutches. He reached for them with his free arm.

The knob turned in his hand. He pushed the door open, stepped inside, and froze. Elizabeth sat on the floor, a bawling baby in each arm.

Impossible.

He blinked and looked again. The wooden object had not been a box, but the end of a cradle. If he wasn't mistaken, it was the cradle they'd dropped off at New Beginnings. How had it gotten here?

Elizabeth appeared to be as stunned as he felt.

"What's going on?"

"I, um, the babies are crying."

Luke looked from one squalling red face to the other. His questions could wait. She needed help, not his curiosity. "Do they need to be fed or something?"

"I think so. The formula and bottles are beside the cradle."

He bent and picked up the formula can. "Should I do it? Or help you up? Or what?"

"I'm all right here on the floor for now. If you could make the bottles, that would be a big help."

"Sure." Except for one thing. He had no idea how to do it. But Elizabeth had her hands full with bawling babies. He'd have to figure it out.

Carrying the can and two bottles, he headed for the kitchen, trying to appear competent. But inside he whispered a silent prayer, *Lord, I need help here.*

Calmness descended on him. He'd been in the kitchen when one of his cousins fixed bottles. She'd boiled water to sterilize the bottles. He could manage that.

While the water heated, he read the can. This part appeared easy. Mix warm water and a scoop of the powder. After rinsing the bottles with boiling water, he filled them almost to the top with warm water. Then he added the formula and shook. So far, so good. Well, except for the babies' cries, which had reached earsplitting levels.

He screwed the tops onto the bottles and carried them out to Elizabeth. "Wouldn't you be more comfortable on the couch?"

She nodded. "Maybe we can put the babies in the cradle for now."

Setting the bottles on the floor beside her, Luke reached for the first baby, his heart pounding. And not just because he was so near to Elizabeth. He had visions of dropping the infant. Or hurting the tiny little girl.

"They're newborns, so you need to support their heads," Elizabeth warned as he took the closest baby.

He cupped one hand around the baby's head the way she directed and lifted the tiny girl from Elizabeth's shoulder. His other hand brushed the bare skin of her arm. He sucked in a silent breath to steady himself and concentrated on the baby.

He laid one crying baby in the cradle and returned for the other. Then he leaned Elizabeth's crutches against the wall beside her. When she placed her soft fingers in his outstretched hands, electricity shot through him. Luke fought the longing to take her in his arms.

He'd been so focused on the babies he hadn't paid much attention to Elizabeth. Not that he'd been unaware of her presence. As he helped her up, though, the brightness under her black work apron caught his attention. *Pink.* Instead of black, she was wearing pink. A color that made her glow. Her beauty sent his pulse skyrocketing.

Now was not the time to be thinking of her loveliness, her sweetness, her . . .

She let go of one of his hands, balanced on her good leg, and reached for a crutch. When she let go of his other hand, she left the imprint of her touch on his palm.

He followed her into the living room and waited until she'd settled comfortably on the couch before he brought her one screaming baby. Then he returned with the bottles. He handed her one, and as soon as the little girl latched on to it her cries ceased.

Elizabeth motioned to the other end of the couch with her chin. "Why don't you sit there?"

Luke set the other bottle on the end table and went to fetch the other infant. Once he inserted the bottle in her small, yelping mouth, she drank greedily. And blessed peace reigned at last.

Having such a small, fragile baby in his arms made Luke long for children. But children meant a home, a wife. He couldn't help but stare at Elizabeth, who was gazing down at the infant in her arms with such motherly love, his heart stuttered to a stop.

He drew in a long, slow breath of yearning. All these years, he'd wanted no one but Elizabeth. It might be too soon for her to consider remarriage, but maybe, just maybe, the pink dress was a sign she might be healing. He wanted to stay close, so he'd be there if and when she was ready to move on.

If only he could stay here forever surrounded by the soft, contented sighs of babies sucking, the scent of cookies and cinnamon perfuming the air, and the woman he loved with all his heart sitting nearby. Her contented smile lit a spark that grew into a raging fire. A fire he needed to douse.

＊　＊　＊

Elizabeth sneaked glances at Luke as he encouraged the baby to drink her bottle. *What a wonderful father he'd make!* At that thought, her cheeks flamed.

But Aubrey had been a good judge of character. He'd be the perfect choice for the twins' father. The only problem was he'd never consider her for the role of mother.

That thought lay like a heavy burden on her heart. Today was a day of sacrifice. Years ago, she'd given up her teenage dreams. Dreams of a future with Luke.

Pictures of Luke avoiding her when they were teens flitted through Elizabeth's mind. He'd been her good friend. Then suddenly one day, he'd acted more like her enemy. Well, maybe not an enemy, but he definitely avoided her. No more joking around. No more conversations. No more friendship.

In fact, it started after that fateful day, the one when Owen drove her home. Luke had been calming her bucking horse, so she'd needed a ride. She'd never considered that it might seem like she and Owen were courting. Everyone knew the circumstances.

But after Luke had brought her horse and buggy back to the house—and she'd stared out the window at him longingly—he'd grown cold and distant. Once he backed away, Elizabeth gave in to the inevitable.

Everyone looked at Owen and her as a couple, and things progressed from there. Because she had no chance with Luke, she settled for Owen. Like most of their friends, she and Owen courted for a year and then married.

He'd been a good husband, and she'd tried hard to be a good wife. But guilt always niggled inside her because what she'd felt for her husband was fondness. Nothing like her nail-biting crush on Luke.

All those old feelings came rushing back. Elizabeth peeped

over at Luke, his muscular arms gently cradling the tiny baby, and Aubrey's note ran through her mind. What if the teen had been right? Elizabeth hadn't realized her own emotions had been so unguarded. But had Luke really looked at her with love? Or had Aubrey been mistaken? Or overly starry-eyed?

As if sensing her eyes on him, Luke looked up. Elizabeth avoided his scrutiny by turning her attention to the baby.

"Now that both babies are quiet," he said, "can I ask some questions?"

"Of course." She appreciated the fact that he'd put the babies' needs ahead of his curiosity.

"So, who are these babies and how did they get here and why? How long will they be staying? And—"

Elizabeth raised a finger to stop him. "One question at a time. First of all, the twins belong to a teen mom from New Beginnings. Do you remember that girl Aubrey who came to the counter while we were there?"

"Vaguely. After all you donated to them, you also agreed to babysit?"

"Not exactly." This would be easier to explain if she showed him the note. "I have a letter that will answer most of your questions, but—" She tilted her head to indicate the baby in her arms. She lifted the little girl and patted her tiny back. "Maybe we should read it after we take care of the babies." Luke followed Elizabeth's lead and burped the twin he held. "It might be easier to talk if we put them into bed first."

The little one dozed on his shoulder. "Let me get the cradle."

Cuddling the baby close, Luke headed into the hall and returned with the cradle in one hand. Elizabeth had barely been able to drag the heavy cradle into the house, but he'd lifted it with one hand.

He placed the cradle beside her, and she almost swooned at his nearness. Then he knelt beside the cradle and lowered the baby from his arms into the nest of blankets. When he gently tucked a blanket around the sleeping twin, her pulse played a double-time rhythm that her heart matched.

"I have an idea." Luke stood. "Can you hold that baby for a few minutes? I need to run to my house, but I'll be right back."

Elizabeth hoped he'd hurry. Not because she was tired of holding the sweet little bundle in her arms, but because Luke had taken some of the warmth and sunlight with him when he left. At the same time, she was reluctant to tell him about the letter. And to see the death of her dream.

Chapter 12

Outside, the temperature had dropped and snow swirled around Luke, stinging his face. He rushed to his workshop, where he'd been making the two cradles for New Beginnings. Even though he'd worked late last night, one still remained unfinished. He was glad he'd completed the other. The second baby needed a place to sleep temporarily.

He had no idea how long Elizabeth would be caring for these little ones, but he doubted she'd need the cradle for more than a few days. The babies only had one can of formula.

It seemed odd the young mother would leave her children on Christmas Day. Perhaps if her family didn't know about the babies or had been angry about her pregnancy, she didn't want to upset them by bringing the babies for the holiday. Did she plan to stay away long? If so, Elizabeth would need extra help. Why had she agreed to care for twins when she had a broken leg?

Right now, he needed to get back as quickly as he could. But he wanted to give her the nativity set. Balancing the box in one arm, he picked up the cradle with the other.

At Elizabeth's, he left the nativity set in the entryway. He'd wait for the right time to give it to her. Then he walked into the living room to find Elizabeth with a scrunched-up face.

"What's the matter?"

"I think both twins need to be changed, and the diapers are still in the hallway."

"*Jah*, they are." Luke set the second cradle near Elizabeth. "Let me start a fire first. It won't take long. I don't want the babies to catch a chill."

He knelt by the fireplace, put two logs on the grate, and crumpled some paper. Then he added kindling and more wood before lighting a match. The paper caught fire immediately, but the kindling steamed a little from the snow on it. After it burst into flames, Luke headed for the hallway.

When he picked up the pile of diapers, a blue envelope fluttered to the floor. Luke scooped it up. The script on the front said: *To the twins' future father.*

How odd.

He carried the letter into the living room with him and held it out to Elizabeth. "You might want to put this in a safe place. Does the twins' *mamm* plan to marry the babies' father?"

Elizabeth had been basking in the heat from the fireplace as the logs blazed. Toasty warm, she reached languidly for the envelope Luke held out. "I have no idea of her marriage plans."

The only thing Elizabeth knew for sure was that she and Luke had been chosen to be the babies' parents. At that thought, her cheeks heated. She hoped Luke would assume her redness came from the fire.

The minute she took the envelope, the writing jumped out at her. *To the twins' future father.* Could her face get any hotter?

"Isn't it rather odd to address an envelope like that?" Luke asked. "Surely she'd know the name of the babies' father. Although the word 'future' makes it seem as if she has someone else in mind."

She did have someone else in mind. You. How did Elizabeth break the truth?

"Umm." Flustered, she focused on unwrapping the baby she held. "The letter in my pocket explains that too."

Reading it from a piece of paper would be a little easier than looking Luke in the eye and saying, *The blue letter's meant for you. The teen mom wants you as the babies' future father.* If she held the other letter, she could keep her gaze on the message rather than Luke's face. She'd have enough trouble holding back her tears.

"I really need to change the babies first." The longer she put off discussing the teen mom's intent, the better.

"Of course." Luke opened the package of diapers and handed her one. "I'm guessing you need pins for those."

Unable to look at him, she only nodded. "And—and some diaper cream."

He picked up the tube and two diaper pins. When he passed them to her, their fingers brushed, and sparks flashed through her. She almost dropped both items. For a fleeting moment, she wished she'd stocked her nursery with disposable diapers. But then she would have missed out on that thrill.

The diapers brought up the memory of choosing this package in the secondhand shop with Mamm and Sarah. How excited she'd been that day!

And she'd dreamed of holding her baby on Christmas Day, surrounded by family. Now here she was on Christmas Day, changing diapers on a stranger's twins. Babies she'd soon have to give up. And she didn't even know their names.

Elizabeth blinked back tears.

"Are you all right?" Luke asked. He still stood there, staring down at her as if studying her every move.

She couldn't lie. She wasn't all right, and maybe she never

would be. Giving a noncommittal shrug, she unsnapped the legs of the pink sleeper.

"I guess it's hard for you to care for babies when . . ." His voice trailed off.

"It is." Her words came out thick with tears.

"I'm sorry."

She waved a hand to show he didn't need to feel sorry for her, but then she wondered if it appeared as if she were dismissing his kindness.

Rather than taking offense, Luke knelt beside the cradle and lifted the other twin. Once again, his big hand cradled the tiny head, and the fluttering that started in Elizabeth's chest spread to her stomach. She forced herself to look away.

"I'll take care of this one."

"You don't have to." Was he doing it because he pitied her?

"I want to." His firm answer made it clear he wouldn't yield to protests.

He followed along clumsily step by step as she diapered the first baby until he came to the pins. "What if I stab her?"

"Slide two fingers inside to hold the cloth away from her skin." Then once again his large hands drew her attention. "Or for you, maybe just one finger."

He poked a pin tentatively into the cotton fabric. "Most of my sisters and cousins prefer disposable diapers. Mammi calls it laziness, but it makes sense." He closed the pin. "If I had twins, I think I'd definitely want disposables."

Elizabeth sucked in a breath. *If he had twins* . . . Little did he know he'd just been given twins.

Luke wrestled with the second diaper pin. How did people avoid pricking babies with these sharp points? He'd already poked himself twice.

Elizabeth held out a neon green diaper cover decorated with cartoon animals. He was pretty sure she hadn't donated that.

He watched her fold a matching one around her twin and snap it into place. Then he did the same.

He couldn't wait to hear more about why she had these babies. He'd been patient long enough. He snapped his baby back into her pink sleeper. No easy feat with his large fingers. Why did they make these fasteners so small?

Replicating Elizabeth's blanket-wrapping technique to make his baby as snug as hers proved even more challenging. Was this what they meant by "swaddling clothes"?

Expelling a long breath, Luke leaned back against the sofa cushion, the baby cuddled in his arms. Being a parent was a difficult task. He couldn't imagine doing this all day, every day.

Doing it for twins would be more than twice the work, although . . . it might be worth it if he could do it with the beautiful woman sitting beside him. Maybe.

Actually, he'd prefer to have her all to himself at least for a year or two. He'd love to have time alone—just the two of them. Luke shook his head. A dream that would never come true.

When she'd had a choice, she'd picked Owen. He couldn't compete with the love they'd had. He wouldn't even try. And if she favored someone else when she was ready to date again, he'd step aside even if it destroyed him.

Elizabeth leaned over to set the baby in the cradle, but he hadn't placed it close enough. Elizabeth started scooting toward the edge of the couch.

"Wait. I'll move it nearer." He didn't want her pitching forward onto the floor. "Let me put this baby in first."

She sat back while he knelt by the cradle he'd brought. Supporting the baby's head with the crook of his elbow, he smoothed down lumps in the small blanket he'd bought to line the cradle. Paper crinkled under his hand.

Ach! He'd forgotten about the baby ornament in the cradle. The one he'd originally bought for Elizabeth but now intended to donate to New Beginnings. His back to her, Luke slipped the small bag from under the blanket and smuggled it into his pocket.

Then he eased the baby into place and covered her with the blanket Elizabeth handed him. Guiltily, he placed a hand in his pocket to keep the paper from rustling as he stood. He nudged the cradle closer to her.

Once she'd settled the other baby in snugly, he took a seat on the opposite end of the couch. "So, tell me about this letter."

Swallowing hard, Elizabeth pulled the paper from her pocket. She had no idea how Luke would react. Even worse, she worried about whether she could get through the letter without breaking down.

Just concentrate on the paper. Don't even glance at Luke.

She killed a few seconds by smoothing out the wrinkled page, but the words had been burned into her mind. She could recite most of the message from memory. Steeling herself, she cleared her throat.

Then she read. Her voice faltered when she reached *"lost your own baby,"* and she took a few seconds to compose herself. But she found it even harder to read, *"I want my daughters to experience something I never had—two loving parents."*

Luke might not know what was coming, but Elizabeth did. She choked on *"you and your husband have a deep bond."*

"Your husband?" Luke echoed, his voice faint but husky.

Had he understood the implications? Maybe she should skip the next sentence. If Luke hadn't realized her feelings for him, she'd be better off not pointing them out.

"What else does it say?" he asked when she paused.

Keeping her head down, Elizabeth mumbled the dreaded words, *"I've never seen two people so much in love."* She rushed on to the next paragraph about the adoption papers.

After she finished, she sneaked a sideways glance at Luke. He sat there motionless, looking stunned.

Several minutes passed before he spoke. "That blue envelope's for me then?"

Her voice barely above a whisper, Elizabeth pushed out a *jah* before handing it over.

"I see." He reached for the envelope.

When their fingers touched, he jerked back as if . . . as if it pained him to touch her. As if he couldn't bear to be near her. As if he couldn't get away fast enough.

Elizabeth bit her lip and lowered her head. She didn't want him to see the hurt in her eyes.

A log tumbled from the grate, sending off a shower of sparks and making both of them jump. Luke turned his back to her and, without opening the letter, headed for the hearth. Did he plan to burn the envelope?

His thoughts a jumbled mess, Luke paced over to the fireplace. To buy himself some time, he picked up the fallen log with the tongs and then poked at the fire, prodding the embers and dislodging ash.

He had to compose himself before he faced Elizabeth. But how long could he keep his back to her without raising suspicion?

Aubrey had judged his feelings precisely, but she'd been mistaken about Elizabeth. The way Elizabeth had muttered the words "I've never seen two people so much in love" made it clear she found the whole idea distasteful.

That had crushed him. And now he needed to read this letter clutched in his hand. It would only drive the knife in deeper.

Another jab at the burning wood stirred up a cloud of smoke. Luke's eyes stung. He coughed and choked. Afraid he might drop the envelope into the flames, he propped it behind the pine bough draped along the mantel.

The words scraped his heart raw. *Future father.*

He'd never be a *daed*. Never. He'd only ever loved one woman. And she was the only woman he could ever love.

But she'd never been interested in him. Not back then. And not now.

How could he face her with all his feelings so raw and exposed?

He bent and placed a fresh log on top with great precision and care. But he couldn't spend all day tending the fire. He had to turn around.

He reached for the envelope. Reading the message would bide him a little more time. He slid a finger under the flap, lifted it, pulled out the folded paper, and opened it.

> *Luke,*
> *Melva rattled on about you when she returned from collecting donations. The armoire you gave for the auction was the most beautiful piece of furniture I've ever seen. I was impressed by your generosity, and then I saw you were part of the couple who donated all of your baby furniture.*
>
> *I saw the pain in your eyes as Elizabeth told Mrs. Hess about losing the baby, and I knew deep inside that you'd be a loving dad. I'm entrusting my girls to your care and want you to raise them to love God.*
>
> *I chose you because of how deeply you love your wife. I pray that you will continue to cherish her as much as you do now. I want my daughters to see that a strong man can be tender, caring, and loving.*
>
> *I haven't named the babies. I'll leave that up to you.*
>
> *Praying God's blessing on you as you lead your family,*
> *Aubrey Lundeen*

Luke choked back the lump in his throat. Both of Aubrey's letters had touched him deeply. How had this teen read his desires and emotions so clearly? All he'd ever wanted to do was love and cherish Elizabeth.

But he'd kept that to himself all these years. At least he thought he had.

He'd finished the letter, so he couldn't make any more excuses to stand here and avoid her. Although he still hadn't sorted out his feelings or decided on his reactions, he had to face her. When he did, he'd do the hardest thing he'd ever done in his life.

He'd tell her the truth.

Chapter 13

"Elizabeth—" he began as he turned around. The rest of his sentence died on his lips.

Tears slipped silently down her cheeks.

"What's wrong?" He'd been so focused on himself he hadn't even noticed she'd needed comfort. He went over and knelt beside her. Was taking care of these babies too much for her to bear?

The letter from Aubrey drifted to the floor as he took Elizabeth's hands. She pulled away and only cried harder.

"Tell me," he begged.

"I can't. You'll think I'm foolish."

"Never. No matter what you say, I'd never think that."

"I-I . . ." She shook her head. "W-when you went over there"—she gestured toward the fireplace—"I thought you were . . . upset . . . with me."

"*Ach*, Elizabeth, I wasn't upset with you. Why would I be?"

She waved a hand to the letter on the couch beside her and the one on the floor. "They said—" She winced and pinched her lips together for a moment. "Aubrey said I-I looked like I was in love with you."

"It's all right. I know you're not. Aubrey's young and made a mistake." Perhaps he could let her think Aubrey had been wrong about him too.

Again, she shook her head. "No, she didn't."

So, she'd realized the truth. Luke lowered his gaze. "I'm sorry. I couldn't help it."

"What?"

At Elizabeth's sharp question, he raised his eyes. She'd drawn her brows together and appeared confused.

"I'm sorry I said, 'I'm sorry.' I know you don't like it, but I truly am. I didn't mean to fall in love with you, but I promise—"

She cut him off with a sharp intake of breath. "What did you say?"

"I'm sorry."

This time a half smile curved her lips. "Not that."

"*Jah*, well, I regret falling for you."

"You do?" Elizabeth sounded hurt.

Ach, she must think him a fool. "*Neh*, I don't regret loving you. I just didn't want to bother you."

"And you think loving me will be a bother?"

She kept turning his words around, making him even more muddled than he already was. Maybe it was time for him to question her. "Is it?"

Elizabeth dabbed at her eyes with a cloth diaper. "Do you know why I was crying?"

Although he suspected it had something to do with the babies, he didn't want to venture a guess.

"I thought"—she swallowed hard—"that you couldn't stand to look at me because . . ."

"Not stand to look at you?" Now it was his turn to be astonished. "Why would you think that?"

"Because you found out I'm in love with you."

"You are?" Luke couldn't believe what he was hearing. "But—but that can't be."

Twisting her hands together, Elizabeth stared down at her lap. "I have been for a long time."

"Months?" It seemed almost impossible.

"*Neh*," she said miserably. "Years."

"But Owen?"

Elizabeth pleated the fabric of her apron. "I went out with him because you ignored me. Once you start dating someone, it's hard to break up. I grew fond of him. And I had no other marriage prospects."

"If only I'd known." How long had he wasted by hiding the truth? He'd almost walked out of her life again today, assuming she didn't want him. "I'm sor—" Luke stopped and started again. "I wish I'd been honest."

"So do I," Elizabeth mumbled without looking at him.

Luke still needed an answer to one question, though. "But what about Owen?"

Elizabeth hung her head. Her words when they finally came were tinged with guilt. "I put you out of my mind and did my best to be a good wife. But being around you the past few weeks has brought all those old feelings flooding back."

If only he hadn't backed away after Owen took her home. He'd made assumptions. Assumptions that had been completely wrong. He'd let hurt pride get in the way.

All that wasted time.

One baby whimpered, and Elizabeth gently rocked the cradle with her foot until the *gretzing* ceased. "I don't understand what happened between us. We were good friends. Then you avoided me."

Should he admit he'd been trying to impress her by calming her bucking horse? If this relationship had any chance of working, he needed to tell the truth.

Luke took a deep breath. "That day I calmed your horse, I was showing off. I hoped you'd notice me."

"I couldn't believe you dove in there. I'd never seen my horse so wild. I worried you'd get hurt."

"I wanted you to stay and see me succeed." He'd endangered his life, but he'd been foolhardy and seventeen. "Instead, you rode off with Owen." Luke still ached inside from that old wound.

"I begged Owen to stay, but he took off."

"You did?" Another thing Luke wished he'd known. That would have given him hope. "By the time I got to your place, you were nowhere around."

As a prideful teen boy, he'd expected praise. Maybe even a chance to take her to the next singing. "I was so disappointed."

Her cheeks pink, Elizabeth ducked her head. "Daed made me go inside, so I watched you from my bedroom window. If you'd looked up, you would have seen me staring at you admiringly."

"I wish I'd glanced up." One thing still bothered him, though. "But you agreed to go to the next singing with Owen."

Elizabeth shook her head. "*Neh*, I was so upset and *ferhoodled* about the horse and wondering when you'd come, I didn't answer him. But after you were so cold to me"—her wounded eyes pierced him—"when he asked again the following Saturday, I agreed."

"But he told me you'd said yes."

"Owen was confident that way. I didn't turn him down, so he took it as a yes."

Luke heaved a huge sigh. He'd let his wounded ego dictate his actions. So many misunderstandings that could have been straightened out by being honest. His pride and fear of being vulnerable had kept them apart.

* * *

Elizabeth wanted to echo Luke's sigh. If she'd had even the slightest idea he'd been interested, their lives would have been different.

Neh, she shouldn't question God's will. She'd surrendered her will to the Lord this morning. Now she needed to believe He'd brought her each step of the way for His purpose.

"God has a reason for all this," she said in a quiet voice. When Luke glanced at her in surprise, she explained, "This morning I let go of my anger at God and told Him I'd accept His will." And he'd blessed her with Luke and two darling babies. If Luke was willing to father them.

"You know," Luke mused, "maybe it's better we didn't get together back then. I had a lot to learn about love and giving. I still do."

"I think you already know a lot." Not only had he donated generously to others, but he'd also done so much for her.

"I have plenty more I want to learn about love." He paused. "With you." He looked deeply into her eyes. "If you're willing?"

Elizabeth's breath caught in her throat. *If she was willing?* God was giving her the man of her dreams. She was more than willing. Except . . .

Her gaze strayed to the cradles. She couldn't answer Luke's question until he answered hers. "Do you want these babies?" Her whole body tense, she waited for his response.

"Well, I didn't expect to have children before I got married." He grinned. "But in this case, I'm happy to be a father first, a husband later."

She laughed. "Oh, Luke, I'm so happy I could cry."

He picked up the diaper she'd used before. "Go ahead."

Elizabeth burst into giggles that woke the babies. One began to bawl. Then the other followed. Elizabeth sighed. "I guess we won't have much time for dating."

As she bent to pick up the nearest baby, she said, "Maybe

you could calm that one, Daed." *That one?* "I'm going to be a *mamm* and I don't even know their names."

Luke could help with that. "Aubrey asked me to name them."

"She did?" Elizabeth glanced at him in surprise.

He nodded. "I'm going to name this one Hope and that one Joy, because that's what you've brought into my life. And so have they."

Her eyes shining, Elizabeth studied the baby in her arms. "Joy is a perfect name." Then she peeped up at him through her lashes. "And you've brought me Hope too."

Her shy look set Luke's pulse on fire. He could hardly believe God had given him this second chance at love.

The little girl in his arms sucked on her fist, and a sobering weight settled over him. He was taking on a huge responsibility. What if he didn't measure up?

He'd need God's strength and support to care for all three of them.

Dear Lord, thank You for this wonderful gift. Please help me to be the husband and father You want me to be.

He had so much he wanted to give Elizabeth and his soon-to-be daughters. For now, he'd start with the nativity set, because he wanted to show Elizabeth his love. And, most important, keep his new family focused on the real meaning of Christmas.

Shifting Hope over his shoulder and patting her back, he headed for the entryway. Doing deep knee bends with a fragile baby in one arm tested his strength. But he managed to scoop the box in one arm.

"What's that?" Elizabeth asked when he entered the living room.

"A present." He crossed the room to set the box beside her. "For you."

"But—" A look of confusion settled over her face.

"Open it. You'll understand."

She unwrapped the first figure wrapped in soft cloth and sucked in a breath. She stared at the shepherd with the lost sheep.

The first figure Luke had ever carved. He'd refined it a little, but the man—who had originally been Jesus—stared down at that little lamb with a deep, abiding love. Then she ran a finger over every line Luke had carved in agony.

Her eyes aglow, Elizabeth whispered, "It's even more beautiful than the ones in Yolanda's shop. Look at his expression. It just about breaks my heart." Without looking up, she added, "This set is much too expensive. I can't take it."

"Yes, you can. This is the original set. You're the reason I carved these figures."

"Me?"

"After I lost you, I had to keep busy, do something to bury my feelings. I carved my heartbreak into every line."

Tears sprang to Elizabeth's eyes. "I'm so sorry. I never meant to hurt you."

"You didn't hurt me. I hurt myself by being self-centered and hiding my feelings. I could have risked being honest. Unfortunately, I chose pride."

"So did I. Not only with you, but also in being angry with God."

"We both learned some hard lessons. You much more than me. We may never know why everything happened the way it did, and we can't go back to change the past. We can only walk forward, trusting God to lead us."

"That's true." Elizabeth rocked Joy back and forth to stop her fussing. "And we're going to need a lot of divine guidance to raise these two."

"I've already prayed about that."

"You did?"

At the admiration in her eyes, Luke's stomach flipped over. "We've taken on a big responsibility. We will—or at least I will—need a lot of help from God."

"We both will." Elizabeth smiled down at Joy. "She's quiet now. Would you be able to hold both of them for a few minutes?"

"Of course." Luke sat on the couch, supported Hope's head with the crook of his elbow, and took Joy in his other arm.

Elizabeth swallowed hard. A short while ago, her heart ached at the thought he'd be a good father. Now it overflowed with joy. She still couldn't believe Luke loved her and wanted these two babies. And she still hadn't opened his Christmas gift.

She reached into the box and unwrapped the carvings one by one. The longing expressions on their faces clearly showed how deeply Luke had loved her. Still loved her.

Her eyes stung as she balanced on crutches to arrange the nativity set on the mantel. She inhaled the fragrance of the pine boughs and placed baby Jesus in the manger. The real meaning of Christmas.

But God had given her so much more.

Elizabeth settled back on the couch beside Luke. "Shall I take Hope this time?" She reached for her other baby daughter. Luke slid closer and wrapped his free arm around Elizabeth's shoulders.

Paper crinkled in his pocket. "I forgot about this. He pulled a tiny gift-wrapped package from his pocket. "I got this for you before I knew about"—he waved a hand in the direction of the nursery—"but now I wish I'd bought two."

Elizabeth lifted Hope to her shoulder and awkwardly unwrapped the small package.

"*Ach*, Luke," she breathed, holding the ornament.

The sparkling baby swayed in the slight breeze, and Elizabeth's heart almost shattered into a million pieces.

She'd always miss her unborn child, but God had given her two new babies to love and care for, along with the most wonderful man in the world. And the Lord had started gluing all those shards of her heart back to wholeness.

"I saw you holding that ornament," Luke said, "the day I dropped off the nativity sets, so I sent Alan to buy it for you."

Luke had sent that *Englischer?* If only she'd known that two weeks ago. Back then, it had been too agonizing even to touch that glittering baby. Now she considered this ornament a blessing.

Taking it from her, Luke stood. "I know the perfect place for this." He headed to the fireplace mantel and hung it from the small central nail holding the pine garland. The baby shone in the light from the dancing flames.

Elizabeth's eyes stung. God had turned the pain she'd experienced that day into a thing of beauty. And he'd filled her life with Hope and Joy. And, most important, Luke.

But best of all, God had forgiven her anger and rebellion, allowing her to have a fresh start. And she and Luke and the babies each had been given their own new beginnings.

Twins Times Two

LOREE LOUGH

Twins Times Two is dedicated to Larry, best friend and real-life hero, who suggested I incorporate my maternal grandfather's "I was gored by a bull!" story into this novella. I hope you'll agree that it made a cool opening scene!

Acknowledgments

Heartfelt thanks to Jody Teets and residents of Pleasant Valley (New Order Amish community near Oakland, Maryland) for sharing fascinating facts and details about life in their picturesque mountain town; and to Carolyn Greene, who, during one brief brainstorming session, helped me iron the wrinkles from a pivotal scene.

Chapter 1

Late September, on the shores of Lake Broadford,
Oakland, Maryland

As he had every day for the past three years, the boss waved
from the inn's covered porch. "See you in the morning, Abby!"

The shortened version of her name never failed to remind
her of Ira—more accurately, her failed marriage—but over-
looking it was a small price to pay to work for a man who fully
accepted her Amish lifestyle. So, as she had every day for the
past three years, Abigail smiled and returned the wave.

The driver's door hinges squealed, and as he had since her
first day at The Broadford, Bill said, "I could fix that with a few
squirts of motor oil . . ."

Although the pickup rattled and creaked and used too much
gas, it was all Ira had left her. Unless the squeal got so bad that
the door wouldn't open, she'd keep right on replying with,
"Thanks, Bill. Maybe tomorrow."

The engine turned over on the first try, and she sent a silent prayer of thanks heavenward. Unlike its former owner, the old Chevy had never let her down. Abigail whispered another prayer, because if her New Order Amish community hadn't re-laxed the no-gas-powered vehicles rule, she wouldn't have been able to get to work. And without the steady paycheck, she'd have to sell the house she'd inherited from her parents.

Life, she thought, merging with traffic on Route 291, some-times felt like a row of toppling dominos.

She cranked down the window and inhaled the thick, peat-like scent of the wood-fired smoke gently puffing from rooftop chimneys of homes scattered on the mountainside. In the dis-tance, sooty clouds hung low over Keysers Ridge. Today, they carried rain, but in a month, maybe less, they'd deliver snow. Beautiful as it looked, draped across the Alleghenies' peaks and valleys, it would make the trip between The Broadford Inn and Pleasant Valley anything but pleasant.

Ten minutes. If the rain held off for just ten minutes, she'd get home in time to gather several armloads of dry wood, enough to start a fire in the wood stove. The perfect end to the crisp autumn day.

Her mood deflated, though, when she spotted Jubal Quinn's big red mailbox, half a mile up the road. Twice a day, she passed it on her way to and from The Broadford Inn. And twice a day, it raised guilty memories. The accident hadn't been his fault. She'd known it even then, and yet she'd hurled hateful accusa-tions at him that night in the ER. "A decent person," Abigail muttered, "would apolo—"

Movement up ahead captured her attention: Four boys straddled the top rail of Jubal's paddock gate. She recognized them as Paul and Peter Briskey and their cousins, James and Thomas Hartz—two sets of twins, born to twin mothers—with a knack for attracting trouble. Just beyond the gate, Jubal's prize bull, Goliath, patrolled the fence line. *They've earned the nickname Double Trouble*, she thought.

Abigail slowed the truck, yelled through the open window, "You boys! Get away from there!"

All four blond heads turned, treated her to impish smirks, and went back to drawing straws. Evidently, they believed, like several Amishmen she could name, that God had created women to submit to men's orders, not the other way around. An annoying mind-set . . .

Abigail beeped the horn, and just as she'd hoped, the noise roused the bull's protective nature. He now paced near Jubal's dairy cows, grazing in the shade of a maple tree. She honked a second time. If nothing else, maybe the boys would realize that she had no intention of giving up and they *would*. They stayed put. Didn't they realize the dangerous situation they'd put themselves in? She leaned on the horn yet again. And again. Would Jubal hear it and come running to put a stop to the racket that might interfere with his cows' milk production? Abigail hoped so, because if anyone could rein in a foursome of unruly twins and an aggressive animal, it was the man who'd kept her wayward husband out of trouble so many times.

Then the unthinkable happened. . . .

Pete dropped into the pasture and, laughing, dashed across the grass. It must have surprised Goliath even more than Abigail, for the bull spun around so fast that his rear hooves scattered dirt in a high arc.

Pete made it safely to the other side and, breathing hard, said, "Your turn, Paul! I made it—so can you!"

His brother stood stone-still, watching the bull wag his head from side to side.

"Jump," Pete goaded. *"Jump!"*

"No!" she yelled, braking the truck. And then she shouted it: "No!"

Ignoring Abigail, Paul obeyed his twin, and ran. And so did Goliath. The boy had barely cleared the top rail when the animal crashed, headfirst, into a fence post.

Now Pete and Paul stood side by side, taunting their cousins. "Do not just stand there, fraidycats!" Pete bellowed. "Come on over! He is big and fat and slow. You can outrun him, same as we did!"

When James and Thomas hesitated, Paul added, "It looks like rain. Better hurry up!"

"Stop!" Abigail shouted. "Are you *trying* to get trampled?"

Like Pete and Paul before him, James dropped and zigzagged across the field, just inches ahead of Goliath's menacing horns. He scrambled over the fence while the bull circled back, as if he sensed that Thomas, too, intended to intrude upon his turf.

"All of you are *gek*," Thomas said.

"Yes, they are crazy," she agreed. "Do not listen to them!"

He met her eyes, and for an instant, Abigail thought the boy might listen to reason. He glanced across the field, at the spot where the others stood chanting, "Doubting Thomas, Doubting Thomas . . . little girl, little *girl*!"

"Pay no attention to them, Thomas. Stay put and . . . and stay *safe*!" To emphasize the warning, she pointed. "Look at that monster. When they crossed his turf, they made him feel threatened, worked him into a frenzy. Why, he is angry enough to kill!"

The boy's blue eyes widened as he took note of the bull, snorting, pawing the ground.

And yet Thomas shoved off the rail, as his brother and cousins before him had, and ran.

Unlike the others, Thomas stumbled, fell to his knees . . .

Goliath tossed his head, widened his stance, and cut loose with a manic, guttural, *Rrrumph-rrumph!*

Somehow, she had to distract the bull, lure him away from Thomas. Abigail whistled. Shouted. Clapped her hands. But the animal remained focused on the now-cowering boy. What choice did she have but to climb over the fence?

The bull, sensing her behind him, jerked around and, facing *her* now, continued grunting and stomping.

She whipped off her apron and moved forward, praying with every step that God would see fit to perform a miracle. Because if He didn't . . .

Jube stopped working and turned an ear toward the door.

No, he hadn't been mistaken. Someone was out there, honking like an angry goose. Annoyed, he tossed the hammer onto the workbench and clomped toward the door. If the lazy, crazy fool kept that up, the cows wouldn't give milk for . . . who knew how long!

He heard shouting. Frantic boys' voices, and . . . and a woman?

Jube raced from the barn to the road. It didn't take long to figure out what had been going on down there: Double Trouble had decided to try to outrun Goliath. From the looks of things, only three of them had safely made it to the other side. The fourth—Thomas—knelt in a puddle of mud and dung, smack-dab in the middle of the pasture. "When I get hold of that bunch, I intend to—"

That's when he saw Abigail Fletcher, black-booted feet planted shoulder width apart, waving her white apron. Brave, he thought, putting herself between the bull and the boy that way. Brave, but stupid: She'd succeeded in diverting the bull's attention from Thomas . . . to *her.*

"Stop that infernal flapping!" Jube roared, leaping over the fence.

He closed in on the bull and smacked his butt, hard.

"Whoa!" he commanded. "Whoa!"

Goliath nearly knocked him over when the animal turned to face him. Instinct compelled Jube to grab him by the horns and hold on tight. "Run, woman!" he bellowed. "You, too, boy! Hightail it out of here!"

Neither woman nor boy moved. In minutes—seconds, even—

Jube would lose what little control he'd gained over Goliath. Desperate to break fear's hold on their minds and bodies, Jube kicked dirt at them. "I. Said. *Go!*"

From the corner of his eye, he saw Abigail jerk Thomas to his feet and half-drag him to the fence. He heard two muffled *thumps*, telling him they'd jumped to safety on the other side. God willing, he'd join them. *Soon.*

But the instant he released his grip on the horns, the bull seized his chance for revenge. In one minute, Jube stood on solid ground. In the next, he somersaulted through the air and landed, hard, on the other side of the fence. It took a while to catch his breath, and when he did, he rasped, "Are you all right?"

Abigail nodded. "I am fine. And you?"

He'd cracked ribs before and had a feeling he'd done it again. "Where is Thomas?"

"Right here," she said, helping the boy to his feet.

"Are you hurt?" Jube wanted to know.

By now, the other boys had gathered round. "He looks all right to me," Pete said. His twin agreed, while James walked a slow circle around his twin. "Well? Answer the man. Are you hurt or not?"

Thomas, on the verge of tears, squeaked out, "No, I do not think so."

Jube rolled onto his back and closed his eyes. "Thank the good Lord."

He heard Goliath exhale one last, satisfied snort. Levering himself onto one elbow, he watched the bull join the seemingly oblivious cows clustered in the opposite corner of the paddock. It wasn't easy, getting to his feet, but he managed it. Fixing an angry glare at each boy in turn, he tried to ignore the ache in his chest and opened his mouth, intent on giving them the scolding of a lifetime.

Pain stopped him cold.

"Jubal! You're . . . you're bleeding!"

He looked from the bright red stain on his shirt to her face, and couldn't decide which touched him most . . .

. . . the fright in her voice, or the look of genuine concern in her lovely eyes.

Chapter 2

Thomas's heart beat in double time as his father walked back and forth in front of the cookstove. Hands clasped at the small of his back, he stopped, stared at him, at his twin, at his cousins. They'd been in trouble before, but this time? This time they'd gone too far. Why else had the parents gathered, looking more angry than usual?

"Care to explain," Ben began, "why you went to Jubal Quinn's and harassed his bull?"

Staring at the toes of his boots, Thomas heard his pulse beating in his ears. When none of the others spoke up, he said, "It will not happen again, Daed. You have my word."

"That does not answer my question," Ben said. "And how many times have your *moeder* and I heard that, eh?"

Thomas's uncle Noah grabbed their jackets from the wooden pegs in the entryway, passed them out, and opened the door. "You boys reek of muck and dung. Wait outside while the four of us pray about what to do with you *this* time."

One by one, the boys shrugged into their coats and filed

onto the back porch. As soon as the door clicked shut, Thomas grumbled, "*Told* you it was a dumb idea."

"Yeah, well, who asked you?" his brother said. "Besides, you are the only one who fell down."

Thomas, realizing the futility of arguing with them, moved closer to the window. "Be quiet for once, and maybe we can hear their plan."

Shoulder to shoulder, they listened.

"It keeps me up nights," Priscilla began, "wondering what kind of men they will become if they keep getting into trouble. What if next time, the trouble is truly serious?"

"I worry about that, too," Leora agreed. "Sometimes, all I can do is cry."

The words hit like a punch to his gut. From this day on, Thomas decided, he'd refuse to go along with the others' schemes. They'd call him chicken. Sissy. But better that than worrying his aunt and mother to the point of tears, ever again.

"Now, now," his father said. "It seems you have forgotten what people called both of *you* when you were girls."

Thomas's mother's voice trembled slightly when she said, "They called us terrors."

"Yet you grew up, became good wives and mothers . . ."

"If we are so good," his aunt said, "why are our boys so *bad*?"

In the ensuing silence, the boys began to fidget. "Stand still," Thomas whispered through clenched teeth, "or they will add *snooping* to our list of sins!"

"Remember what turned us around, Leora?"

"*Ach*, I will never forget. . . ."

And then the whispering began. The boys held their breath. Pressed closer to the window. But the silence went on for what seemed like five whole minutes.

The door opened with a *whoosh*, startling the boys, and they plowed into one another. Ben waved them inside, ordered them to sit at the table.

"As we see it," Noah began, "you boys have too much time on your hands. Time that you waste, thinking up ways to get into trouble. You behave like little children, selfish and concerned only with yourselves. This must stop. Now."

"First," Ben continued, "we will visit Quinn. You will apologize, offer to milk cows, muck stalls, and—"

"For how long?" James interrupted.

The question earned a silencing glare from their mother. "For as long as it takes. You caused the bull to cut his head when he rammed the gate. And poor Jubal cracked three ribs, trying to save you. Why, Abigail said it took eight stitches to close the wound!"

Thomas stiffened at the memory of the bloody tear on Mr. Quinn's shirt. He also remembered how the ground had quaked with every stomp of the bull's hooves, and the strings of saliva that whipped right and left with every shake of his shaggy head. Thomas pictured Mrs. Fletcher, too, waving her apron . . . until Mr. Quinn grabbed the bull by the horns. Goliath could have killed any one of them. Maybe even all three of them. *Why didn't you try harder to talk some sense into the others!*

"If you had stayed home, where you belong . . ." His aunt shook her head. "Yes, you will work for Jubal, doing whatever he asks of you, until he has healed."

Mr. Quinn owned dairy cows. Thomas exhaled a shaky sigh, because the sum total of what he knew about milking wouldn't fill his mother's thimble.

Paul got up. "May we go now?"

Pete stood, too. "The sooner we start, the sooner it will be over."

"Ah, but that is only Phase One of your punishment. When Jube is through with you," their father said, "you will begin Phase Two."

The boys exchanged worried glances.

"It will require serious thought," Leora said. Looking at Thomas, she added, "As the most responsible one—and I use the term loosely—we trust you to lead the others in prayer, so that together, you will make a wise decision."

"A decision?" he echoed. "About what?"

"About who in the community needs something."

"What kind of something?" Paul asked.

"Pray, Nephew, so that God will guide you."

Ben nodded. "You will recognize the need when you see it."

"The person, too," Priscilla said.

"You will fill that person's need by Christmas Eve," her twin added.

"Come," Ben said. "It will be dark soon. Jubal will have rounded up the cows by now."

Leora reached for a pie. Tiny holes in the top crust formed the letter *A*. "Bring this to him. He is a bachelor. No telling when he last had home-baked apple pie."

"Well," James said grumpily, "he is far from skinny, so he must know how to cook."

From the now-open doorway, Ben said, "Scrambled eggs and sandwiches. That is what a busy, unmarried man prepares for himself. Easy to make, easy to clean up. But pie? I think not."

The men led the way to the van, and the boys followed.

Paul said, "I want to get this *apology* over with."

His twin agreed. "And find out what dirty jobs he will—"

"Stop, you two!" came Thomas's harsh whisper. "Are you trying to get us into *more* trouble?"

The panel van served one purpose . . . to deliver baled hay and firewood to neighbors and townsfolk when the twins' fathers weren't working at Max Lambright's construction company. The heater barely functioned, and the floor and seats were littered with bits of hay and sawdust. Thomas considered offering to hitch Chester to the buggy, but by the time he got the job done, they could be at Mr. Quinn's. Besides, admitting how much he disliked the cold, smelly vehicle would only prove his father right: He *was* self-centered and immature.

The ride to the dairy farm was silent, but when the big mailbox came into view, James pressed his nose to the window. "He's right there, fetching his mail."

The other three looked over his shoulder, saw Jubal Quinn, flipping through a stack of envelopes.

"Slide open the side door, boys," Noah said. Rolling down the window, he called to Quinn, "Hop in, and we will drive you the rest of the way."

Quinn's expression said, *Why are you here?* But he issued a one-word greeting and climbed in, wincing as he slid onto the bench seat.

"How long before that storm hits?" Ben asked Jube.

"Cows are easier to milk when things are quiet and calm, so I hope it passes us."

Ben parked alongside the back porch, and as Quinn's boots hit the ground, he grimaced again. Once in the kitchen, he tossed the mail onto the counter. "Make yourselves comfortable."

Noah handed Quinn the pie. "The wife baked it this morning. Thought you might like it."

Both eyebrows disappeared beneath dark blond waves. "Thank her for me," he said, placing the pie beside the mail. "I will slice it, and we can have coffee."

Ben raised a hand. "No, we cannot stay. Would you join us outside for a moment?"

Jube went with them, but only in the hope of getting the lot of them out of his house, sooner rather than later.

The men took turns explaining why they'd brought their sons here. Jube didn't like the idea and said so.

"Look at it from a practical viewpoint," Noah said. "You are injured and need help, at least until you heal."

"He is right," Ben agreed. "In reality, you will be doing us a favor. We are at our wits' end with those four. God willing, the process will teach them to consider the consequences of their actions."

"What about their schoolwork, and chores at home?"

"This is more important. Everyone admires you, Jube, including our boys. We hope they will learn from your good example."

He and Ben and Noah had known one another all their lives. Was that a backhanded reminder of the man he'd been before Ira died?

Jube still felt largely responsible for the accident. Other than the dressing down Abigail had doled out—and the way she'd treated him since that night—he hadn't really paid a price for what he'd done. Maybe at the end of "the process," he could stop punishing *himself*.

"All right," he told them, "but only for a few days."

"You are a godsend," Noah said. "How can we thank you?"

"By not saying things like that."

He returned to the kitchen with Noah and Ben close on his heels, then sat at the table and waited.

Thomas spoke first. "We are sorry, for everything."

"Especially the goring," Pete said. "Did Goliath's horn poke a deep hole in your side?"

He bit back a grin. "More like a scrape."

James wanted to know if Dr. Baker had been too busy to fix him up. "Is that why Miss Fletcher had to do it?"

"No, it was late in the day. Interrupting Emily's family time would not have been neighborly."

Noah cleared his throat. "Speaking of neighborly, finish up, boys. Jube has things to do."

"We can start working tomorrow. There is no school on Saturday."

Jube stood and faced the boys. "All right, but just so you know, the day begins early on a dairy farm."

"How early?" Pete ventured.

"Four o'clock."

"*In the morning!?*" the boys asked in unison. "But why so early?"

"Because the cows are easier to handle at that hour. They are sleepy. Sometimes, they doze while I milk them. But even when they do not, I talk to them, quietly, which not only protects me from being kicked, but from being smacked by wagging tails." He paused. "Have you milked cows before?"

The boys chorused, "Never."

"Get a good night's sleep, then. You will need your wits about you in the morning."

As they walked back to the van, Jube heard Thomas say, "Milking cows requires wits?"

"I suppose so," his twin said, "if you do not want to be kicked or whacked with a swishing tail."

The next days would be a lot of things, Jube thought, but boring would not be one of them.

It took longer than anticipated to scrub the blood from Jubal's shirt. Frayed threads on either side of the rip held the stain, despite hours of soaking in white vinegar. Rubbing bar soap into the cloth made her fingers ache, but Abigail kept working. Achy fingers seemed a small price to pay for being saved from the furious bull.

Abigail wrung icy water from the shirt, hung it from the laundry room clothesline, and headed outside to rake leaves from the front lawn. Swept them from the covered porch, too, then piled them onto an old blanket and dragged it to the

stacked stone fire pit her grandfather had built using rocks unearthed from his vegetable patch.

Which reminds me, I have not fed Patch today.

The calico cat met her at the door and walked a figure eight
around her ankles. "I know, I know. You are hungry."

The cat chirruped happily, and while she ate, Abigail mixed
up a batch of sugar cookies. After they'd baked, she moved the
sugar bowl, creamer, and salt and pepper shakers to the counter,
and replaced them with her sewing basket. She had just started
snipping loose threads from either side of the rip when someone knocked.

"What a nice surprise, Willa," she said, greeting her friend at
the door. "Please, sit. Coffee for you, milk for Frannie?"

"I'd love that," Willa said, and began closing doors. "Frannie gets into everything these days, so this is more for your
protection than hers."

At the mention of her name, the child looked up, saw the
cookie-covered counter, and said, "Oooh . . ."

"Sugar cookies," Abigail told her, "fresh out of the oven.
But first things first . . ."

A shallow wooden box served as a booster seat, and a table
runner became a safety restraint. "There," she said, "all set!"

"Big!" the girl said, clapping. "F'annie big!"

"How long before the big day?" Abigail asked Willa.

"Too long!"

"I take it Max is still driving you crazy with 'are you all
right?' and 'what do you need?' "

"Yeah, but just between you and me, I love it."

Not that long ago, Willa had been gaunt, angry, and suspicious. Now she glowed with joy and good health. Marriage and
motherhood, Abigail believed, had been responsible for the
changes. If Ira had lived, would a child have inspired a change
in him, too?

"Little birdie told me you had a run-in with a bull yesterday and a white knight came to your rescue."

"It has barely been twenty-four hours. How did you hear about it already?"

"Just so happens that I ran into Priscilla at Hannah's shop. She says you're a hero, too."

"Stop, please. You would have done the same, under the circumstances."

"No way! What you did was bold and brave, so I won't listen to any 'sin of pride' talk. You probably saved that kid." She sipped her coffee. "And if that wasn't enough, you stepped in for Emily and me, took care of Jube's wound. How many stitches?"

"Six. Eight." Abigail shrugged. "I did not count."

"Was he a good patient?"

The scene flashed through Abigail's mind: Jubal, shirtless in his kitchen, making small talk about the weather, unfinished chores, had she heard about Matthew Yoder's new plow—small talk, she assumed, to distract him from the sting of antiseptic, the prick of the needle, the pressure as she taped the bandage in place.

"He was truly brave. You know that old saying, 'grab the bull by the horns'? Well, that is exactly what he did . . . and why Goliath was able to throw him over the fence."

"Wow. Amazing. Bet you'll see that every time you close your eyes."

Yes, if last night was any indicator. She'd also remember standing close enough to Jube to inhale a whiff of fresh hay, the way his big, warm hand blanketed hers, and his voice near her ear, whispering, "*Thank you, Abigail.*"

"Mama?" Frannie said, interrupting her thoughts.

The baby aimed a dimpled forefinger at Patch. "Wook, Mama. Kitty!"

Abigail felt a bit like she'd spent the past moments in a trance.

"Yes, isn't she pretty?" she heard Willa say. "Her name is Patch. Can you say 'Patch'?"

"Pash?"

The connection between mother and daughter was a beautiful sight to see. *Lord*, Abigail prayed, *if it is Your will, bless me with love like this.*

"You okay, Abigail?"

Blinking, she said, "Yes. Of course. Why?"

"I dunno. . . ." One shoulder lifted. "You looked kinda sad and far away just now."

"No, I was just thinking."

"About your husband?"

She'd been a widow more than a year when Willa came to town. Had someone told her about Ira's less-than-Christian conduct?

"No, not Ira."

"Sorry," Willa said. "Didn't mean to intrude." She patted Abigail's hand. "But I'm a great secret keeper . . . if you ever need to talk."

"I know." Abigail threaded her needle and placed Jubal's shirt in her lap while Willa helped herself to another cup of coffee.

"Mind if I ask why you keep to yourself so much?"

Abigail poked herself with the needle. She'd just spent an hour removing blood from the shirt, and to protect it from the droplet clinging to her fingertip, she popped it into her mouth.

"There are half a dozen eligible bachelors in town. Why hasn't one of them snapped you up?"

Abigail took a stitch, pictured Jubal, bent at the waist, clutching his bloodied side, putting on a brave face for the boys, who looked at him with adoring puppy-dog eyes.

"I am content with my life."

"Content. Mmm-hmm." Willa winked again. "Wonder what he'll say next time he sees you."

"Who? Jubal?"

"Y'know, he's *Jube* to the rest of us."

"Jube," Frannie echoed. Willa untied her, eased her to her feet. "Pash," the baby said, wiggling her chubby fingers. "Come, Pash."

"You were about to tell me why you're the only one who calls him Jubal."

"I was?" She surprised herself by saying, "It's respectful. I owe him that after . . ."

And like vinegar from an overturned bottle, the truth spilled out: Three, sometimes four nights a week, she told Willa, Ira had gone into town to gamble and drink. "Ira and Jubal were best friends since childhood. There were no secrets between them. I was never good at arithmetic, but I could add two and two: Jubal knew about all of it, even Ira's affair with that widow. I think he tried to stop him from entering her house that night. Ira hated being told what to do. That, I believe, is why they fought, why Ira drove off like a madman and . . ."

Eyes closed, she pictured the bustling, brightly lit ER. Tubes and wires everywhere. Ira's hand atop hers. "Not Jube's fault . . . mine."

Jubal, saying, "Be quiet so the healing can begin."

And Ira, shaking his head. "No more lies." He'd looked at her then and said, "I am so sorry. You deserved better than me, Abby." Then his hand went limp and—

"It's okay, Abby. Don't say any more. Sorry I roused all those awful memories."

Awful memories were all she had. Maybe if she shared them with a friend, they wouldn't seem so horrible.

"Jubal knelt beside the gurney, tried to say something—

good-bye, I suppose, since they were so close—but I would not let him speak. I was furious. With Ira, for . . . for everything. With God, for not answering my prayers. With Jubal, for keeping so many secrets from me. The things I said . . ." Abigail exhaled a shaky sigh. "Hateful, horrible, heinous things. Things that hurt him. I saw it in his eyes. *Still* see it in his eyes."

She looked directly at Willa. "I keep to myself because here, alone in my house, I need not face him and remember all the ugly things I said."

Willa sat back and, arms crossed over her chest, said, "I don't know him well, but Jube seems like a good and decent man. I'm sure he understands that you didn't mean those things, that grief made you say them."

Frannie chose that moment to climb into Abigail's lap. Pudgy hands bracketed her face. "Aw, Abby sad?"

Hugging the child tight, she forced a smile. "I am happy, see?" She grabbed a cookie and took a bite. Frannie did the same . . . right before she released a long, whispery yawn.

Willa got up, collected the mugs and Frannie's tumbler, and put them into the sink. Brushing cookie crumbs from the table into her cupped palm, she said, "This li'l girl needs a nap. And I have a mountain of laundry to do. Supper to start—I promised Max a pot roast—and housekeeping. I could write 'Willa Loves Max' in the dust on the end tables."

"Let me wrap some cookies for you to take home."

"Okay. But only because poor Jube can't eat *all* of 'em." She punctuated the comment with a girlish giggle. "Hey, why don't you join us for supper? There'll be plenty, and I know Max would love to see you."

"Maybe some other time. I have laundry to do, too." Abigail patted Jubal's shirt. "And this to finish."

Hours later, she inspected her work. The shirt looked almost as good as new. If someone didn't know where to look, it wasn't likely they'd notice the mend. She decided that as long as the ironing board was out, she might as well iron her blue dress and the aprons in her laundry basket. Tomorrow, on her way to the inn, she'd deliver the shirt, along with a tin of cookies.

Between then and now, she could work on a suitable opening line.

Chapter 3

It was their first day on the job, and Jube stood behind the boys as they watched the van grind down the driveway. If they asked what was discussed during the private conversation between him and their fathers, he intended to quote 1 Thessalonians: ". . . mind your own business, be quiet, and do your own job." When the red glow of taillights faded into the early-morning darkness, he said, "Did you boys have breakfast?"

"I think so," Thomas said around a yawn.

" 'Course we did," James said. "Maem made egg sandwiches, remember?"

"Us, too," Paul said. "With ham and cheese."

He slid a cast-iron skillet onto the left-front burner, dropped in a pat of butter. "You will find mugs in that cabinet. Help yourselves to coffee."

As they ate the scrambled eggs he'd made them, the boys struggled to keep their eyes open. "How late do you usually sleep?"

"Six or seven."

"Or eight."

Thomas yawned again.

If this was a sign of things to come, it promised to be a long, tedious morning. Jube made more noise than necessary, putting the dishes into the sink, hoping to snap them to attention. On the way to the barn, he said, "There is a sink on the back wall. That is where you will wash up."

"Wash up, to *milk cows*?"

"Yes, then you will wash their udders, and wash up again before you will filter and bottle the milk. Can't risk contamination, now can we?"

While they took turns at the utility sink, Jube checked on Goliath. "That gash is nearly healed already. This is good. I am glad." He stroked the bull's forehead. "Maybe you will remember this next time you decide to have a temper tantrum."

He heard one of the boys say, "He said more to that animal than to us!" No surprise there. Since Ira's accident, he hadn't exactly been talkative. Over time, he'd come to realize that the less he spoke, the fewer things he had to apologize for, and by now, he rather liked his quieter, less complicated life.

"Do you always keep Goliath in here with the cows?"

"Only at night. Not even he could withstand a black bear attack."

"But people say bears are more afraid of us than we are of them. . . ."

"People are wrong."

"So, if a bear showed up, you would shoot it?"

"Only if it posed a threat. Last week, I fired warning shots into the air when a sow and cubs came too close to the pasture."

"I heard people say bears are not meat eaters."

"People are wrong," he said again, and lined up two hay bales. His plan was to recite a quick lesson in washing cow udders, then show the boys how milking was done.

But before he could begin, Pete said, "I expected it to stink in here."

"Cleanliness is key. While the cows are out, I shovel dung, spread fresh hay. Once a week, I hose down the stalls."

"What do you do with the dung?"

"Load it into a wheelbarrow and dump it on the back lot."

They looked none too happy about the prospect of hauling manure, so he launched into the cleaning-and-milking lecture.

"Sounds time consuming."

"Not really." Jube filled a shiny stainless bucket with warm water, dropped in a clean, dry rag, and pocketed a small spray bottle of iodine teat tip. "Besides, it is necessary work, and best for the cows. A very satisfying expenditure of time, in my opinion."

Thomas nodded. "And it is not like you have a wife or children taking up your time."

The comment stung, Jube admitted, because he'd given up on the idea of having a wife and children of his own. Giving up, however, hadn't smothered the dream.

Instantly, Abigail came to mind. Once, and only once, Jube had seen her with her hair down. He'd stopped by to talk with Ira, caught a glimpse of her at the kitchen sink. Thick dark hair, unbound by braids, spilled down her slender back like a mahogany waterfall, and long-lashed brown eyes grew big and round when she peeked over her shoulder and saw him. "Ira," she'd scolded, "are you out of your mind, letting Jube in here while I am still in my nightclothes!" Ira had quickly shut the door, but not soon enough to keep Jube from seeing her flushed cheeks and embarrassed smile. He'd always liked Abigail, but at that moment—

"If the cows fall asleep while we are milking them, will they fall over on us?"

Pete's question snapped him back to attention. "No."

All four youthful faces relaxed.

"What say we get started, eh?" Carrying the bucket, he stepped up beside the first cow. "This is Daisy. She is the most fidgety, so I will milk her myself."

"They all have names?"

As he recited them, each cow turned toward him.

Thomas said, "They recognize their names?"

"Of course. Cows are intelligent and can be trained to do many things. They have excellent memories, too, and never forget a person who mistreats them."

"Then I guess we had better be gentle!" Pete said.

When the laughter subsided, Paul asked, "Why are they all named after flowers, except for Robin?"

"As a calf, she made noises like a baby bird."

It dawned on Jube that he only had one stool. Turning in a slow circle, he looked for something that could do double duty. There, in the barn's far corner, he'd stashed several orange crates he'd bought last week. Fastened to the stall walls, they'd act as storage shelves for grooming brushes and hoof-trimming tools, but right now they could be milking stools.

"Each of you grab a box," he said, and after each boy returned with an improvised milking stool, Jube entered Daisy's stall. Squatting, he tucked the three-legged stool under him. "The job will take about ten minutes, and she will give me about three gallons. But first things first . . ."

He wrung out the rag and wiped Daisy's udder. "We cannot allow mud—or, worse, dung—to fall into the pail." He then spritzed each teat with iodine. "This helps avoid infection and reduce any chance of bacteria spreading. Some hand milkers wear gloves, but I find them cumbersome."

Peripheral vision told him that he had their full attention. Sliding the bucket directly beneath the udder, he said, "I will start with the teats farthest from me, take hold, and squeeze, sort of the way you get toothpaste from the tube. Steady, even pressure that is not too tight or too loose."

"What if Daisy gets really fidgety?"

"He will talk to her, quietly," James said, repeating what Jube had said.

"Yes, good. And if that does not work?"

No one spoke.

"Then I might have to postpone milking for a few minutes," Jube said, filling the silence. "I might feed her, or stroke her forehead." Standing, he scratched between Daisy's ears. "Good girl," he crooned. "You are happy now, right?" She answered with a quiet grunt.

On the stool again, he leaned his cheek against Daisy's side. The first squirt echoed in the empty pail, and before long, he sat up straight.

"How do you know when she is empty?"

"If the udder feels slack, your job is done. Almost." He gave each teat another squirt of the iodine and got to his feet.

As they moved to Robin's stall, Paul asked why Jube still milked by hand.

"My grandfather and father milked this way. Here in Pleasant Valley, we have adapted to the New Order ways, with our washing machines and pickup trucks, running water and electric lamps. I like doing some things the Old Order way. Now, if I had dozens of cows, instead of only thirteen, I would use machines. For just these few, it is not worth the expense."

"But you have pasteurizing machines, right?"

"No. The Department of Agriculture approved the sale of my raw milk to a handful of stores and restaurants that cater to what people call 'health nuts.' As soon as we have collected the milk, we will cool and filter it, and pour it into sterilized bottles, and take it to town."

"It will not spoil?"

Of all the boys, James seemed most interested in the process. "Not nearly as quickly as pasteurized milk. We will still get it into town as fast as possible, and then my customers will refrigerate it."

An hour later, with only a minimum of problems, all thirteen cows had been milked. Jube and the boys used towels to keep the bottles from clinking against one another, and while loading the crates into Jube's truck, Pete asked about the unfinished buggy in the big shed beside the barn.

"I make them in my spare time," Jube explained. "It takes months and costly materials, and because people know that, they are willing to pay five or six thousand dollars for one."

"No wonder our folks are doing all they can to hold on to their squeaky old buggies," Thomas said. As his twin and their cousins nodded, he fist-pumped the air. "I just had *the best* idea for Phase Two: We're supposed to find someone in need and I know just who it is—our parents—and what they need are buggies!"

Jube didn't understand; neither did Thomas's brother or cousins. The boy explained that in addition to working for him, their parents had given the twins a second assignment . . . to give to someone less fortunate . . . which they hoped might cure the boys of the immaturity and self-centeredness that had inspired their many transgressions.

"We still have last year's birthday money, and everything we earned doing odd jobs last summer. This summer, too," Thomas continued. "If we pay for the materials, will you teach us to make buggies for our parents?"

"Listen to him," James said, "spending all of our money without even asking us!"

"Yeah, but it really is a great idea," Pete said, and Paul echoed the sentiment.

Their harmonic pleading prompted Jube to say, "I admire you for wanting to help your folks out, but as I said, it takes months to complete just one buggy. And you hope to make two? Before Christmas?" He shook his head. "I am a 'where there is a will, there is a way' sort of man, but, boys, in this case, there might not be a way."

"Because of chores and school and what we still owe you in work hours?" Thomas wanted to know.

Jube appreciated that the Hartzes and the Briskeys wanted their sons to trade boyhood pranks for responsible behavior, but he'd already committed enough of his own time to that plan.

"Would you teach us? Please?"

Four young, fresh faces stared up at him. Jube didn't want to say no, but how could he say yes?

"If we had more time—"

" 'Where there is a will, there is a way,' " James quoted.

Not all that long ago, Jube had been a wide-eyed, eager boy who didn't believe in "impossible." "If we have any hope of succeeding, we need to ask if this idea is *God's* will," Jube said. But what they heard was *Yes*.

During the drive to Oakland, they talked nonstop about the project. The discussion continued as they delivered bottled milk to Jube's customers, and all the way back to his place. Half a mile from his driveway, he asked if they'd like him to drop them off at home.

"No, thank you, Mr. Quinn. We will walk."

"Thomas is right," James said. "That will give us time to talk about what to say if our parents ask about the Christmas project."

He had to hand it to them. They'd tackled the milking, and everything that went with it, without a word of complaint. Something told him that, even without this unusual assignment, they would become responsible, productive men. What sort of man would *he* be if he didn't help them meet the fast-approaching Christmas deadline?

"Need us to do anything before we head home?" Pete asked.

"No, but thanks."

"What about firewood?"

Before he had a chance to reply, all four boys were racing back and forth, carrying logs and stacking them neatly beside the wood stove, and on the porch, where they would stay dry in the event the clouds over Backbone Mountain had a mind to drench the Alleghenies. They built a fire, too, and when they finished, Jube invited them into the kitchen for sandwiches to tide them over until suppertime.

"It is hot in here," Pete said, and opened the door.

The temperature outside had dipped into the high thirties, but the inside thermometer now read seventy, and Jube gladly agreed.

As they ate, the boys pummeled him with buggy-building questions:

"What kind of wood do you use for the carriage?"

"How do you make the wheels?"

"Is the chassis iron?"

"Will the seats be cloth or leather?"

Jube laughed, and promised that as they worked tomorrow he'd give them a step-by-step how-to lesson. "We will work out the details of your work schedule, too, because it would not be right to let the project interfere with your other responsibilities."

They got up to leave, and as they slipped into their jackets, Thomas extended a hand.

"Thank you, Mr. Quinn, for . . . for saving my life, and . . . and for *every*thing today."

His brother and cousins did the same.

"See you in the morning," he said.

Odd, he thought, stacking the sandwich plates, that he'd already grown accustomed to their incessant chatter.

But wait. . . .

Her heart fluttered in response to his admiring expression. "Oh, I have never needed a full eight hours' sleep."

"Burning the midnight oil, eh?" He turned, draped the shirt over a chairback, and winced.

"Let me look at your ribs," she said.

"I'm fine," he said, pressing a palm to his side.

"I will be the judge of that." And without waiting for his agreement or permission, Abigail moved closer. "Untuck your shirt." When he hesitated, she met his eyes. "Would you rather I do it?"

Jube groaned quietly but complied.

Bending at the waist, she examined the bandage. "The tape seems to have held, but the gash bled a little. Not so much that it stained another shirt, thankfully, but enough that you need a clean dressing." Straightening, she said, "Tell me where you put the gauze and tape I used yesterday, and—"

"I appreciate the offer, but I can take care of it."

Jubal was visibly uncomfortable in her presence, and that bothered her, but if she let him have his way, infection could set in. *And you've already hurt him enough.* "We went all through this yesterday. The wound is in a hard-to-reach place. You simply cannot do it yourself."

A certain sadness dimmed his eyes—eyes as blue as wild chicory—as his frown deepened. *Lord, if this is the moment You have chosen for my apology, show me a sign!*

"The things you need are right where you left them yesterday."

He nodded toward the dining room, and there on the sideboard was the platter where she'd assembled gauze patches, adhesive tape, peroxide, and scissors. Fetching it before he had time to change his mind, she slid it onto the table.

"Please. Sit," she said, pulling out a chair, "while I wash up."

After arranging the materials in the order she'd use them, Abigail knelt beside him.

"Does Bill ever schedule you to work weekends?"

"Not usually," she said, removing the existing dressing. "Only during the July Fourth and Valentine's Day weekends."

"Englishers. What a peculiar celebration. A day for expensive chocolates, greeting cards, and flowers?" Jubal harrumphed. "I am glad to be Amish!"

Abigail tilted the peroxide bottle until it saturated a gauze pad. Gently, she cleaned dried blood from his skin. "Yes. Seems to me a couple should show affection every day, not just once a year."

He nodded.

"The stitches are holding nicely." Standing, she attached tape to a large gauze pad, spread antiseptic ointment onto it, and got onto her knees again. "I can probably remove them on Monday or Tuesday," she said, pressing the pad into place.

His muscles tautened under her touch. "No need for that. I will visit Emily or Willa at the clinic, first thing Monday morning."

Disappointment shot through her like a hot arrow. "Why? You do not trust me?"

"Yes, of course. I just . . . I hate to impose."

"Imposing? I am happy to do it. Need I remind you that the only reason you are hurt is because *you saved my life*!"

Abigail got up so quickly that if Jubal hadn't reached out, slid a hand behind her waist, she might have stumbled. The sudden movement strained his bruised muscles and cracked ribs, and seeing the flash of pain in his eyes made her feel even more guilty.

"You saved me. Again. And hurt yourself doing it. Again. Will you forgive me?"

She followed his gaze to where her fingertips rested lightly on his forearm. Until that moment, Abigail hadn't realized that she'd touched him. She snatched back her hand, hid it in her apron pocket.

"I was only too happy to do it," he said, echoing her words. "Believe me, there is nothing to forgive. If anything, I am the one . . ."

He stepped back, tugged at the hem of his shirt until it covered the bandage.

"Well, I should go. There is laundry waiting for me. And leaves to clear from the gutters, before they clog the downspouts and cause a leak. I have to sweep the porches, too, or the leaves will stain the floorboards." She was rambling and knew it but couldn't seem to stop the nonsensical flow of words. "Plus there is the ironing. And Patch to feed, of course."

"Of course." The hint of a smile lifted one corner of his mouth. "And vegetables to pick and put up."

A nervous giggle popped from her lips. "Yes. That, too."

"When the job is finished, I volunteer to help carry the jars into the root cellar."

This time, she quoted *him*. "Thank you, but I hate to impose."

She'd meant to tease him, but his wounded expression told her that the joke had backfired. *You are such a* domoor! It also told her that the apology she'd been planning to make was not God's will. At least, not today. If He wanted her to do it at all, He'd have to present an opening that not even a simpleton like her could miss! Feeling clumsy and stupid and cruel, Abigail grabbed her shawl.

"Time to go. Rest well, Jubal."

All the way home, she prayed that between now and tomorrow, when she returned to check his bandage again, she'd find the strength to set embarrassment aside and concentrate on what was best for Jubal.

Because God knew she'd already hurt him enough.

Chapter 4

Abigail left so quickly, Jube could have sworn he felt a breeze. Left so quickly, in fact, that there hadn't been time to thank her for mending his shirt, or baking cookies, or changing his bandage. He'd thought about it while washing dishes, while changing into his nightclothes, and still couldn't decide if he was more angry than hurt, or the other way around. If he had to choose a word to describe the way he felt, it'd be "exasperation."

"Three years is a long time to hold a grudge," he muttered around his toothbrush.

Tomorrow, as soon as the boys finished milking, he'd send them home. They'd asked for a buggy-building lesson, but that could wait a day. A visit to the bishop could not. Micah Fisher had been first on the scene the night of Ira's accident, and while waiting for the EMTs to pry Ira from the mangled wreck, the man had heard a full confession. Perhaps, as the only other person who knew the whole truth about that night—and the events leading up to it—Micah could help Jube make sense of things.

After a night of disjointed dreams about Abigail, Jube woke tired and achy. Even after he chased a fried-egg sandwich with two cups of coffee, irritability hung clung to him like old cobwebs.

The boys arrived early, wide awake and in good spirits. At one point last night, he'd considered telling Ben and Noah to find some other way to teach their sons a lesson. But he'd given his word, and not even the younger, more unreliable Jubal had ever broken that. As he'd told Abigail, he enjoyed the boys' company. And if their remaining days unfolded as this one had, their unending questions would keep his mind off her.

"Rose has a calf in her belly, doesn't she?" Pete said.

"As a matter of fact, she does."

"Violet, too?"

"Only Rose. I try to keep it to one calf a season."

"But more cows mean more milk, and more milk means more money, right?"

Jube chuckled. "The more cows I have, the longer it takes to run this place. And not all calves produce milk."

They gave that a moment's thought before Paul said, "Ah. I get it. Bulls."

"And as you discovered yesterday, bulls are not easy to handle."

"But Goliath is your only bull. What do you do with other males that are born?"

"Sell them." He didn't think it necessary to admit that some ended up in stewpots.

"When will Rose's baby be born?"

"Mid-January is my best guess. I prefer spring for calving, but sometimes nature—and Goliath—has other ideas."

Their fathers worked in construction, so Jube had no clue how much the boys knew about livestock breeding. It was a lesson he had no business teaching them, so he quickly added,

"Winter is hard on the little ones. They are not very surefooted, and their ears are susceptible to frostbite."

"But I see cows outdoors, standing in deep snow all the time," Thomas said.

"Yes, and some farmers think I pamper mine. I disagree. They raise beef cattle. Dairy cows," he said, grinning, "are a horse of a different color."

On their own, the boys decided that Pete and Paul would scrub buckets, while James and Thomas helped filter and bottle the day's collection. They'd been at it for all of ten minutes when Thomas said, "Can I ask you a question?"

The timidity in the boy's voice reminded him that many folks saw Jube as gruff and standoffish, and although he accepted his self-imposed solitary status, he didn't enjoy it. He missed being with people, but joining in the fun meant that sometimes Abigail would be among the crowd. Abigail, whose disdain for him was palpable.

"What question?"

"Does Jethro ever work here?"

"Not often." He'd been eighteen when his younger brother was born ... with Down's syndrome. As Jethro grew and learned, he endeared himself to everyone, but none more than Jube.

"You know that he has Down's syndrome, right?"

"We know that he is different. But that is okay. We like him!"

"A couple of times, Jethro tried helping out, but cows are big and clumsy and noisy, all things he dislikes. When he visits, I do my best to keep him away from the barn."

"You are a good big brother," Pete said.

"I hope so. Jethro deserves only the best."

"Can I ask another question?"

Jube started to suggest that he get back to work when Thomas asked, "Are you in love with Miss Fletcher?"

If he'd asked what caused Down's, well, that might have made sense. But *that*?

James said, "I think *she* is in love with *you*."

The sky was starry black, and the barn's lighting turned the windows into ebony mirrors. Jube caught sight of his own reflection . . . slump shouldered, gap jawed, wide-eyed. *You look as stupid as you feel*, he thought, clamping his teeth together.

"She looks at *you* funny, too. . . ."

Too? When had he ever looked at her *funny*? And when had Thomas—when had anyone, for that matter—seen him and Abigail together long enough to notice the way they looked at each other?

"How old are you boys?"

Shoulders back and chins up, they stretched as tall as their five-foot frames would allow. "Thomas an' me will turn fourteen come February."

"Thomas and *I*," Pete corrected, and, ignoring his cousin's dirty look, said, "We were all born in February, but Paul and I are a whole week older."

As girls, their mothers—twins born on Christmas Eve thirty-some years ago—had gotten into plenty of trouble. Had Priscilla and Leora filled their boys' heads with silly, romantic notions?

"So you are thirteen?"

All four nodded.

"Old enough, then, to know better than to poke your noses into other men's business." He stabbed the air with a forefinger. "Have you finished your jobs?"

Pete said, "Buckets are scrubbed."

"And the cows have all been brushed."

"I am still filtering."

"And filling bottles."

"We want to finish the work fast," Thomas said, "but we want to do it well, so that you will help us with the Christmas surprise."

He didn't have the heart to make them wait. If there wasn't time to talk with the bishop today, well, there was always tomorrow.

Abigail had been up most of the night, first tossing and turning, then pacing the floor. Would she summon the courage to say what must be said? *You had your choice, you ninny, and you let it pass you by!*

What she needed, Abigail decided, was time spent in earnest prayer. Where better than at church, during the Sunday service?

She managed to pay attention during the first hymn, as the preachers and deacons quietly deliberated who'd deliver the sermon. When it was decided, she joined Bishop Fisher and the rest of the congregation in giving thanks that they no longer needed to hide in caves and forests to worship God.

Her mind wandered to the days when her community had met in one another's houses. Farming required the Amish to work long hours, but they'd done more than make ends meet. They'd prospered. The community had grown so much that it became impractical to meet in one another's houses . . . homes that now featured indoor plumbing, electricity, and modern-day appliances.

Despite the sweeping changes, they held tight to many Old Order ways, keeping boys and men on one side of the church, girls and women on the other. If Abigail leaned right, just a bit, she could see Jubal, looking handsome, as always, on the other side of the room.

Beside him, his younger brother looked adoringly up at him. And no wonder. For every one of Jethro's seventeen years, Jubal had doted on him, bringing him to town, treating him to ice cream, buying books for him to read. Their mother once shared that she didn't dare compliment another woman's dress material, tea towels, or window curtains. "If Jube hears it," Judith had said, "he buys it!" If any member of the community needed a ride into town, help with fence repair, or chasing down a runaway horse, Jubal was right there, offering assistance.

He is a good man, that Jubal Quinn.

Jubal, in a white shirt that brought out the blue of his eyes, whose beautiful baritone made it all the way to her side of the building, and who'd forever wear the mark of Goliath because he'd put himself at risk to save her and Thomas Hartz.

The mark of Goliath, indeed! Even in her mind, the description sounded overly dramatic. If she wasn't careful, a fit of giggles would disrupt the service.

In her eyes, he was more handsome than Ira, whose dark, rugged good looks had made him the center of every Pleasant Valley girl's dreams. How many times had she caught Jubal staring, as if he thought she'd hung the moon? And how many nights had she lain awake, wishing he'd come courting? *Dozens,* she thought. *Maybe more.* After months of futile hoping and praying, she told herself it must have been thoughts of the sister and father he'd buried that painted the forlorn expression on his face. She'd been two years past optimal marrying age when Ira asked for her hand, and fear that she'd end up like Spinster Nelson prompted her to say yes. Jubal had attended the wedding, and although he'd seen plenty of Ira, Abigail could count on one hand the times he'd seen *her*.

Willa elbowed her, and when Abigail looked over, she winked. It meant she had caught her friend wool-gathering in the middle of the service.

Get your mind straight! Heart thumping and pulse pounding, she bowed her head and joined in the hymn, "Blessed Redeemer." And right in the middle of singing, "Seems now I see Him on Calvary's tree," a disconcerting thought popped into her head: If Willa had noticed her daydreaming, had Jubal noticed, too?

One peek, and she'd know—

Exercise some self-control! Isn't his opinion of you already low enough?

A long, shuddering sigh escaped her, and when Leora heard it, she squeezed Abigail's hand. Her twin, leaning around her, said, "Everything all right, friend?"

Abigail answered Priscilla with a nod as Willa elbowed her again. Now two things distracted her: how to explain yesterday's hasty departure to Jubal and what to say when Willa asked why she'd been gawking at him.

Two hours later, the service ended and church members gathered out back. It was sunny outside, and unusually warm for October. A westerly breeze had kicked up, propelling a few tablecloths and napkins into the air, and they floated back to earth like blue-and-red-checked parachutes.

When the meal ended, the men gathered for a game of cornhole while the women stacked plates and bowls into wicker carriers. On the way to the parking lot with her basket, Priscilla caught up with Abigail. "Oh, how I dread riding home in that rickety old buggy. On the way here, the lurching and bumping chipped my favorite serving bowl!"

The Hartzes and Briskeys lived side by side in identical houses and shared a huge panel van. When it wasn't in use, delivering boards and other construction materials to Ben and Noah's job sites, Leora and Priscilla used it to transport their goats, chickens, and hares to customers. Since its floorboards were always covered with sawdust and hay, it didn't surprise Abigail that they rarely drove it to church.

"Ben and I, and Leora and Noah, are saving up to buy horses for the boys, to surprise them for their birthday." Abigail didn't think she'd be as generous with sons who, for years, had run amok all through town.

"But that is not why I hurried to catch up with you." Standing in Abigail's path, Priscilla said, "I wish I knew how to thank you for saving Thomas."

"No need to thank me. It was Jubal Quinn who saved him."

"But he told me that *you* were in the pen when he got there. I said to Ben, we ought to insist that Jube put that monster down. The whole community could enjoy a barbecue! But you know how men are." She deepened her voice. " 'Mind your business, Prissy.' " Shaking her head, Priscilla added, "Have you had nightmares about it? Being face-to-face with that slobbering beast, I mean?"

"No." She could tell the truth, that the incident hadn't been the bull's fault. Goliath had been right where he was supposed to be when the boys showed up. Why, he could have ground them into dust if he'd had a mind to! "But I am grateful, too . . . that Jubal jumped the fence when he did." *Now* that, Abigail thought, picturing the moment, *is something I will dream about!*

"Speaking of Jube . . ." Priscilla moved in closer, lowered her voice. "I saw the way you were looking at each other from across the church. Oh, what a perfect match you two would be. And it is high time, if you ask me."

What had she said? A perfect match? And high time for *what*?

"No need to worry, Abigail. Your secret is safe with me. I doubt anyone else noticed. But even if they did, what could they say? Ira has been gone for years. I hate to speak ill of the dead, but he was hardly a stellar husband. Now *Jube* . . ." She exhaled a dreamy sigh. "He would make an exemplary husband!"

Hardly a stellar husband? Did that mean Jubal wasn't the only one who'd been aware of Ira's carousing?

By now, the women had reached Priscilla's buggy, and again, she blocked Abigail's path. "You are both young. Strong. Good-looking. Just imagine the beautiful children you would have!"

"Who would have what?" Ben said from behind her.

"Goodness, Husband. I will have to put a bell on you." Giggling, she said to Abigail, "Now I ask you, how does a man this size move about as quiet as a cat!"

He relieved his wife of the basket, slid it behind the buggy seat. "Thank you, Abigail, for what you did for Thomas."

How many times would she have to say it? "Jubal deserves all of the credit."

"The boys are to blame for his injury, and they will work for him until he has healed. Although no physical harm came to you, they also owe you a debt, so start thinking of things they can do around your place."

"No need for that. Really."

"Oh, but there is," Priscilla said. "We have to impress upon them, once and for all, that everything they do impacts others."

The old "pebble in a pond" theory your opa *was so fond of?*

"They are becoming young men," Ben continued. "If we let them run roughshod over everyone and everything they come into contact with, what kind of men will they become?"

Abigail understood, but even if she had a notion to agree with the offer—and she did not—her house and yard were small and easily maintained.

The Hartz twins raced up just then. "Thank you again," Thomas began, "for—"

"I thank God that I was in the right place at the right time."

It's what she'd tell Jubal next time she saw him. The decision made her feel strong. Brave. More confident than she'd felt in a long, long time. So yes, that's what she'd tell him.

That . . .

. . . and a whole lot more.

Chapter 5

"You were not at the gathering yesterday," Pete said.

Jube didn't look up from his milking. "I had work to do."

Paul's brow furrowed. "I thought we were here so you can have fun once in a while."

Thomas's expression bordered on arrogant, and Jube wondered what kept the others from taking him down a peg or two when he said, "That is only part of it, *grote babe*."

"I am not a big baby," his brother argued. "I know why we are here."

"Yeah? Why?"

"To keep us too busy to get into trouble."

"And," Jube stepped in, "to help you learn that from an honest day's work comes self-respect."

"Our parents must really hate us," Thomas whined.

Jube shook his head. "Not true. They are disappointed, in you, *and* in themselves. They believe if they were better parents, you would not cause so many problems."

If he'd ever seen more miserable faces, he didn't know where.

"Look. Boys. You have shown me what you are capable of.

Soon, they will see it, too, and they will be proud, and so will you."

"But pride is a sin!" Paul said.

"Pleased, then. Yes, that is better. You will be pleased with yourselves." Seeing that his words had improved their mood, Jube smiled, and for the first time in a long time, he *felt* like smiling. "Rose needs water."

They filled her tub. Filled the rest of the tubs, including Goliath's, then got busy with the milking.

"He is not so big and bad, tied up in here, is he?"

"He is not big and bad in the pasture, either," Jube said, "when there are no interlopers around, threatening his cows."

Shrugs, frowns, and quiet muttering told him they understood: Even Goliath behaved well . . . when doing what was expected of him.

"Why do you avoid the gatherings?"

"I have attended my share."

"I have never seen you."

Leave it to Thomas to ask the tough questions, and follow them up with equally tough comments.

"So many questions! Are you writing a book, Thomas?" He grinned, so they'd know he was kidding. On a more serious note, he added, "Mine is not the largest farm in Pleasant Valley, and until you arrived, I worked alone. Staying on top of things leaves very little time for partying."

"Still, everyone needs to have fun, even a man like you."

A man like him?

"Serious," the boy said, answering Jube's unasked question. "If I ever write a book, I will quote the old 'all work and no play' saying!"

They all had a good laugh over that, and for the rest of the day, the boys worked and smiled and stood a little taller than when they'd arrived. Again, he offered to drive them home, and again, they said no. "I'll go with you, see what is in the mail-box," he said, joining them as they departed.

"It is Sunday," James said. "The mail does not come on Sun-days."

"Forgot to fetch it yesterday."

As they walked, Pete asked, "How long is your driveway?"

"Thirteen hundred feet from road to porch."

Squinting, Paul did the math in his head. "A quarter mile." Then, pointing, he added, "Is that Miss Fletcher's truck?"

Jube's heartbeat quickened.

James gave his twin a brotherly shove. "Just look at his face!"

"Yeah. No need to answer our question."

If only he could forget what they'd asked . . . and what they'd said.

"I think it is true." Thomas's thumbs and forefingers formed a heart. And then he exhaled an exaggerated sigh.

"I think you are right, Brother." James formed the heart, too.

"Stop it, boys," Jube chided. "It is warm for October and her windows are open. She could hear you."

"How would you explain *that*?"

"Easy. I would simply say the four of you are *gek*."

"Lower your voices," Thomas warned. "She has heard the stories and will believe we *are* crazy!"

They were still laughing as she turned into the driveway. Abigail waved, and so did they.

"See you tomorrow, Mr. Quinn," one said.

"Maybe a buggy lesson?" asked another.

"Shoo," he said, smirking, which prompted a new round of laughter.

They'd stepped onto the roadside when he approached her truck. "I did not expect to see you today."

Long lashes fluttered. "Why?"

"It is Sunday. Plus, yesterday you rattled off a to-do list as long as my forearm."

"One thing on the list was 'Check Jube's side.'" She smiled. "May I drive you back up to the house?"

He moved to the truck's right side, grimacing at the door's high-pitched squeak. "Before you leave, remind me to give those hinges some oil."

A second, perhaps two, passed before she faced forward, shifted into Drive. "All right."

Why the hesitation? he wondered. But after the way she'd run off yesterday, Jube decided not to press the issue.

Side by side, they climbed the porch steps. "The boys really like you, Jubal. That, I think, is a wonderful thing."

"I like them, too."

"Do you think you can turn them into dairy farmers?"

If her impish smile hadn't told him she was teasing, her glittering eyes would have. "No, but if they ever find themselves stranded in the desert . . . with a cow . . . what they know will save them from dying of thirst."

She let out a giggle, reminding him how much he enjoyed the musical sound of it. He hadn't heard it often, because Ira gave her very little reason to laugh. If Jube had acted on his feelings before Ira made his move . . .

He shook his head, because not once in all those years had Abigail done anything to indicate interest in him.

"The coffee is hot. . . ."

"That sounds good. But first, I will take care of your side. Are the bandages in the dining room, still?"

"They are," he said, reaching for mugs. She was quick and agile, and not even the loose folds of her apron could hide her slender waist. She'd worn a black mourning dress for a full year after Ira's funeral. The first time Jubal had seen her without it, about two year ago, he'd wanted to shout, *Finally!* Today, dark curls had escaped her bun and peeked out from under her cap, reminding him of the vision she'd been that early morning in her kitchen.

"Coffee before or after the bandage?" he asked.

She thought about it for a minute before answering. "Before."

In case he said something stupid, as he had yesterday, and sent her running?

"Cream and sugar?"

"Just black, thanks."

"Something else we have in common."

She sat across from him. "Something else?"

Ach. *Now you have put your foot in it, fool!* He cleared his throat. "We both grew up here. Neither of us has missed a church service. Despite the bishop's sometimes bossy, prying ways, we like him." He stopped himself from saying, *And we both loved Ira. . . .*

"And we both love black coffee."

Jube wished the mug were bigger, so that he could hide his foolish face behind it.

"Am I to understand that in addition to teaching the boys about milk cows, you will show them how to hitch a horse to a buggy?"

"Noah and Ben have likely given that lesson." Leaning forward, he said, "Can you keep a secret?"

She mimicked his action, lessening the space between them. "As long as it does not involve a crime," she whispered, "yes."

Sunlight, slanting through the window, lit the top half of her face, highlighting the faint freckles that dotted her nose and casting spiky shadows on her cheeks. *Lord, but she is lovely*, he thought.

If anyone came to the door right now and saw them, nearly nose to nose, they might face a reprimand. A lot of things had changed when the community traded Old Order for New Order ways, but an unmarried man and a woman, alone, still violated the rules of propriety.

He sat back, and so did she.

"Well? The suspense is killing me. Tell me all about this deep dark secret you are keeping."

He loved the way her eyes glittered when she teased him. Loved the way she smiled, and tilted her head, and . . . But who was he kidding? He loved *Abigail*, had loved her from the moment she'd walked into their one-room schoolhouse so many years ago.

"Secret?"

"The buggy lesson?"

He filled her in on the punishment that, in the hope of convincing the four teens to stay on the straight and narrow, included finding a neighbor in need and fulfilling that need by Christmas Eve.

Faint lines formed between her brows. "What does that have to do with buggies?"

"They selected their parents as the neighbors in need, and—"

"I get it!" she said, slapping the table. "Just this morning, Priscilla complained about their buggy. Said it rides so rough that it rattled things in her basket, chipped her favorite serving bowl." Hands clasped under her chin, she sighed. "How sweet of the boys. How thoughtful. They want you to teach them how to build one for the Hartzes, don't they?"

"You are half-right."

The furrow returned. "Oh?"

"Turns out the Briskeys' buggy is in sad shape, too. And since neither family can afford to buy a new one . . ." He shrugged, extending his hands, palms up.

"I am confused. Priscilla also said they will buy horses for the boys. Surprises, for their birthdays. If they have money enough to buy horses, they can afford buggies."

Now she looked worried, and, oh, how he wanted to comfort her!

"I hope the plan to build buggies . . . does it mean they know about the surprise?"

"Probably not. But then, I have only been with them a few days."

"Maybe you will find out before they have served their sentence. . . ." She giggled, waved a hand in front of her face. "*Sentence.* That sounds so serious!" Abigail grew serious as she asked, "Will you help them build the buggies?"

"I intend to try." He outlined the cost of supplies, the tools and processes—some dangerous—and hours of meticulous attention to detail required to turn the materials into safely functioning, eye-pleasing vehicles. "They cannot meet the deadline unless I pull a few all-nighters while they are home, sleeping."

"You would do that for them?"

"I will try," he repeated.

Abigail inhaled a deep breath, let it out slowly. "Well," she said, walking to the sink, "that bandage is not going to change itself. While I wash up, untuck your shirt?"

As she had yesterday, Abigail arranged the supplies in the order she'd need them, then knelt beside him, wincing with every tug of the tape. It reminded him of how he'd laughed, watching his mother's lips part with every spoonful that went into baby Jethro's mouth. He wanted to pull Abigail close and thank her for being empathetic . . . for being *her*.

He resisted the impulse.

And made a decision.

Jube saw no reason to traipse all the way to the bishop's house for advice, because he knew exactly what he needed to do: Before she left here today, Abigail would know the details of that awful night. Afterward, she might resent him even more, but it was a chance he had to take.

She made quick work of tidying the table and returned the

tray to the sideboard. Abigail sat beside him, and he prayed for the strength to tell the truth.

"I need to talk to you," she said, "if you have a few minutes."

"I will always make time for you, Abigail."

"I have been meaning to say this for a very long time, and—"

A loud, guttural bellow stopped her.

"What. Was. *That?*"

"Not Rose, I hope. It is much too soon for her to drop that calf." He'd checked, just before the boys left, and seen none of the telltale signs: swelling, discharge, restlessness . . .

"What can I do?"

"You can go home. I appreciate the offer, but if Rose is calving . . ."

If she was calving, there wasn't a moment to waste. Jude nearly shoved his palm through the screen, opening the door, and made a beeline for the barn. Somehow, Abigail kept up with him. Stood beside him. Helped slide the big doors aside.

"Could be messy," he warned. *Especially if the calf is breach. Or worse, already dead.* "You sure you want to see this?"

"What I want is to help her. She sounds terrified, and in horrible agony. Tell me what to do."

Rolling up his sleeves, he approached, saw blood covering the cow's hindquarters and rear legs. Covering the walls. Spattered on the stall walls. "The calf's hooves must have nicked an artery or shredded the birth sac." Jube had only seen such a thing once. That cow hemorrhaged so badly that she was dead within minutes.

The other cows, upset by Rose's bawling, had started mooing, pacing, thumping against their stall boards.

"They sense that something is wrong," Abigail said. "I wish there was a way to let them know things will be all right."

"There is a way. You will find clean buckets against the back wall. Fill them with water and put one in front of each cow.

God willing, that will distract them, settle them down, at least until I can calm Rose enough to find out what is going on."

Abigail turned so quickly, the cap slid from her hair. How odd to see it roll lazily left, then right, before coming to rest against Goliath's gate. Normally, the bull would've been in the pasture at this time of day, but with the milking and deliveries, church services, showing the boys where they'd build the buggies, Jube hadn't had a chance to move him outside.

Feet planted shoulder width apart, Jube wrapped his arms around the cow's neck, tried to ease her down and onto her side. "You are okay. It is all right," he chanted. "Lie down, now, so I can . . ."

As if by God's design, Rose's legs buckled, first the front, then the back. She hit the hay-strewn floor hard, pinning Jube's leg beneath her. She'd stopped screaming, which could only mean one of two things. . . .

Chapter 6

When she approached Rose's stall, Abigail found Jubal sitting on the floor, forehead pressed to a bent knee. The only other time she'd seen Jubal look more defeated had been that night in the ER.

Abigail knelt beside him again, this time plucking bits of hay from his hair. "You were right. Putting water in front of the cows quieted them." *If only humans could be comforted as easily.*

He looked at the blood on his hands, his trousers and boots, and the floor and walls around him. Using the hem of her water-soaked apron, Abigail wiped a streak from his cheek. Wiped away a stray tear, too.

"You did everything humanly possible for her, Jubal. If she suffered . . ." Rose's chilling wail echoed in her mind. "At least it was quick," she amended.

"Yes. There is that."

Hett iss Gott's wil. She'd keep the thought to herself, because at this moment, he didn't need to hear that Rose's death was God's will.

He met her eyes as one corner of his mouth lifted in a faint, sad smile. "Thank you for staying."

If he hadn't chosen that moment to get to his feet, Abigail would have thrown her arms around him.

"Jubal! You are limping!"

"Just a pulled muscle." He glanced at the lifeless cow. "I must take care of her."

In other words, he needed to bury Rose.

"But your leg . . . We will need help."

"*We?* No, Abigail. She weighs nearly two thousand pounds. This is not something you can help me with."

Abigail ignored his dictatorial tone, putting it down to shock and misery. "I can, and I will. Let me drive you to the Hartzes'. Noah and Ben will be in their shop."

He gave the idea a moment's thought and, frowning, limped closer.

"We have to pass the clinic on the way. Emily has a new X-ray machine, and we can have her look at your leg."

"No time for that. Once Rose has been taken care of, I will think about it."

Oh, he would do more than think about it if Abigail had anything to say!

"Lean on me," she said, sliding an arm around his back. And to her amazement, he did.

Jube remained quiet all through the short drive, and she could only imagine what might be going through his mind.

The men met her at the workshop door. Ben took one look at her wet, bloody apron and said, "What happened?"

On the heels of her hasty explanation, Noah said, "Give us a minute to tell the wives and we will meet you there."

Ten minutes later, Noah and Ben and their sons joined her and Jubal in the barn.

"What is the plan?" Noah asked.

They'd chain Rose to the skip loader to pull her from the

barn, and once outside, he'd lift her into the bucket, and drive her to the back lot. From the looks on their faces, Abigail knew that even the boys understood what would happen after that.

Having noticed that Jubal was favoring his right leg, Noah took charge. "I will drive the loader, and Ben and the boys will ride over there in the van."

Abigail tensed, waiting for Jubal to insist he was capable of doing it himself. Instead, he joined Ben and the boys in the van.

She had plans of her own.

Scrubbing away all evidence of what had happened in the barn left her filthy, sweaty, and exhausted. The men and boys would feel even worse when they returned. After filling the teakettle, she tossed her dirty apron aside and washed up. Abigail was setting the table when Jubal limped into the kitchen, alone.

"Where are the others?"

"They had to get back to work."

She followed his gaze to the platter, plates, and mugs on the table, and felt silly for having made so many sandwiches. Her biggest concern wasn't waste, but Jubal's sad and weary face.

"Is that . . ." He pointed. "Are you wearing my shirt?"

It hid most of her torn, stained skirt. "I was afraid grit or bits of hay might fall into the food."

"Makes sense."

She pulled out two chairs, told him to prop his leg on the second. Too weary to disagree, he sagged into the first.

"Try to eat." Abigail pushed a plate closer to him.

Again, he complied without protest.

Abigail darted up the stairs and began opening doors. Two sets of bunkbeds on the right side of the hall, a double bed on the left, and straight ahead a sink, toilet, and tub. Shoving the stopper into the drain, she turned on the hot water and, after setting towels and a washcloth on a stool, returned to the bedroom on the left. She selected a set of clean clothes, hung them on the hook behind the bathroom door, then tested the tub water's temperature. A tad too hot, but by the time he got upstairs, it wouldn't be.

She found him hunched over an empty plate, shaking his head. Although he'd devoured a sandwich and emptied his mug, fatigue dulled his eyes and sagged his shoulders.

"I ran you a bath. It will ease your sore muscles."

Yet again, he was compliant. "Thank you," he said, and went upstairs.

She'd fed him. Cleaned Rose's stall. The bath she'd prepared would wash away physical evidence of the heartbreaking job he'd just completed.

But Abigail had no idea how to mend his aching soul.

When he returned to the kitchen, Jube found her at the sink, rinsing suds from the cocoa pan.

"Sorry to see it is gone."

Turning, Abigail smiled. "There is more. In the refrigerator. Let me heat a cup for you."

"You have already done enough. Too much."

She rolled her eyes. "A few sandwiches is hardly too much."

"I stopped by the barn on my way inside. . . ."

She shrugged it off. "I wanted to spare you having to see it."

Her thoughtfulness was touching, but not the least bit surprising. She'd been good to Ira, who'd never deserved her kindness. It was high time he delivered his confession.

Jube pulled out a chair, and using his good leg, inched one out for her, too. "Will you sit and talk with me for a moment?"

Her fingers were still red from all her scrubbing as she gripped the chair's back. "We can sit after Emily has taken a look at your leg."

"Soaking in that hot tub helped it."

Abigail answered with a snort of disbelief. She looked tired. Disheveled. And determined to take him to the clinic.

"If it still hurts in the morning, I will go."

She didn't look convinced, so he raised a hand, as if taking an oath. "You have my word."

"I have been meaning to tell you something, too."

His revelation could wait a few minutes more. "Ladies first . . ."

Her lips parted, came together as she pulled out the chair, pushed it back under the table. "Let me fix us both a cup of that cocoa first."

Abigail moved through his kitchen as if she'd been doing it for years. He was glad that she felt comfortable enough to make herself at home. Would she feel that way after he'd 'fessed up? *Tell her now, while she is in a friendly frame of mind.*

"Might as well kill two birds with one stone," she said from the dining room, "and change your bandage while the cocoa heats up."

Like a happy pup, he got to his feet, slid the suspender from his right shoulder, and untucked his shirt.

And she went right to work.

"Oh no. You popped a stitch." Within seconds, she'd unspooled a length of the silk thread, placed it on a napkin beside the needle, and drenched both with alcohol. Dampened a gauze pad, too, and used it to clean the wound.

"This might sting a bit," she said, threading the needle.

While she worked, Jube thought of the patient, tender way she'd stitched up Ira's forehead when he came home bleeding after a bar brawl in Oakland. He wondered if Ira had realized what a gift she was, if he appreciated all the tender, wifely things she'd done every day of their married life. *God knows she deserved better*, Jube thought.

Precisely why anything more than friendship between her and him was out of the question.

"There," she announced, tugging his shirt back into place, "good for another day."

"Thank you," he said again.

She waved his thanks away. "Now then, you were saying?"

Give me strength, Lord. . . .

A verse from Isaiah came to mind: "*. . . no eye has seen, nor ear heard, nor the heart of man imagined what God has prepared for those who love him.*" God's way of assuring him that it was safe to tell her?

"Well, ah, I . . . I thought we decided ladies first?"

Her smile disappeared, like shadows exposed to light.

"All right. I suppose it is long past time," she said, and folded her hands on the table.

Memory of the accusatory words she'd snarled that night in the ER came to mind. "Irresponsible." "Uncaring." "Weak." "Dishonest." That last one, Jube thought, stung like a razor cut, even now. Jube braced himself for the worst and hoped for the best.

"I owe you an apology," she began.

"What? No. I owe *you* an apology."

She looked mildly surprised but continued as if he hadn't spoken.

"I said terrible things, things you did not deserve. I called you dishonest when, in reality, I was the dishonest one. Because I suspected. For months before the accident. And yet I pretended . . ."

What, exactly, was she saying? That she'd known about the things—and the women—that had lured Ira to town? He'd heard it said that love was blind. The writer of that cliché should have tacked on an addendum: Love had the power to veil the truth.

He didn't want to believe that Abigail . . . his sweet, beautiful Abigail . . . had let him spend three long years punishing himself for Ira's death.

"A hundred times," he began slowly, "I almost told you everything that Ira had been up to." A bitter laugh punctuated his statement. "You were right about one thing. I *was* weak. Too weak to risk hurting you. And the whole time, you knew. *You knew!*"

Abigail, crying now, said, "Jubal, let me explain why I—"

He began to pace. "That fistfight. The accident. Neither would have been necessary if . . ." He drove a hand through his hair. "I kept telling myself if I had confronted him sooner, if I had never promised to keep his secrets . . ." Whirling around to face her, he said, "I told myself it was my fault that he got so angry, that he drove off like a madman and . . ."

He couldn't bear to finish with the truth: . . . *crashed head-on into a tree, where he* died.

Seeing her there, hiding behind her hands, made his heart ache. Made him almost sorry for what he'd just said. Made him want to hold her close and promise that nothing, no one, would ever hurt her again.

Almost.

Three years, he told himself. Three long years of beating himself up, of feeling guilty for changing her from a happy young wife into a lonely, bitter widow. And to think that even before the accident, *she'd known*.

He needed time. To separate fact from fiction. To make sense of the anger—and love—that battled inside him.

He grabbed her shawl from the hook in the mudroom, thrust it in her direction. He pretended not to notice when her hand shook as she took it from him.

"I appreciate everything you did today. Everything you have done since I was injured." He barely recognized his own voice. "But I am tired, Abigail. I need some time alone."

A pea-sized silver tear slid down her cheek. Its silvery track glistened in the late-afternoon sunlight that slanted through the window. She looked so small. Vulnerable. Miserable. Yet again, he fought the urge to comfort her.

"I should have told you the truth when I admitted those hard truths, a year ago."

He barely heard her. When Jube opened the door, a blast of cold air blew into the room. It ruffled her hair, free now from the constraints of the cap, stained beyond salvation, that she'd added to the rubbish pile. Had the truth stained their relationship, too?

In the doorway, silhouetted by the setting sun, she whispered, "I will return your shirt tomorrow, when I come back to change your ban—"

"I can manage on my own. And the shirt is old. I only wear it to fetch wood. Keep it."

Jube hoped she'd read between the lines: *Stay away from me, for now, anyway.*

Standing on the top porch step, she said, "I am sorry, Jubal."

Jubal remained in the open doorway as a frosty blast of air battered the curtains, sent napkins skittering across the floor. Napkins she'd carefully placed beside his cup and hers. Cups that held the cocoa she'd made. He hadn't given her a chance to put away her self-made first-aid kit, and sunlight glinted from the needle. Tears stung his eyes, and he blamed them on the wind. On having just buried Rose and her calf.

It wouldn't be easy, facing the boys. They'd seen the bloody mess. Watched Noah tilt the loader's dirt-filled bucket, completely blanketing the cow and her baby with rich, loamy soil. Would they ask him to explain how and what had gone wrong? If so, he'd quote Ecclesiastes: "... *what happens to the children of man and what happens to the beasts is the same; as one dies, so dies the other. All have the same breath, and man has no ad-*

vantage over the beasts. All go to one place. All are from the dust, and to dust all must return."

What would he say if they asked why Abigail—who'd made regular appearances to deliver cookies and lemonade as they worked—had stopped coming around?

He hoped they wouldn't ask about either.

Because God help him, Jude didn't understand any of it.

Chapter 7

Weeks ago, Abigail had washed and pressed Jubal's shirt, and hung it in the entryway. Every time she passed it, going in or out of the back door, it made her heart ache. So she'd moved it to the front hall. *Out of sight, out of mind, right?*

Wrong, she thought, driving toward the inn.

The thermometer on the porch post said fifteen degrees, and now it was snowing, too. Tiny, frosty flecks stuck to the windshield and painted the road's edge white. She gripped the steering wheel so tightly that her fingers ached, and her heartbeats kept time with the wipers.

Calm down, she thought. *By the time you make the return trip, the road crews will have salted the pavement.*

After Ira's death, waiting tables at The Broadford eased her adjustment to widowhood. Just as the work had helped then, it would help now. At the start of her morning break, she asked Bill for more hours. Any shift, any job, even the one she liked least. Even shoveling ashes from the fireplaces was better than going home, where Jubal's shirt hung like a plaid flannel reminder of his sad face and angry words.

"Are you good with numbers?" Bill asked.

"I suppose. . . ."

"Ever used a computer?"

"Only the one that runs the cash register in the dining room."

"That'll do. Marybeth can teach you what you don't already know. This is perfect timing. Stella fell and dislocated her hip, and can't leave the house for a month, at least. If you'll come in early and stay late to balance the checkbook, pay bills, write checks, I'll pay you double time."

Even without the offer of overtime pay, she would have said yes.

"Come in early, stay late, whatever works for you. Beggars can't be choosers, y'know!" He laughed, then handed her a key to the back door. "Don't forget to keep track of your hours." Winking, he turned his attention to the couple who approached the check-in desk.

Despite the weatherman's prediction of three feet of snow by suppertime, the guests were in good spirits. In the dining room, laughter and spoons, clinking the sides of soup bowls and coffee cups, blended in an off-key song. A hearty discussion about the upcoming election filled the parlor, while in the library two gentlemen debated: checkers or chess? And in the kitchen, Marybeth hummed as she arranged sliced cheese and crackers on small serving platters.

Bill entered through the back door.

"As I live and breathe," Marybeth said. "If it isn't Nanook of the North."

"I give up." He brushed snow from his shoulders and stomped clumps from his boots. "It's coming down so fast that I no sooner get a path cleared than it's covered up again."

His wife waved away the flakes that had whirled in and landed on the table. "Close the door before you have to shovel a path through the miserable stuff *in here*!"

"Ingrate," he teased, kicking it shut. "May I remind you that without that miserable stuff, we'd have to shut down during the winter months?"

She popped a piece of cheese into her mouth. "I stocked the fridge and pantry, so I guess the guests won't mind waiting until tomorrow to hit the slopes."

He dropped his parka and knit hat onto the floor. "Al will help," he said, adding snow-crusted gloves to the pile.

"Home. With a one-hundred-and-two-degree fever."

Grinning at Bill's unintelligible response, Abigail looked out the window. He hadn't exaggerated. The snow was falling so hard and fast that she could barely see the inn's big red barn, rented during warmer months for weddings, corporate parties, and fundraising events.

"I can help with the shoveling."

"No, you can't. You're sweet to offer," Marybeth said, "but we're booked solid. I need you inside."

"She's right, Abby. But even if we weren't full up, you'd freeze out there. It isn't just snowing to beat the band; it's windy, and cold as a mother-in-law's kiss, too!"

"Hey, watch it, buddy." And smiling at Abigail, she said, "Would you mind delivering these trays? And let everybody know there's tea, coffee, and hot chocolate on the way."

When Abigail delivered the snacks, one of the ladies said, "What a lovely surprise."

Her friend said, "Yes, and tea sounds lovely, doesn't it, Marie?"

"Be right back," Abigail told them.

She started for the hall as the first woman said, "Isn't she just adorable?"

"Yes. I just love listening to the Amish speak." She met Abigail's eyes. "Are you married, dear?"

"My husband died three years ago."

"Oh, what a shame. Children?"

"No."

She glanced at her husband, who sat with Marie's husband,

playing Double Solitaire. "That's number three for me. So don't worry. Pretty as you are, your number two will come along soon."

"She's right," said Marie. "Has some handsome young Amishman set his cap for you?"

Abigail pictured Jubal, and the way he'd looked the last time she saw him.

"If any man has set his cap, I am not aware of it." She smiled. "I will be back shortly with your tea."

It was true, she thought, filling teacups and coffee mugs. Jubal had looked angry. Disappointed. Hurt. But on other occasions, she remembered, placing the sugar bowl and creamer on a big wooden tray, he'd looked anything *but*. Would he have reacted so strongly if he *didn't* feel a certain warmth toward her . . . feelings that had nothing to do with his friendship with Ira?

The longer you tell yourself things like that, the longer it will hurt.

While here at The Broadford, she'd concentrate on the job. At home, she'd catch up on things she'd been putting off: Refinishing her mother's rocking chair. Painting the porch swing her father had built. After all, taking care of the house they'd left her was important for reasons that had nothing to do with Jubal Quinn.

The ladies were deeply involved in a game of Gin Rummy, and barely noticed when she delivered their tea. *A good thing!* Abigail told herself, and made her way to the dining room to clear the tables. Several guests had gathered at the windows.

"Guess we can forget about a night ski," said one of the men.

Silhouetted as he was by fast-falling snow on the other side of the glass, he reminded her of Jubal . . . tall, broad shouldered, trim waisted—

Stop it, she scolded. *And do your job!*

"To be honest, I'd rather stay inside," his wife said. "We'll ask Bill to build a fire in our room."

Hand in hand, the couple climbed the curved staircase as Abigail cleared tables. While she was loading the dishwasher, the wind drew her attention to the windows, where snow had blocked the bottom panes. *Poor Jubal*, she thought. He'd have to trudge through the stuff to tend his cows, fetch firewood, with still-healing ribs and an injured leg. "Stop it," she mumbled to herself. He'd made it through last year's back-to-back snowstorms, and those that had closed Pleasant Valley's roads every year before that. He'd survive this one, too.

And the boys? She hoped they'd gone straight home after completing their milking chores, and were by now engaged in an exhilarating snowball fight. But what if, instead, they'd talked Jubal into letting them work on the buggies? *Then they'd be trapped there now.* The image of Jubal plumping pillows and gathering blankets to make them comfortable inspired a smile.

She carried those good thoughts all through the next hours, as she folded laundry, pressed tablecloths, and folded bed linens. "Let me know when you've brought fresh towels to the guests," Marybeth said, "and I'll introduce you to the office equipment."

It was nearly five o'clock when they wrapped up the first session, and as they moved from office to kitchen, the boss's wife stood at the back door. "Good grief, Abby, look!"

Abigail peered over her shoulder, saw her truck nearly buried in a drift. "If it is this bad here, what do the roads look like?"

Her boss tuned a small radio to WKHJ. "... and if you don't have to be out," Terry King was saying, "stay home, or you'll end up stranded, right, partner?" Jim Shaffer, the other morning DJ, said, "Yep. We're stuck here, subbing for the afternoon crew, 'cause we can't get out, and they can't get in." He went on to describe icy, snow-covered roads, where drifts had turned I-68 into a one-lane highway.

"You can't drive in this mess."

"I know." Abigail sighed. "But there are no rooms at the inn."

Laughing, the boss's wife gave her a sideways hug. "Very funny, honey. But not to worry. You can bunk down in the office. Thanks to Bill's snoring, I know that couch is comfortable. And anyway, it's only for one night, right?"

She'd only left Patch enough food and water for one day.

"I hope so."

Lord, watch over Jubal, please?

Snow in late October was nothing new for the Oakland area. The three feet that had fallen throughout the day, inconvenient as it was, didn't really surprise Jube. Several years ago, when an unexpected storm trapped him at his mother's house, he'd shared Jethro's room. His kid brother, happy for the company, had jabbered for hours, and Jube barely slept a wink. He had a feeling that was nothing compared to what he'd face between now and morning.

As usual, Noah had dropped the boys off at four, and after milking the cows, they'd all gone into town for the daily milk delivery. Nearly every merchant asked if Jube had heard about the forecast. He'd responded by assuring them that at this time of year, an inch or less would accumulate. And it would melt before the plows hit the roads. So when the boys asked to stay and work on the buggies, he'd said yes.

They took turns loading coal into Jube's forge. Took turns operating the bellows, too, to maintain the heat. If he'd allowed them to, they would have put his tongs to use, steadying steel rods and sheets in the belly of the forge. Instead, they watched, wide-eyed and silent, as he carried red-hot metal to the anvil, where he snipped it to size and hammered it into shape. In six hours, he'd created one of the buggy chassis.

"We need to get home. I am starving." When Thomas opened

the door and saw how much snow had fallen, James said, "Oh. My. Goodness. Gracious."

The cousins pressed close, staring slack-jawed at the white stuff that had blanketed everything in sight.

Pete groaned. "It will take us three hours to walk home in this!"

"We had best get started then."

"No, Paul. You will stay here tonight."

All eyes were on Jube when he added, "I cannot drive you, and your fathers cannot pick you up."

"You have four extra beds?"

"As a matter of fact, I have five. One in the front bedroom, and two sets of bunk beds in the back."

It was Thomas who said, "But you live alone. What do you need with that many?"

"One is mine. The others are for when Jethro stays the night." *And for any children God might someday bless me with.*

Thomas frowned. "Our mothers will worry."

"No," Jube said again. "When you are not home by the usual time, they will say a prayer of thanks that we had the good sense to stay put." He put on his jacket. "Better button up, though. It is fifty yards from here to the house." Stepping outside, he said over his shoulder, "Be sure to latch that door behind you."

Jube dragged his feet, plowing an easy path for them to follow, and laughed to himself when he heard them grunt and groan as the heavy doors slid together.

On the porch, they stomped snow from their boots. "Good thing we stacked wood up here yesterday," Paul said. "I would hate to hunt for logs under a mountain of snow!"

Inside, they hung snow-covered jackets on pegs near the door.

"How about breakfast for supper?" Jube asked.

Four voices chorused with, "Sure!"

"Pancakes, with sausage and eggs?"

"Sounds great!"

"Good. Wash up and I will get busy."

"I guess Daed does not know much about bachelors after all."

Paul's twin deepened his voice. " 'Scrambled eggs and sandwiches,' " he quoted.

"We have yet to see what his pancakes and eggs look like," Jube heard Thomas say. "Or what they taste like."

The boys set the table without being told to, and before long, Jube delivered the food. "Good job," he said, nodding at the way they'd arranged plates and flatware in front of each chair.

"You did a pretty good job, too," James said, forking a pancake.

Paul closed his eyes and folded his hands, and the others did, too. After a quick, silent prayer over the food, the questions began: How soon would they make buggy harnesses? Would the seat covers be made of cloth or leather? Should they attach lanterns up front? Jube provided answers, and asked a few questions of his own: Now that both chassis had been assembled, what came next? What sandpaper grit was best for the buggies, themselves? Which would their parents like best, flat or satin black paint?

There were two pancakes and one sausage left when Thomas asked, "Where will we buy the wheels?"

"No need to buy what we can make."

They exchanged puzzled glances. "Make them? *Ourselves?*"

Chuckling, Jube said, "It is time consuming, but not as difficult as the work you have already done."

By nine, they'd cleaned the kitchen and stoked the fire, and seemed to have talked themselves out. "You have been up since before dawn," he said, leading the way upstairs. "Time for bed."

After loaning each a clean white T-shirt to sleep in, he showed them how to squeeze toothpaste onto their fingertips and brush their teeth.

"We would not get cavities by skipping just one night," Thomas grumbled.

"But you would wake with breath foul enough to melt the griddle."

They lined up at the sink, then again to whisper bedtime prayers. Then the squabbling began. All of them, it seemed, wanted the top bunks.

"Which twins were born first?" Jube asked.

"Me," Thomas said.

"And me," echoed Paul.

"Then you two get bottom bunks."

"Hey, wait," Thomas whined. "Older should get first choice!"

"That might be how you settle disputes at home, which is why here, we will err on the side of fairness."

Satisfied or not, they climbed into bed as he stood at the door.

"We were thinking," Pete said.

"Uh-oh. . . ."

"We want to announce the ree-rah-rih—"

"Recipients," Thomas helped him.

"Yeah, that," Pete said. "We want to announce the recipients of our good deed at a Christmas Eve supper."

"Where we will do everything. Decorating. Cooking. Wrapping," his twin added.

Thomas said, "Except for the buggies. But we know just how to hide them until the right moment."

"We have saved up some money from the work we did over the summer." James smiled nervously. "Last night, we put it into one pile and counted it. It should be enough to pay for the food."

And if it wasn't, Jube decided, he'd donate a few dollars to the cause.

The boys recited their grocery list: canned ham, green beans, and sweet potatoes, dinner rolls, butter, and pies for dessert. Jube anticipated the next question and offered to drive them to the market.

"Can we store the food in your refrigerator?"

"Of course."

"And heat everything up on your stove?"

He nodded, and they cheered.

"I do not know what we did to deserve a friend like you, Mr. Quinn, but if we ever find out, we will do it over and over, to show God that we appreciate you."

Jube felt the heat of a blush creeping into his cheeks and, to hide it, turned off the ceiling fixture.

"Get to sleep. You need to be well rested, because come morning, we will move mountains." He laughed. "Of snow."

The hall lamp provided just enough light to let him see four blond heads nestle into pillows. By his best guess, they'd be fast asleep before he made it to the parlor. In the weeks they'd worked together, Jube had learned a lot about them. He didn't know what inspired the pranks that had prompted adults to dub them Double Trouble, but he knew this: The Hartzes and the Briskeys had nothing to worry about. Their sons were well on their way to becoming good and decent men.

"You have worked hard, as hard as any man I could name," he told them. "In my opinion, you've more than paid for your childish transgression. My side is mostly healed, so tomorrow will be your last day working for me."

He could almost hear the wheels of their minds, grinding out more questions, so he quickly added, "Instead of milking and deliveries, chopping and stacking wood, you will spend your time here finishing the buggies. If you do not, Christmas

Eve will come and go and you will not have fulfilled the second portion of your punishment."

All four levered themselves up on an elbow. "Really?" they said in unison.

"Really." He'd started pulling the door closed when he heard: "Mr. Quinn?"

He stepped back into the room. "Yes?"

"Would it be all right if we used the big shed, where we are building the buggies, for the supper? We will clean up before and after, set up the tables, everything. You only need to show up and eat."

"My dining room table will seat ten, easily."

"But . . ." James leaned over the top bunk. "But we hope to feed more than that."

"How many more?"

They recited the names: Jube's mother and brother, the bishop and his wife, Dr. Baker and her family, Max, Willa, and Frannie, their parents. "When we add the four of us, and you and Miss Fletcher," he said, "that makes twenty-two."

The number got lost as he mentally repeated her name. *Miss Fletcher. Abigail.* Frowning, he ran a hand through his hair. They'd grown up together, and since Pleasant Valley couldn't rival New York's population, they'd keep right on running into each other. Even with twenty others in attendance at the party, the big shed would feel smaller than his five-by-five bathroom, seeing her face-to-face for the first time in more than a month. During the four weeks between now and then, he'd pray. Pray long and hard for the strength not to behave like a stumbling, bumbling idiot.

"Something wrong, Mr. Quinn?"

"No, no. I am just wondering where you will find enough tables and chairs."

"Like you said, why buy what we can make? We will use

hay bales for chairs, and cover them with clean sheets. Our mothers will not miss them for just one day, and we will launder them afterward. We will eat on paper plates, and use plastic utensils and cups. Sweet tea is easy to make, and—"

Jube laughed. "Sounds like you've given this a lot of thought!"

Paul said, "We have a lot to prove, not just to our parents. Our behavior caused a lot of trouble, and we want to show everyone that we have left childish pranks behind, that we are grown-up enough to care for horses. When we get them, of course."

"Our folks will be shocked," his twin said, "when we tell them we do *not* want horses for our birthdays . . . that we want the money, instead, for another surprise."

Jube didn't understand and said so.

"The bishop's buggy is in sad shape, too," Thomas said, "so we want to use that money for materials, and build him a new one."

Jube shook his head. Had he fallen asleep, standing up? Was all of this a pleasant dream?

"If God should bless me with children one day, I hope they will be like the four of you."

"Hoo-boy," Thomas said, slapping a hand to his forehead. "We had better pray for forgiveness."

"Forgiveness?" his twin echoed. "For what?"

"For the sin of pride." He paused, then added, "But thank you, Mr. Quinn, for your kind words."

"We are friends—you said so yourself. So please. Call me Jube."

They were still whispering happily when he hit the top step. And when he hit the bottom, he grabbed his Bible. "No time like the present," he said to himself, "to start asking for help in dealing with Abigail."

Outside, the snow was still coming down, hard and fast. As

far as he knew, she'd never missed a day of work. He hoped she'd left early, that she was home now, safe and sound.

Was he a hypocrite, hoping such a thing, especially with his own angry words still ringing in his ears?

Admit it. You want her safe because from that first moment in school until this, you have loved her.

So maybe, just maybe, the Almighty would help him find a way to bridge the wide gap he'd put between them.

Chapter 8

"I was wondering if you have a few moments to talk. . . ."

Micah Fisher removed his wire-rimmed glasses, placed them beside his Bible. "Of course, Jubal." He gestured toward the chairs in the front row. "Sit, sit."

The confession spilled from him faster than water from a bucket. "Were my years of silence a sin of omission? Should I have told Abigail what I knew?"

Micah stroked his long gray beard and, nodding, said, "No, I would say it was not sinful to protect her from Ira's actions."

"But she was angry, so angry, in the ER that night."

"It was a terrible night, to be sure. And now that Ira is gone, I do not feel it violates my promise to protect his confession."

The words surprised Jube. "You mean he told you . . . everything?"

"Not willingly. Too many times, I smelled alcohol. Too often, I saw him lurking behind the widow Miller's house. One day, I dragged him into the church and made it clear: If those things continued, he would be shunned."

And yet, Jube thought, *it continued.*

Micah smiled. "You know, it is odd that you stopped by this morning. I had a visit, just yesterday, from another worshipper, who had similar concerns."

Jube wouldn't ask who that worshipper might have been, because if the bishop named Abigail it would awaken hope and Jube didn't dare hope for more than civil interactions with her.

"I want to say something, son, and I pray God will open your mind to receive it, that He will bless you with discernment, that you might understand my intent.

"Your relationship with Abigail requires teamwork. You worked together to save those boys. To mend your wound. She nourished their bodies with food, while you nourished their minds by teaching them the value of hard work." The bishop paused, then said, "Do you love her, Jubal?"

He stared at the floor.

"No need to answer, for I have seen the way you look at her, the way she looks at you."

He met the bishop's clear blue eyes, magnified by thick far-sighted lenses.

"Have you asked God's guidance on this matter?"

Jube had prayed, often and fervently, but couldn't be sure he'd prayed *correctly*.

"And the answer?"

"If He answered, I did not hear it."

"Because you are stubborn. Too stubborn to set aside hurt feelings and guilt and admit the truth. *To Abigail.*"

Abigail, who'd looked at him in a way that led the bishop to believe she cared about him. Could he believe it? *Dare* he believe it?

Eyes closed tight, Micah quoted Genesis: " 'God said, "It is not good that man should be alone; I will make him a helper . . ." Then the Lord God caused a deep sleep to fall upon the man, and while he slept, God took one of his ribs and closed up its place with flesh. And the rib that the Lord God had taken from him, God made into a woman, and He brought her to the man. The man woke, and when he saw her, he said, "This at last is bone of my bones and flesh of my flesh; she shall be called woman, because she was taken from man."'"

Was it a coincidence that, at that very moment, Jube's injured side ached?

"Be honest with her, Jubal."

Instantly, a list of reasons he shouldn't materialized.

"I am getting old and forgetful." One shoulder lifted; one hand reached out. "Sometimes, the elderly say things they do not intend to." The hand now turned, its fingers forming the *shoo* gesture.

You have been dismissed, Jube thought.

"Thank you, Bishop," he said, donning his hat. "I will pray on what we discussed."

"See that you do," Micah said, wiggling his eyebrows.

A week before Thanksgiving, the congregation decided to gather in the church basement following the service. It was cold and snowy outside, but the sun was high in the sky, warming the air and inspiring a deacon to prop open the back door.

From where she sat, Abigail could see dozens of buggies, parked side by side along the drive. Cars, too, and a few pickup trucks, including her own. Beyond the vehicles was the plain white fence that surrounded the graveyard. She hadn't visited Ira's grave since the funeral, and although it looked identical to every other, she knew it was four from the front, five from the path. And, like every other, Samuel Yoder had carved three lines into the granite slab: name, marital status, years of birth and death.

"Abigail?"

Turning, she saw Priscilla and Leora approaching the door. It was widely known that the women were twins, but blond hair, blue eyes, and stout stature were the only similarities Abigail could see.

"Your shoofly pie was delicious," Leora said. Leaning closer, she lowered her voice. "I had two slices!"

"I am happy you enjoyed it."

Priscilla moved closer, too. "We . . ." She glanced at her sister, then began again. "We couldn't help but notice you, staring into the graveyard just now. It must be difficult, without Ira."

"I have adjusted, thank the Lord."

"How long were you married before—" Leora stopped herself short.

"Nine years," Abigail said. If he'd lived another month, it would have been ten.

"I say this as a friend," Leora continued. "You are still young and vital, young enough to have children!"

"She is right, Abby. We have seen the way you look at Jube."

"And the way he looks at you," her sister agreed.

"We had hoped that time spent with him while our boys were at his place might encourage both of you to acknowledge your feelings."

"Speaking of the boys, we thank you for all you did for them. Bringing food. Making lemonade. Bandaging blisters."

"You will make a wonderful mother. . . ."

Abigail stiffened. The things she'd told Jubal at Ira's ER bedside felt like a shadow, following her every step, darkening every dream she'd had. She'd give anything to step away from it, to stand in the light of love. *Jubal's* love.

"If it is God's will," she said.

"I would be miserable, living alone for . . . how long has it been now?"

"Three years."

"Are you not lonely?"

"I have my job. The house and yard to care for. My gardens.

And I have started a quilt." Abigail laughed. "It is my first, so it is taking longer than I had expected."

"I cannot imagine life without Noah and the boys."

As if he'd heard his name, Leora's husband called out to her, then waved her closer.

"We hope you will arrive early to service next week," Priscilla said, "so you can sit beside us again, instead of in the back row."

Abigail wasn't about to admit that tardiness had nothing to do with her seat selection.

When they walked away, Abigail folded her tablecloth and packed it among pie tins and serving utensils in her basket. Their words, spoken in friendship, had unearthed feelings she'd tried hard to bury. And now, despite their good intentions, she knew it would take hours of prayer to lay those feelings to rest again.

Abigail slipped into her jacket, hung the basket's handles over her forearm, and hurried to the truck. Yes, the door still squealed, but at least the engine had never failed her. She wasn't exactly living her dream, but she had much to be thankful for. Good health. A good job. A good house. Good food. What right did she have to feel sorry for herself?

Chapter 9

It was wedding season in Pleasant Valley, but since no ceremonies were planned this fall, seamstress Judith Quinn had outdone herself preparing for Thanksgiving. The turkey looked good enough to earn the November page in a wall calendar. She'd spent two days cooking and making her sons' favorites. Stuffing. Sweet potato casserole. Broccoli-cauliflower salad. Dutch green beans. Mashed potatoes and gravy. Homemade biscuits. Applesauce cake. Banana bread. And of course, her Pleasant Valley–famous pumpkin pie.

Yesterday, Jube had helped her extend the dining table to its full twelve-foot length and dragged chairs from all around the house to seat the in-laws and cousins she'd invited. Her mother's linen tablecloth and napkins were out, and so were the "for special occasions only" brown stoneware plates.

She opened the oven door. "I sort of hoped you would invite Abigail Fletcher."

Good thing she was busy, basting the turkey, Jube thought, because it kept her from reading his expression. "Now why would I do that, when I have never invited her to family functions?"

Using a potholder to fan her face, she said, "You have been together nearly every day for weeks and weeks." Judith shrugged. "Naturally, I thought this year was different."

Jethro strolled into the room, smiling as always, and announced, "Jube and Abby had a fight. I think he hurt her feelings."

Judith looked from her younger son to the elder. "Jubal." Clucking her tongue, she shook her head. "What did you do to that sweet girl?"

This was a day to give thanks, for family and friends, good health, provisions, a well-built home, and money enough to get by, all by the grace of God. Jube didn't want to tarnish it by rehashing the harsh words that had started new troubles between him and Abigail.

"Who will join us today?"

Jethro snickered and gave him a playful shove. "Aw, Jube is changing the subject, Maem."

"What a surprise," she said, and rolled her eyes.

Slanted blue eyes grew serious. "I think," Jethro lisped, "it is because he wishes they did not fight. He likes her. And she likes him. You can say it, Jube. You miss her."

If he hadn't been so efficient before leaving the house, he could duck out now, with the excuse of completing an undone chore.

"Have you made your bed, Jethro?"

Both hands flew to his mouth. "Oops! No, I forgot." He shuffled from the room, muttering, "I will do it. I will hang up my clothes, and make sure there is toilet paper in the bathroom."

Judith stared after him, and sighed. "He is such a joy."

"That he is," Jube agreed.

Years ago, when friends and family heard that Jethro had

Down's, they'd offered help and sympathy. In typical Judith fashion, she took it all in stride. "He is a gift from God, and I will enjoy him, as the Almighty intended." Jethro's big heart and loving spirit more than made up for any extra work he'd caused her. And without him to care for, Jube didn't know what might have become of his mother after the massive stroke took Jeremiah.

"You are just like your father," she was saying.

She hadn't meant it as a compliment. He braced himself for the explanation that would follow.

"Jeremiah was bullheaded, too. Why, if I had not taken the initiative, he never would have asked me to marry him." Her forefinger wagged, like a flesh-and-bone metronome. "You had better make some hard decisions, Son, because Abigail does not strike me as a take-charge girl, like I was."

If his mother had heard what had happened in the ER that night, she wouldn't say that!

"She has all the makings of a good wife and mother. I would love a few grandchildren while I am still young enough to bounce them on my knee."

Implied: Jethro would not marry, would not make her a grandmother, so it was up to him. Jube didn't much appreciate the added layer of guilt.

"God knows best. He took Bess and Lemuel so they would not have to see what that boy of theirs became." She went on, listing Ira's sins: Drink. Cards. Women. Adding, as usual, the times he'd led Jube into temptation, too.

"Any trouble I got into," he said, "was my doing. Ira did not hold a gun to my head, you know."

"When you say things like that," she said, giving his cheek an affectionate pinch, "you make me happy. You are a good man, and you will be a good husband and father." One brow rose high on her forehead. "If you stop behaving like your father, that is."

Dinner was lively and festive, and he would have enjoyed it even more if Abigail hadn't come to mind so many times. Everyone loved her, so it wasn't likely she'd spent the day alone. At least, he hoped not. Still, the image of her, wandering through the empty rooms of her house, tidying doilies and repositioning candlesticks, perhaps stopping now and then to pet her cat, caused an ache in his heart, because if he hadn't been—as the bishop and his mother pointed out—a stubborn fool, she could have been *here.*

Once the others left, Jube hung back to help his mother and brother clean up. While Jethro washed dishes, Jube dried and put away and their mother filled containers with leftovers.

"The whole time we ate," she said, stretching plastic wrap over sliced turkey, "I thought of poor Abigail, all alone over there in that big house."

Please, Lord, show me a sign that those containers are not for Abigail.

A smart man, he told himself, wouldn't wait for a message from heaven. He'd find a way to leave, before his mother turned him into a delivery boy.

"Dry those hands, little brother," he said, "and help me shorten the table."

Together, the brothers stacked and stored the leaves in the hall closet, then joined their mother in the kitchen.

"On your way home," his mother began, "I want you to drop this off for Abigail."

How would she react to blunt honesty?

"I would rather not."

"Funny," she said, "but I do not recall asking what you wanted. I am not young and spry anymore. If I have to do it myself, tomorrow, who knows what might slip from my lips?"

Had she and Micah talked? How else could he explain that their threats were nearly identical?

"All right. Fine. I will go." He shoved an arm into his jacket sleeve, then kissed her cheek. "But you owe me a chocolate cake."

"Choc-o-lit cake is my fay-voh-rit," Jethro said. "Can I go with you? To Abigail's house?"

Saying yes meant a return trip to bring him home, but Jube had never said no to his brother. A positive thought popped into his head. With Jethro there, Jube wouldn't have to work so hard, looking for safe topics . . . and avoiding risky ones.

"Sure, buddy. Grab your coat."

"You are a good man," his mother said as Jethro slipped into it. "A good brother, too." She handed him the basket.

"And a good friend?"

"If it is God's will, she will be more than that. Soon." She gave him a gentle shove. "Now go. Jethro is waiting out there in the cold."

With Emily's mother-in-law running the show, dinner at the Bakers' promised to be a fun, festive event that would keep Abigail's mind off Jubal.

"Your pies look perfect," Sarah said, placing them on the sideboard. "The children will love the sugar cookies, and I cannot wait to dig into that noodle casserole."

Emily fed the baby another spoonful of oatmeal. "You really didn't need to do all that. Marybeth told me you're putting in a lot of overtime hours at the inn, so I know you're busy."

Abigail stopped peeling potatoes long enough to say, "Listen to the pot, calling the kettle black! This big house, a husband and two children, beautiful flower gardens, long hours at the clinic, and you still have the energy for get-togethers like this? Tell me your secret!"

The baby stuck his finger into the bowl, and laughing, Emily blew a kiss into his chubby palm.

"I remember a song from my Englisher days. 'All You Need Is Love.' When everyday life threatens to overwhelm me, I sing a few lines. Sometimes it takes the whole song to put my head right again, but it works."

Abigail had loved Ira, or thought she had, anyway. But it seemed to her that it took more than that to achieve Emily's level of happiness. The pretty young doctor had traded city life for the Plain life, walked away from the praise of peers, and didn't seem to miss stylish clothes or other Englisher trappings. *Instead of praying for a similar life, Abigail thought, maybe you should ask God for the wisdom to choose a similar husband.*

Someone like Jubal?

The meal was everything she'd expected, and like everyone else, Abigail had enjoyed the food and good-natured jokes, so much that returning home felt anticlimactic. Concentrating on her quilt ought to get her mind off what a life with Jubal might be like. She spread the batting across the kitchen table, and placed her scissors, thread, and the shoe box she'd filled with colorful scraps of material on a chair seat.

"Only a raw beginner, an absolute ninny," she complained to Patch, "would believe she could fashion a proper quilt from triangles, squares, and rectangles. Why didn't I start with just squares?"

Patch meowed and rubbed against her mistress's legs.

Someone rapped on the back door, startling the cat and causing Abigail to prick her forefinger. Popping it into her mouth, she saw Jethro Quinn's friendly face staring through the window. Just behind him, Jubal was looking west, toward the mountains. Oh, but he was handsome, even in profile!

Abigail glanced at the wall clock. Why would anyone come calling at six thirty on Thanksgiving night?

"Well, hello," she said, opening the door.

Jubal turned, removed his black hat. "What are we interrupting?"

"Nothing. Come inside where it is warm. I stoked the fire not ten minutes ago."

"Why are you sad?" Jethro asked, sliding a box onto the table.

"Frustrated is more like it. That quilt . . ." She frowned at it. ". . . is testing my patience." Abigail rolled her eyes. "Who am I fooling? I bit off more than I can chew. I have never made one before, and . . . and . . . and only stubbornness keeps me from throwing it into the fire!"

"No!" Jethro said. "You should never quit. No matter how hard things get." He looked up, into his older brother's face. "Right, Jube?"

Jubal shifted his weight from one foot to the other. Shrugged. "Yes, I have said that on occasion."

Jethro said into his palm, "Not on occasion. You say it all the time!"

Jethro's simple statement intensified his brother's tense expression.

"Maem sent you turkey," Jethro said. "Stuffing. Mashed potatoes and gravy. Baked beans. Pumpkin pie. Her famous apple butter, too. She said since you live alone, you probably did not roast a turkey." He grinned, jerked a thumb over one shoulder. "There is another box of food in the truck. But that one is for Jube."

"Why, I will not have to cook for a week!" *For two weeks, thanks to the leftovers you brought home from the Bakers'.* "Be sure to thank her for me. Thank you, too, for delivering it."

Jubal met her eyes, but only briefly. "Well," he said, donning the hat, "I should get Jethro home, let you get back to work."

"I thought Maem said Abigail would not have any pie. I guess she was right. Abigail does not have *a* pie; she has *three* of them!"

"I made a few things to bring to the Bakers', a thank-you for including me in their Thanksgiving feast. I had bought a peck of apples and worried they might rot before I had a chance to eat them all. And since pies last longer . . ."

"They look good," Jethro said, licking his lips.

"Please, sit, and we will have a slice together." *And if an opening presents itself, you will tell Jubal you are sorry.*

"I really ought to get Jethro home."

"Oh," he whined, "can we stay for one slice? Please, Jube?"

She watched the stern expression soften as he met his brother's eyes. "You ate enough to satisfy a horse," he teased. "If we stay, where will you put it?"

Jethro patted his round belly. "Right here!" he said, and took a seat.

Abigail gathered up the quilt and draped it over a parlor chair, placed the shoe box there, too, then slid plates from the cupboard.

"Coffee?" she asked, grabbing forks and a knife from the drainboard.

"I love coffee!" Jethro said as Patch sauntered into the room. Bending at the waist, he held out a hand and made kissing noises. "Are your feet cold?"

"She has built-in fur slippers," Abigail said. "I doubt her paws are cold."

"Not the cat," Jethro said, pointing at her socks. "You!"

It seemed Jubal hadn't noticed her white-socked feet, and now that he did, he smiled. It was good to see, and she smiled, too. "The wood stove keeps me warm and toasty from head to toe," she said, delivering coffee and pie.

Patch leaped onto Jethro's lap. "She is happy," he said. "I know because cats purr when they are happy."

"Yes, they do," Jubal said. Directing his attention to Abigail, he added, "You are working double shifts at the inn?"

"Only until Stella heals up. Office work is challenging but makes time pass quickly."

"We should have a cat," Jethro announced.

"You know how Maem feels about animals in the house."

"But cats, they kill mice. I saw one in the basement, next to her washer. In the barn, too. If we had a cat, we would not need traps." Grimacing, he shuddered. "I hate seeing them in a trap."

"And I hate emptying them," Jubal agreed. "Tell you what, buddy. First chance I get, I will talk to her about getting a cat. She might say yes quicker if you promise to take full responsibility for it, so you should start practicing your speech."

Still more proof, Abigail thought, watching and listening, that Jubal would make a wonderful father someday.

"Good idea, Jube! I practice!" In his excitement, Jethro startled Patch, who jumped down and disappeared around the corner.

"Aw, I scared her."

"She is easily startled," Abigail soothed. "I scare her, too, all the time, by laughing!"

His brows drew together as he gave that a moment's thought. "But you live alone. What do you laugh at?"

"My own clumsiness, mostly. I sometimes take corners too fast and bump into doorways. Once, I stumbled over my shoelaces. And have you noticed that when it is dark outside and the lights are on inside, the windows look like mirrors?"

Jethro nodded.

"Well, just this morning, I saw my reflection, and scared myself!"

Laughing now, Jethro got onto his hands and knees. "You are funny, Abigail." A moment later, he sat cross-legged, stroking Patch's cheeks.

"He is right," Jubal said. "You have a good sense of humor."

His expression had warmed. Did it mean that his anger had thawed, too?

"How are the boys' buggies coming along?" *Coward!* she scolded. "Will they finish before the deadline?"

"Yes, I believe so. Once they sand and paint, they can attach the buggies to the chassis. All that will remain after that are the headlights and rear reflector."

"They? You are not helping anymore?"

"I try, believe me." A slow smile softened his features. "They like to have me nearby to answer any questions that come up, but all four of them seem determined to do the work themselves."

"They are good kids. And you are largely responsible for the positive changes in them."

"Goodness was in them all along."

"But who knows how long it might have taken to come to the surface without your example, without the patient lessons you taught?"

"Nice of you to say."

"It is the truth. And so is this." Abigail leaned forward to add, "I am sorry, Jubal. For what I said in the ER, and for not apologizing right away, once I figured things out. It was unkind and unfair to let you think I blamed you for things Ira did, before and after the accident. It is a lot to ask, I know, but I hope you can find it in your heart to forgive me."

He held her gaze for what seemed a full minute, and when the words she longed to hear didn't come, she added, "Someday."

"We have both made mistakes. You are sorry; I am sorry. We can call it even."

Jethro stood between their chairs and, looking from one to the other, said, "You are friends again." He slid an arm across Jubal's shoulder, across Abigail's, too, and drew them into a three-way hug. "This makes me so happy!"

Not as happy as I am, Abigail thought as tears of joy stung her eyes. *Not nearly as happy as I am!*

Chapter 10

Driving away from Abigail's house tonight had been harder than ever. And she hadn't made it easier by sending them on their way with a pie.

"I once heard Judith say that Dutch apple is her favorite," she'd said. "Tell her this is my lazy way of saying thank you, without having to write a note."

They'd barely left her drive before Jethro said, "You and Abigail should get married. I like her. She would be a good sister-in-law for me."

Jube laughed. "Is that right?"

"Yes, it is. She is pretty, and funny, and smart, and very kind. All the things that Maem is. Maem was a good wife. She is a good mother. Abigail will be a good wife and mother, too."

Jube didn't know how to respond, so he remained silent.

"Have you been pretending to like her, just to be polite and nice?"

"Of course not. She deserves better than the likes of me."

"That is crazy, Jube. You are the best man in Pleasant Valley."

"Thanks, buddy, but not everyone agrees with you."

"Abigail does. I just know it."

Even if that was true, a union between them was doomed to fail. Jube saw himself as a living, breathing reminder of every hurtful thing Ira had done to her, and eventually, she'd resent him for his part in every disappointment.

"You take care of Maem and me. You take care of Goliath and the cows. You are even taking care of those twins. You would take care of Abigail, too. I just know it," Jethro said again.

"Jethro, if I was half the man you think I am, well, maybe then I would deserve a woman like her."

"You are making me mad, Jube." He punched the dash.

"Mad? At me? Why?"

"Because you are quitting. Quitting is bad."

"A man cannot quit what he never started."

"Remember when I was six, and I thought I was too stupid to be in the Christmas play? You said I was not stupid. You said I would make the best innkeeper the church had ever seen. So I tried out. I was scared, but I did. And everyone clapped real, real loud!"

Jube turned into their driveway.

"And remember when I was afraid to go to school, because I thought the other kids would make fun of me? You told me to go, and show them that I belonged there, same as them. So I went. And Miss Adams said she wished all of her students worked as hard as me."

Putting the gearshift into Park, Jube said, "I remember. She put a gold star on your report card."

"Did you mean it every time you said I was just like everyone else, only a little slower?"

"Of course I meant it!"

"Then . . . you should take your own advice and *try*."

Side by side, they made their way up the walk. "Okay, I will."

"Thanks, Jube."

I'm the one who should be saying that, he admitted.

"I would hug you right now, except I might drop this pie. And Maem would not like eating pie off the sidewalk!"

"No, she would not." Jube slid an arm across his shoulders. "I love you, little brother."

"I love you more!"

Jethro's stock reply made him feel good, and for the first time since Ira's death, he had hope.

"We will never finish this one in time for Christmas."

James sighed. "Why are you always such a sourpuss, Brother?"

"It is the name," Pete said.

"Yeah," Paul agreed. "He takes the doubting Thomas stuff in the Bible too seriously!"

Laughing, the boys went back to painting their buggies. They whistled and hummed and exchanged good-natured barbs, more relaxed than Jube had ever seen them. They'd spent weeks on the wheels, alone, and today they'd applied a final coat of shellac.

"We are lucky to have Jube as a witness."

"A witness? To what, Thomas?"

"That we actually built these things ourselves."

"I promise to tell anyone who thinks your buggies were factory made to look at your palms. Those calluses came from hard work, not childish pranks!"

Thomas grunted.

"*Now* what, Doubting Thomas?" James said.

"We need to get on our knees and ask God's forgiveness."

Pete frowned at him. "For what?"

"I do not know about you three, but I am proud of myself. Proud of the buggies."

The others nodded. "I see your point," James said.

"Boys," Jube began, "I have a feeling that the Father is pleased with you, and I do not think He sees your reaction as sinful."

"You should have been a teacher," Pete said.

"Or a preacher," his twin agreed.

"We will never forget the things you taught us."

"James is right," Thomas said. Then he pointed. "Look! More snow!"

"We should leave, in case it gets worse."

"What if the weather keeps people from the surprise party?"

"Oh, Thomas," the boys said. "Hush!"

One by one, they filed past Jube. "Let me drive you," he suggested.

"No, thank you. We have to put the final touches on an idea."

Jube laughed. "I am not sure Pleasant Valley is ready for another of your ideas!"

He watched as they plodded up the driveway, and heard James say, "If we pool the money we earned this summer, we *can* get him a Christmas present."

"How many times do I have to repeat myself," Thomas droned. "We will need every penny to buy food for the meal, remember?"

"We will make something for him, then."

When they were out of earshot, Jube closed the shed doors and hiked toward the cow barn. "All is well," he said, peering inside.

And not just in here, either.

The boys had fulfilled every promise, draping garland around the window and doorframes and arranging white-sheeted tables in a big square. In the center, a big, hollowed-out log held holly berries and evergreen branches. Near the back wall stood a separate table, decorated with now-empty serving bowls and platters.

They'd clothespinned more sheets to a rope tied between two support posts. The big sign pinned to them said: KEEP OUT! PRIVATE! ENTER AT YOUR OWN RISK! Jube had helped them position the buggies back there. Now only one question remained: When would they reveal the surprise?

"This is so hard to believe," Priscilla said. "Not just the food and the decorations, but the change in our boys."

Leora dabbed a tear from the corner of her eye. "Makes me wonder why we were in such a hurry to see them turn from rowdy boys into men."

"I trust you will share those sentiments with the boys. Whatever accolades they received today were hard earned."

As the women nodded, Paul moved into the center of the square and clapped his hands to command attention. He waited until his brother and cousins joined him to say, "By now, it is no longer a surprise. We are here to present a gift to someone deserving. So what started out as a punishment turned into something good, something that made us appreciate how hard our parents have worked to help us become good Christians and good members of the community."

All heads turned; all eyes were on Jube. He started to protest, but Paul continued, outlining the details of their assignment. "We gave it a lot of thought. A lot of prayer, too, to come up with deserving recipients of our gift."

"Recipients," Ben echoed. "There is more than one?"

"Yup," Pete said. "There are four."

If Jube's pulse was pounding this fast, he could only imagine how much harder the boys' hearts were beating.

James waved his parents into the center of the space. Paul did the same. The adults exchanged puzzled glances. "What is going on here?" Noah asked.

"Jube, will you open the curtain for us?"

They'd put a lot of thought into every detail, he realized, crossing the floor. Then, just as Thomas had asked, he whipped the sheets aside to reveal twin four-seater buggies that shone bright under the bare overhead lightbulb.

"No more worrying that the axles will crack in the middle of the road, Daed," James said. "Or that the wheels will break under our weight."

Ben took a step toward the buggies, but Pete stopped him. "Wait, please. We have one more gift to give."

The adults looked more confused than ever.

"Mr. Quinn—Jubal—there is something for you, too, behind the buggies. Hardly a proper thanks for all you have done for us, but . . ." He shrugged.

Jube walked to the corner, saw a stack of wooden crates, each with a dozen, perfectly squared interior compartments.

"For the milk bottles," he said, mostly to himself. He looked at them and, beaming, said, "No more towels to keep them from clinking all the way to town. But where did you find them?"

"We made 'em," James said, "with wood scraps from the buggies."

Not only had they mitered every corner like expert carpenters, they'd also painted QUINN DAIRY in red across the front of the boxes.

"I do not know what to say." It must have taken hours, time they could have spent playing or sleeping. " 'Thank you' seems such a paltry thing to say, considering . . ."

"Oh no, Jube. This is *our* thank-you, to you!"

He joined the little group, shook each boy's hand. "Excellent work," he said. "You have made me proud." He met their parents' eyes. "You can be proud, too, with good reason." Then, grinning, he asked the boys, "Okay if they take a closer look at their gifts now?"

"First," Leora said, "I have a question." She rested a hand on her son's shoulder. "Why us?"

"You told us to find someone with a need."

She finger-combed the bangs from Pete's forehead. Paul's, too.

"Well, go ahead," Thomas said. "Get inside. See for yourselves . . . barely a bounce!"

Slowly, Jube walked back to his table, where the bishop sat on his left and Abigail sat to his right. "I am stunned." He faced her. "Can you believe what they did?"

"I can."

Micah smiled, got to his feet, and, as Paul had earlier, clapped to get everyone's attention. "Listen up, friends. I think Jubal, here, has something to say."

He'd practiced and prayed, prayed and practiced, but how could the bishop have known that? Fear pulsed through his veins. What if he stumbled over his words? What if his speech wasn't good enough? *Well*, he thought, *whatever the outcome, at least you are among friends.*

On the heels of a shaky breath, he took Abigail's hand in his own. All eyes were on them; the only sound was the snow, pecking the shed's windows.

"We worked well together," he began, then recited all they had done, together, to help make the boys' Christmas wish come true. "We were teammates."

"Starting on that day in the pasture."

He laughed, squeezed her hand. "I think I will always remember the way you flapped that apron."

"And I will never forget how you grabbed Goliath by the horns . . . right before he threw you into the air." She laughed, too, then sobered. "Teammates help one another."

"And protect one another when the need arises."

"Will you be my teammate, forever?"

She'd stolen his line, and Jube didn't quite know what to say next.

"As in *wedding*?" Micah asked.

A moment of silence passed, and Ben broke it by saying, "We will drive you to the church in our new buggy!"

Things were happening fast. Way too fast. Had he heard correctly? Abigail had actually suggested marriage? Jube's answer came when he looked into her face. All fears that she might one day resent him disappeared. God had orchestrated these events, and God would manage their future.

Jubal was about to wrap Abigail in a hug when Leora leaned out of her buggy's window.

"If all of you are finished waxing poetic," she said, "I have an announcement of my own."

Now all eyes were on her.

"This non-bouncy four-seater will come in handy next year at this time, when we add a little one to the family."

Within seconds, the buggy was surrounded by family and friends offering congratulations and well-wishes.

Jube pulled Abigail to his side. He hadn't yet professed undying love, and neither had she, but they had the rest of their lives for such things.

"It has been a good day."

"A very good day."

"What do you bet," Thomas grumbled, interrupting their kiss, "the baby will be twins?"

Read on for an excerpt from Loree Lough's upcoming release, LOVING MRS. BONTRAGER!

Chapter 1

Despite the wide brim of his black hat, Sam squinted into the early June sunlight. "She was supposed to be here an hour ago." He stamped one booted foot. "If this is her idea of a good first impression . . ."

Matthew, the youngest, held tight to his father's hand and stood still and silent, watching and listening.

Molly elbowed her older brother. "It is not her fault the train is late. Besides, remember what we promised Daed. . . ."

Aaron realized it had been reluctant submission, not a promise, that had compelled his children to agree with his decision. They were well aware that he couldn't keep food in their mouths and a roof over their heads while tending the critters and the garden, preparing meals, and doing laundry and housekeeping. All three of the children, even older-than-his-years Sam, needed a woman's touch, and truth be told, he'd grown tired of being mother, father, and full-time caretaker of . . . everything. During the drive from Oakland to the Grantsville station, he'd lectured them: When Bethel arrived, they were to treat her with the respect they'd show any adult. He'd asked them to help him make her feel at home, to help out around the place, too. "If you'd been more helpful to your aunt Stella," he'd reminded them, "I would not have been forced to take such desperate measures."

Now, faced with his son's resentment, he had to admit: *A man cannot get much more desperate than to hire a wife.*

His sister had done a good job, balancing her household and his . . . until the twins were born. For a while after the babies were delivered, Stella had tried traipsing back and forth between her house and his, and it still shamed him to remember Karl's frantic plea: "If she keeps up this pace," his brother-in-law had said, "I fear I will lose her." Since none of the eligible women in Pleasant Valley wanted to step into Stella's shoes, Karl had suggested his second cousin, Bethel Mast. "If she is such a prize," Aaron had asked, "why is she unmarried?" Karl held his tongue, in part because he worked for Aaron, in part because he avoided altercations whenever possible. "Beth was born with a limp, and everyone thinks it likely rendered her barren."

The distinctive clatter of steel wheels grinding along the polished tracks broke into his thoughts. The train would screech to a stop any minute now, and when it did, he'd stand face-to-face with the woman who would soon become Mrs. Aaron Bontrager. "We cannot condone a woman living in your home without benefit of marriage," Bishop Fisher had said. And so it was decided: He would marry Bethel as soon as possible. But could he really go through with it? *Should* he go through with it?

Molly grasped his forearm and shook him into the here and now. "Tell me again, Daed, why our new mother limps."

"She is *not* our mother," Sam snarled. "She is here to cook and clean and take care of the chickens and goats. And that is *all*."

"Sam!" Molly said. "Daed, make him stop saying such mean things!"

"Your sister is right, Son. Bethel is not a servant or a hired hand. She has a big, caring heart, and if you need proof of it, just think about everything she has given up, coming all the way out here to help us. We will welcome her and treat her like family—because that is exactly what she will be. Is that clear?"

The boy hung his head, but Aaron could tell that he'd pretty much made up his mind not to like Bethel. Aaron hung his head, too, and said a prayer for guidance. Things wouldn't be easy, especially not at first, but they'd be a lot harder until Sam came around. *If* Sam came around.

Lord, I have a feeling I will call upon You a lot in the coming days.

"You never answered, Daed. Why does Bethel limp? I do not want to be rude and stare."

"Why not just ask her?" Sam said. "Since she is so big-hearted and all, I am sure she will be happy to tell you."

Aaron chose to ignore his boy's latest outburst. "The way I understand it, Bethel was born with the limp. No one knows what caused it. But Karl says she gets around as well as the rest of us."

Passengers and those who'd come to greet them shared warm hellos and hearty hugs. It wasn't enough activity to blot his own words from his mind: *She will be family.* In a week, two at most, he and Bethel would be husband and wife. Their union must appear traditional in every sense . . . on the surface. First chance he got, Aaron intended to take her aside and gently explain that he still felt bound by his vow to love Marta until death, and that while he'd happily share his name, his home, and his bed, he could never share his heart.

Aaron chuckled to himself. *What makes you think she wants your too-old heart?*

"Are you looking forward to meeting her, Daed?"

"I . . . well . . ." He cleared his throat. "What makes you ask?"

"You are smiling."

"Yes, I suppose I am looking forward to meeting Bethel." *And living like a normal man for a change.*

"You said she sounds like a very nice lady."

He remembered the slight tremble in her voice, and how edgy she'd sounded, asking and answering questions. To her credit, Bethel had laughed, too. Several times. And the music of it had given him hope that as they worked toward providing a stable home for the children, they might one day develop a companionable partnership.

"Yes, Molly, a very nice lady."

He'd learned a few things about her during their two hour-long phone conversations. For starters, she wasn't a whiner. She hadn't complained about the businesslike arrangement between her father and himself, the hurry-up nature of the final conclusion, or the 26-hour train ride from Nappanee, Indiana. It had been her agreeable attitude that prompted him to reserve the sleeper car for her, rather than a regular seat. God willing, it had made the trip a bit more pleasant.

"I hope she can cook," Sam said. "I am hungry."

"You are always hungry. Why, you eat more than Daed's horse! I am sure that she can cook. But if not? She will learn."

They didn't call her Molly the Peacemaker for nothing, Aaron thought, grinning at his daughter.

"What will we call her, Daed?"

"Anything but Maem!" Sam shot an imploring glance at Aaron, and in that moment, he looked like the carefree boy he'd been before Marta's death. "Please, Daed, do not make me call this stranger Maem."

"Karl calls her Beth. That or Bethel will do. Once she has been with us a while, we can ask what name she prefers." Aaron had already decided to call her Mrs. Bontrager, a factual title that would ensure a respectful emotional distance remained between them.

When the train slowed, little Matthew gasped quietly and pressed his cheek to Aaron's knuckles, pressed so close that he couldn't tell which of them was trembling . . . the boy, or himself.

"Relax, kids." *Who are you reassuring . . . you? Or them?* "In time, everything will be fine. She will be good for us. You will see."

Even Molly, the eternal optimist, looked doubtful. "How can you be so sure, Daed?"

"Because, sweet girl, I have prayed on it, long and hard, and I believe it is God's will." *For us, and hopefully for Bethel, too.*

At last, the train came to a full stop.

And for an uneasy instant, so did his heart.

Connect with Us

Visit us online at
KensingtonBooks.com
to read more from your favorite authors, see books
by series, view reading group guides, and more.

for sneak peeks, chances to win books and prize packs,
and to share your thoughts with other readers.

facebook.com/kensingtonpublishing
twitter.com/kensingtonbooks

Tell us what you think!

To share your thoughts, submit a review,
or sign up for our eNewsletters, please visit:
KensingtonBooks.com/TellUs.